The Road less Traveled to Sanity is art imitating life. A two-book series of an extraordinary tale inspired by true events in the author's life. A young Black boy from a poor family who was caught in the grips of deleterious forces in society, and became a criminal; spending over half his life behind bars.

While incarcerated for the third time for armed robbery, he came to witness the September 11, 2001 attack of the Islamic Taliban on American soil. The date, 9/11, happened to be the last three digits of his prison number and after a dream he became convinced the number was a message from God to change his wicked ways or be damned to eternal hell.

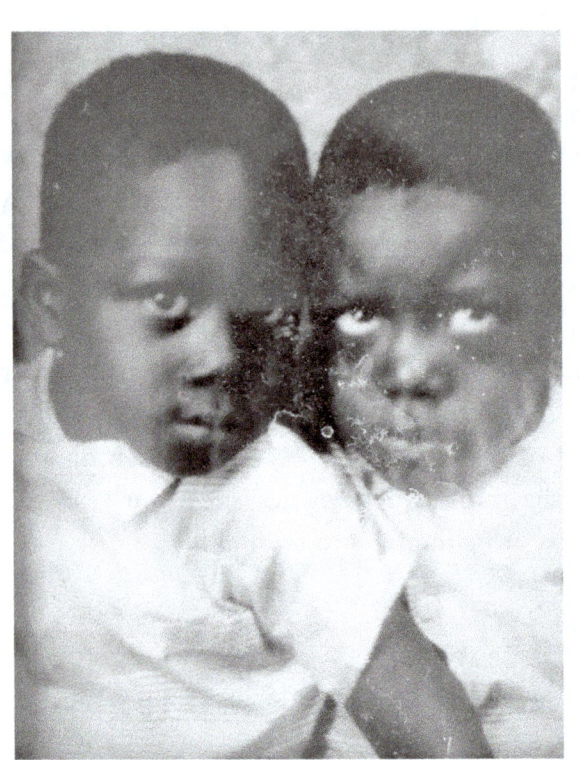

The Road Less Travelled to Sanity

A story about Drugs, Sex,
Crime and Redemption

W. D. SLEEPY

ACKNOWLEDGMENT

I thank God, who for some earthly, unexplainable reasons has given an old wretch like me favor, praise HIM. In loving memory of Willie and Pandora Drake, my parents. To all my author family members whose literary accomplishments gave me the motivation to keep going when the muse seemed to have abandoned me. I thank you all. And to my loving wife, Selisa Tell Drake: what's understood doesn't need to be attempted, here, in this limited space to explain falling short of all that you are, for me. I love you, my queen.

Contents

*The Road Less
Travelled to Sanity*

Epiphany

I was eight years old when I committed my first robbery. I had snatched an old lady's purse and was promptly sent to a juvenile detention home. Thirty-five years later I was still committing robberies and going to jail.

Had it not been forbidden to include my juvenile record in the adult criminal prison system, I would've been a six-time loser, for robbery.

There were two types of prosecution: one for a white criminal and one for a Black criminal. If you were white, you'd get slapped with nothing but armed robbery; however, if you were Black, you'd get a bunch of crimes, such as armed robbery, kidnapping, possession of a firearm, and assault. For every criminal charge given to a white criminal, there were at least two charges stacked on for a Black criminal.

I was charged and convicted with all kinds of violent crimes, such as kidnapping, possession of firearms, and assault with a deadly weapon. I robbed drug dealers and number bookies, and any other crime was usually a function of my Blackness.

My criminal behavior was a manifestation of insanity, repeating the same crime and expecting a different result. I was a "crazy nigga." And it was only fitting that, for my third armed robbery conviction, I would end up in a prison that had been an institution for the criminally insane: the Lima Correctional. Needless to say, no one, including yours truly, was surprised when the judge handed down the maximum sentence: fifteen to thirty-five years.

When I was a kid, the court would say, "He was the ring-leader and he's not remorseful." The courts were right. I really enjoyed breaking the law and doing the opposite of what a society expected out of me. I was raised in a God-fearing, law-abiding household, but did the opposite of what God-fearing family expected. From the time I could remember, there has always been an innate rebellious spirit within me. Each day I would leave the house, I would learn more and more about the world. I learned that being Black was the most disadvantaged color in my world. And the more the world would confirm this fact of life, the more rebellious I became and the harder it was for me to do as the world says, and not as the world did. So, one day when I left the house, I decided to become a criminal. I stole something.

The countless institutional sociologists and personality psychologists would always seem so surprised when I told them I grew up and lived in a two-parent household. They unwittingly let me know their thoughts and beliefs, that they thought poor Black people were incapable of being civilized. Little did they know that I was different, that I was born with a contradictory nature. Whenever one was going right, I would turn left. There was never an absolute for me. I always felt the need to take the road less travelled and test the limits of my fear of God, which I suppose meant that I didn't mind staring the Devil in the eye.

My relationship with God was like that of most criminals: hypocritical. When I was committing crimes, I turned a blind eye to the presence of God. But as soon as the judge slammed his gavel down to pronounce me guilty, I would pray, "God, please, help me!"

In fact, I despised spiritual hypocrisy in others I guess you could call me a spiritual hypocrite. Indeed, I believed my sinning peers who walked the same path as I did and claimed they had a relationship with God were fake Christians. I thought to myself how murderers, rapists, thieves, and robbers like me could ever be in God's favor? I even dared to challenge and suggest hypocrisy in God: Why me and not someone else? I couldn't wrap my mind around the level of love, faith, and forgiveness God was giving to men, men I knew didn't even deserve to breathe the air of a cockroach.

So, here I was again, forty-two years old with yet another fresh fifteen to life, living in that empty space where all sinners find themselves between religious fear and undefined spirituality, questioning others' faith, beliefs, interpretations, and understanding of the Bible dwelling in hopelessness and unwilling to recognize my own spiritual misgivings challenging the truth about God and God's truth about me.

I was comfortable with a simplistic polarized view: pretty and ugly, rich and poor, good and bad, love and hate. I needed a world that wasn't complicated. I needed a world that was explainable and gave no energy to abstract opinions. I had learned to believe in a world that was physical and right in front of me: the cold steel bars and wasted lives ... a world that was unforgiving to the hope seekers who tried to look beyond the bars of their Black reality. The more I lived in this world the more I stopped trying to convince myself I was someone other than what the world had made of me.

After this third conviction, I slid further down into a spiritual abyss. I tried to distance myself from my loved ones because I did not want to infect them with my hopelessness. I had abandoned all thoughts of ever reconciling with my spirituality. Negativity had shrouded my entire being and hung over me like a dark cloud. Yes, this third conviction was different; it took everything I had left inside of me. It felt like a chain had been placed around my entire being.

During that period, the world was meaningless. My only thoughts about the politics of nations, and the religious differences of men were that the foundation of their politics, the premise of their constitutional principles was worthless for the Black race of people. Being in jail was beginning to feel normal.

It was clear the world wanted me to become who I had become … and after this third stretch, and second thirty-five-year sentence, I totally resigned myself to a "fuck the world" mentality. That was my one and only motto. I was ready to resign myself to the man in the mirror, believing that if there were an omniscient God, who was the architect of my world, then He surely had to be in conspiracy against me. I grew up in a household where it was believed that God sent his messages through numbers. I think I was around nine or ten years old when my mother interrupted my childhood games and instructed me on how to play her numbers at the corner store. My mother was a walking numbers player's dream book. Her playing the numbers game was like cooking dinner; it was something I always remember her doing.

If a person wanted to know the number that corresponded to a rainy day or perhaps a cheating lover, they would look it up in a numbers dream book. When a dream book wasn't available, they would ask my mother who knew the meaning of every three-digit number combination there was.

The mob controlled the numbers racket. It was what we had

before the lottery. The final stock numbers were used to determine the winning numbers.

You could count on Black people playing numbers the same way you can count on them cooking greens, corn bread, macaroni and cheese, fried chicken, and candy yams once a month.

My mother planned our life around her hitting the numbers. It was not a question of "if," but of "when" she would hit. She believed, like most Black folks did who played numbers, that hitting the number meant that God's blessing and presence was upon you. At the very least, it was a sign God was trying to get your attention.

Therefore, it stood to reason that I came to believe the measure of one's faith and blessing were the times a winning number produced a brand new, shiny red car, or toys under the Christmas tree. "Lord, please send me a number" was a phrase that I grew up hearing. And when my mother hit, just before a holiday or some important occasion: "Thank you, Jesus! Thank you, Jesus!" No one could tell me the number wasn't sent by God.

911 Straight

On September 11, 2001, my number came out. I was working as an adult education tutor in the prison school when the educational supervisor answered the phone with a loud "Hell, nah!" And instructed me to immediately turn on the classroom television. All the student inmates were gathered around the TV as the events kept repeating like a broken record, believing at first that it was a horrific accident but soon finding it to be a planned suicidal attack by an Islamic extremist group who decided to crash the American passenger airplanes they had hijacked into the World Trade Center buildings in New York City, in the middle of the morning.

I had been too young to understand the Vietnam War but that was the last time war had been a thought in my lifetime. The disagreements between white men, brown men, and Asian men concerning worldly matters and discussed behind closed doors were never a concern of mine. I felt that things that happened around the world didn't concern the Black people, that nothing would change for their betterment. I felt this way at a young age even though I had no idea what hopelessness was supposed to feel like.

But this was different. This was a different statement. This wasn't a behind-closed-doors statement. Everybody was being brought into the conversation, including Black people. Everybody's opinion seemed to matter. Why this infamous moment was different from all the other moments, I couldn't put my finger on it.

I could certainly argue that there had been plenty other earth-shattering situations that happened in my life that were of a greater personal magnitude for change. But for some unexplainable reason, this wake-the-fuck-up moment was different. They say there's a time and place for everything; well, this was my time and place. This was the day shit got serious for me, this was my epiphany and why I made a conscious effort to stop being who I had always been.

I had no plans. I had been aimlessly wandering on the road for so long I had become comfortable with my state of confusion. But on this infamous day, fresh into a fifteen-to-life sentence, I knew I had to stop in the middle of the road.

It was a surreal moment even for a group of men whose lives for the most part had been built around crime and mayhem. We all were frozen in our own moment of disbelief, asking rhetorical questions that no one could answer. The supervisor asked for everyone to be quiet, but his words fell on deaf ears. I turned up the volume on the TV set just when the news commentator was saying, "The date, 9/11, 2001, shall go down in infamy as the most horrific attack on American soil." Moments later, the prison loudspeaker began to blast, ordering all the inmates to return to their cell blocks and dorms immediately.

During a time when most people were mourning death and destruction, a strange indescribable feeling of hope began to take hold of my entire being. Why was I feeling this strange sense of euphoria? It was as though I had just won the state lottery. And then it occurred to me: only a mentally disturbed person could feel as I did in the face of such tragedy.

9

I had known long before I'd witnessed airplanes crashing into a New York City skyscraper that I was mentally disturbed. I was a lifelong criminal, so it wasn't impossible for me not to be off my rocker. In fact, it was more impossible for me not to be crazy.

Nevertheless, I'd rather cut my own throat before I let the prison quacks experiment on my brain, pumping me with every psychiatric medication known and unknown to man. No way, I thought. If I was going crazy, so be it.

When you lock up a man in a cage, at some point that man will be broken by the sheer physicality of his incarceration. And when that happens there will be three paths for him to choose: the path of darkness, the path of light, and the path of inertia. The path of darkness was for those individuals who decided to check out mentally or self-destructively. The path of light was for those who decided to search within themselves for some spiritual/ religious awakening. And the path of inertia was for those who did nothing; they were time masters, people who were experts in doing time.

Each path presented its own set of pros and cons. Each time I had been incarcerated I had resigned myself to doing my time. Somewhere around twenty years of doing time, I became a time master. Time masters believed "Father Time" was undefeated, so you might as well walk slowly and drink a lot of water. Time masters are convinced that all the years spent behind bars were not wasted because the only thing that matters in the end is that you survived. And if you had survived, the time masters believed, you became wiser. I came to find that time masters were wrong.

Each time I had been released from prison, I told myself I was a better man than I had been before. I was in the same place as I had been on the day that I entered the world from the womb. After 9/11, I decided it was time to take a different approach and path. This time I willed myself to be serenaded by the soft whispers that dwell above mental capacity and consciousness. This time I would embrace faith for the things I couldn't see but could hope for.

I was mindful that I would have to be aware of the harlot that lived inside of every man. I have witnessed how strong-minded men lose their mental stability down a spiritual path, finding themselves forever wandering and searching, spiritually hoodwinked, their minds stolen by the harlot who used religion and the spirit of false Christianity, posing as a faith healer, stealing minds, great minds that were never to be found again.

If I were able to ask God one question, what would that question be? The thought took hold of me for days, days turned into weeks, and weeks into months. And one day it struck me that I had been like most men who were afraid to be angry with God, not in a blasphemous way but in the same way a child would be afraid to show anger to their father. I knew there was nothing under the sun that wasn't known about me to God and the very thought of that made me angry. The question I wanted to ask was Why? Why did I turn out into what I am, Omniscient One? Knowing all along that my "free will" would be folly.

It was clear to me that I had been set up for failure, and at some point down this infamous road that I'd traveled, Omniscient One, you knew I would grow accustomed to the path and build up a tolerance like a ghetto rat who had been eating poison for so long he had become inured to it, and instead of killing me the poison nourished my being – in the same way I chose to turn the word "nigga" from one that represented hate, into one about love.

Therefore, you knew, Omniscient One, I would be who I am today.

I was angry with God. These were my thoughts and how I felt before 9/11 and afterwards, realizing I should have been angry with Satan.

The 9/11 death toll was approximately 3,000. The number of those injured was more than 6,000. Most Americans who witnessed what turned out to be the most horrific attack on American soil since Pearl Harbor felt devastated for the victims and underwent some form of political or spiritual awakening. Until this infamous day, I had resolved to do my time and be a normal criminal who didn't give a fuck about the outside world. I had officially checked out. I looked down at the number 293-911 stitched across my prison shirt pocket above my heart and questioned myself whether I was grasping at straws. After all, there were two three-digit numbers that made up my prison number: 293 and 911. I tried like hell to dismiss the idea of the tragedy having any connection to me, telling myself it was just a horrific act of war and it didn't really affect me one way or the other. Let it go, I told myself over and over. But the thought kept coming back like a lost stray dog that no matter how far down the road you leave him, the dog kept coming back to you. What if, I feared, God was testing me? What if my faith was being tested? So, I owned it and cashed the number in.

I began to have conversations with God and God began to speak to me and said, "To know thyself is to be free, find your purpose." The words kept repeating, "Find your purpose." And for the first time in my life I realized every living thing on Earth had a purpose. It was a simple and obvious fact of life but unlike most people it had escaped me. I had understood purpose to be tangible and worldly. After 9/11, I realized it to be much more than that.

I fell into a deep dream, drifting through clouds, weightlessly floating. When I emerged from the cloud or fog, if you will, I found myself in the cockpit of an airplane. The fog hung throughout the airplane and it was hard for me to see two inches in front of me. As I was trying to regain my bearings, my eyes traced my arms and sweaty hands to the airplane throttle, squeezing it in a death grip.

In that moment, my predicament was realized. I tried with no success to wake myself from the dream. I was aware that it was a dream but useless to abort it; a dream that had taken a 360-degree turn into a nightmare. I told myself that if I didn't look out the plane window, perhaps it would all go away. But like a frightened child who's afraid of the dark and hides under his blanket, my curiosity got the best of me. I slowly opened my eyes and looked out the front window of the plane and the ominous World Trade Center towers emerged from the clouds directly in the plane's path. Realizing the outcome, I began to panic even more. This can't be. Why am I here? I began to plead and beg God to stop the plane. I tried to unbuckle the seatbelt, pulling back on the plane's throttle and pressing the control buttons. I was trying everything to stop the plane. It was weird, at no point did I not know it was a dream, or I should say a nightmare, but I still felt that I could die in the dream. At some point I stopped trying to resist and tried to relax my mind. It was as if the dream was toying with me. I knew I was dreaming but helpless to do anything about it. My eyes scanned the cockpit. There weren't any Taliban hijackers. The captain and the co-pilot were gagged and restrained. I didn't feel a thing when the plane slammed into the tower. In fact, if it wasn't for the pieces of airplane debris floating around my head like a scene in a 3D movie, I wouldn't have noticed the plane had crashed at all. After a few seconds trying to duck and dodge the flying debris, I realized nothing could harm my hologram-like body. Everyone in the airplane could see me and they knew that I could see them, but I couldn't do anything to help anyone. I cautiously exited the plane into the fiery inferno and immediately became consumed by the carnage. Mayhem was everywhere. This must be what hell was like, I thought, and was thankful the fire wasn't meant for me. People ran up to me with their bodies engulfed in flames, screaming and pleading for my help. I'd reach for them but ended up grabbing at air. I began to hear a chorus calling out, "911, 911! Help us!" The voices rose higher and higher. I turned to see a line of people on their knees engulfed in flames, arms stretched out toward me. To my surprise, the number 911 was written in big bold red numbers across the front and back of my shirt. I moved through the building and reminded myself once again that it was only a dream.

The morning after, the first thing I thought about was buying a journal. I'd remembered someone saying that keeping a journal and writing down your daily thoughts can be therapeutic. Several weeks later I got a journal and without any pre-thought, I wrote the words, "The Road Less Travelled To Sanity." I didn't know where the title came from; it was as though my hand had a mind of its own.

I was still a criminal with many dark secrets, so I was apprehensive about exploring and documenting my sanity in a self-inquisition that would literally turn my life into an open book. At the same time, I knew I had to face the truth about myself, whatever that truth maybe and and follow wherever it might lead me, even if it meant giving evidence to those whose purpose was my demise. The journal would remain in my locker box for weeks. The only thing I had written was the title. I would get up every morning and just stare at the title and turn the empty pages. My cellmate one day asked me, "Man, when are you going to start writing that book?" I told him, "It's not a book, it's a journal. I just need to find out some shit about my life and explore what makes me tick." Dude nodded his head and gave me a look that implied that he didn't believe a word I said.

I was no different than most Black men incarcerated in America who woke up one day and realized it was more than the crime that put my Black ass in prison. Like most Black men, I felt the underlying systemic dark forces that had aided and abetted my incarceration, but I was unable to articulate the conspiracy or present evidence that could confirm the diabolical plot. For convenience, I began calling the invisible forces the "White Man."

I was never one to go after a low-hanging fruit. I was like an ambulance-chasing lawyer who goes after the deep-pocketed person by default. And on many days, waking up in a cold lonely cell, I would place the blame for my situation at the feet of God.

I remember sitting in church as a child, that age when a child understands their station in life compared with that of the broader population, and having been taught that God was the giver of all things, and rationalized that God had to be aware. God knew we were poor and other people were rich. God knew we were hungry and other people had food. God knew.

After 9/11, I began to understand that the battle between good and evil was real and understood why all my life I had felt comfortable and justified walking in the shoes of criminals and being exiled and excluded from humanity.

I used to be afraid to explore eschatology, my feelings about facing my death, judgment, and the final destiny of my soul. Living was tangible like the bars in front of me. But death well, death was unseen, and certainly not hoped for. All that mattered to me was life, as though I was immortal. Why was I here? It was crystal clear that everything and everyone had a purpose, including a seemingly worthless criminal and each passing day I gained mental strength from that revelation and the pending challenge to find my purpose. If nothing else, the effort would serve as a road map for those lost souls on a less travelled road to sanity.

I would lie awake in my bunk until the wee hours of the morning, asking myself questions that seemed to be unanswerable in the earthly realm. I wondered what humanity would feel like having never participated in "the human race" and whether it was an endless war against Satan. I thought about going to the prison church for answers, but I was still distrustful of criminals who claimed to be born-again Christians. I was still distrustful of myself.

It wasn't rocket science, I told myself. There were only two roads good or evil, and all I would have to do is take either path.

I never thought of myself or aspired to be someone who endeavored to make a difference to mankind. Unselfish thoughts never crossed my mind. I rationalized my life in the first person. If it wasn't my point of view, there wasn't a view at all. Now, I was attempting a 360-degree turn. I was reaching for the highest hanging fruit and trying to accomplish something bigger than myself and I was certain that nothing I could do in the universe would be bigger than defeating the servants of Satan that had lived and moved inside of me.

I stayed in my cell for the better part of 2001, leaving only when ordered to do so. My fellow inmates began to give me that sympathetic look. That look we would give to a death row inmate. I understood that my newly found normality would be the definition of insanity to my peers. At that point I didn't care what people thought because I no longer gave a fuck about the concerns of those who would become invisible.

Most days you could find me pacing like a caged lion for

hours, trying to devise a mental strategy that would be sustainable in my surrounding. How can I mentally not be a criminal and survive in a criminal environment?

I remember this one day I was feeling mentally defeated, and contemplating aborting my plan for reinvention, feeling overwhelmed by the sheer magnitude of what I had conceived and the efforts it would take to bring a life such as mine back from the depths of hell. The more I thought about it on that day, the more my confidence began to fade. By the end of the day, I was on the verge of tapping out. Then it occurred to me that that's what I had been doing all my life, tapping out to Satan. On this day, Good and Evil were perched on my left and right shoulders in a knock-down, drawn-out fight. Doubt was relentless. But I kept reminding myself that doubt was the devil. "Even though I walk through the valley of the shadow of death, I will fear no evil, for you are with me; your rod and your staff, they comfort me."

I began to have this feeling of worthlessness in my spirit, and it seemed to keep building higher and higher during the days and months following 9/11. At first, I couldn't put my finger on it because it had nothing to do with the normal melancholy of incarceration. It wasn't one thing I could point to; it felt like the sum of all the things that made me who I had become, shamefully put on display before the world.

I had no worth, good or bad. I felt that even the infamous martyrs who had flown planes into the buildings had more purpose and significance than me. I was nothing. What had I contributed, offered to the world? I had nothing to give. No legacy worth remembering. What did I stand for?

I began to think of ways I could help mankind, but the magnitude of the task only made me realize just how worthless I was:

a broke criminal, uneducated, and doing a fresh fifteen-to-thirty-five-year sentence.

Then one day I felt a surge of energy that made me rise out of my bunk as though a giant spring had propelled me to my feet. I simply would reinvent myself.

Great men had always had to find their true purpose after trials and tribulations. Mistakes are no more than the road to the truth, I reminded myself. And it occurred to me that I had never tried to do a self-evaluation on myself. I never tried to dig deep down and search for reasons and intentions for the things that defined me and made me who I was. I had never tried to do corrective surgery. I just accepted the cause and effects of my actions. To reinvent myself, I knew that change could only begin after knowing and accepting who I was and who I had been.

I was thankful that God hadn't forsaken me and wondered why God didn't say things plain and simple. Why did God have to speak in riddles, symbolism, and allegories such as 9/11?

My belief behind bars was a lie. My truth behind bars was a lie. I understood my challenge would be to eliminate the bars in my life as soon as possible.

I considered the shit I did stupid, not crazy. When I first got the journal, I was a bit apprehensive to put my thoughts on paper. I would have to admit that my thinking was in fact crazy. Therefore, the journal remained in my locker box for weeks. The only thing I had written was the title. I got up every morning, opened it up and turned the empty pages. I didn't have a clue where to start and what to say. I just stared at the blank pages. So, when my cellmate again asked when I was going to start writing the book, again I told him it was just a journal. "I just need to find out some shit about my life," I told him, "and explore what made me tick. You know what I mean?" My cellmate nodded and replied, "Sounds like some deep shit you about to put down. Like I said, when are you going to start writing that book?"

The dominant factor in the dream was the victims, crying out to me for help. In the dream, I was known as 911. I thought about the victims in the crimes I had committed over the years.

In the beginning, I rationalized my crimes to be legally wrong but morally right, telling myself I'd only robbed numbers runners and drug dealers, people who were themselves engaged in some type of criminal activity. I never jumped on a bank counter. In fact, I only robbed one legitimate establishment in all those years: a bar. So, where was the victim? The only victim I saw was me.

My father was a law-abiding man, a hardworking man who took care of his family and made no excuses for his disadvantages. To maintain some measure of respect for my father's principles, perhaps I convinced myself that I was a modern-day Robin Hood who rid the Black community of the neighborhood parasite.

I was like all the other Black men in America who instinctively felt the systemic forces that dictated our path but were unable to articulate the conspiracy. And even if we could've, nobody would give a fuck. Therefore, like all the other Black men behind bars, I accepted the consequences that rebelling against the laws and the hypocrisy of society had brought us.

All my life I'd been comfortable walking in the shoes of criminals, exiled and excluded from the rest of humanity. I had come to the fork in the road. I reached a place I had never conceived before. I pondered what it would be like and decided to take on the challenge.

I understood God had created two paths for every man to travel and explore with free will. A Gemini, African American, and a child of God, I had never tried to control my dual nature, and never conceded my path to evil nor would I concede it to good, until now.

Indeed, I was hardheaded, I had to feel the heat on my face and reach out and touch the fire before I would certify anybody's truth, my own truth, God's truth. It was weird but it seemed to me that infamous criminals like the pilots of 911 or Adolf Hitler were just as significant to the collective consciousness of humanity as were Dr. Martin Luther King Jr. I don't know why the other side was so intriguing, but it was. For me, bad press was good press.

How must a man prove his noteworthiness to himself but most importantly to humanity? Must every man become a saint or an infamous sinner? If no one knows your name and deeds, how significant are you to humanity? Does a man have to fly an airplane into a building or invent a cure for cancer to think of himself as significant? Can a good rich man enter heaven? Jesus Christ died for the sins of humanity; did it not relieve all of humanity of significance? Can a sinner truly become a saint?

I wasn't a religious man by a long shot, but I am and always have been a deeply spiritual man. I wouldn't say my faith was weak as it was demanding. I would challenge God, in a spiritual realm as though the Father were a man with flesh and bone. Belief in Him had never been a question for me. I read this profound line awhile back that said, "If you want to hear God laugh, tell him your purpose and plans." That, in a nutshell, was my relationship with God. The man with the audacity to make God laugh, sarcastically. Now, my purpose, my challenge is to be an unwavering champion for all of humanity. Just for the challenge of reaching the high-hanging fruit. For me, it must be conquering the world or nothing. The challenge of giving voice and space to the adversary was no longer challenging. It was time for change.

I picked up my pen and grabbed my journal off the locker box and read the title slowly. "The Road Less Travelled To Sanity." It will be difficult, what if I ended up like a blind man wandering in the wilderness of his own making? I knew that the only way for that not to happen was to become an expert on myself, and it dawned on me that I didn't even know who I was. I knew there were a lot of things I was carrying around that never belonged to me, those things that I had picked and wore just because they were fashionable. I knew I would have to tell the truth about himself. And I knew facing the man in the mirror would be a hard thing to do, but not as hard as it would be to change him. Who the hell was I, stark naked before the world?

Same Dirt

My family lived in a two-room shack owned by a white man, in the middle of a cotton field, in a place called Sledge on the Mississippi Delta. It was one of those one-stop-light, dirt road towns that seem to exist only to the people who live there. The kind of town you would see in an old made-for-TV cowboy movie where Black people didn't exist, and life appeared to be normal without their presence. What I remembered most about Mississippi perhaps came to me from repeated family folk tales. At least that was what my parents believed. They said there was no way I could have remembered Mississippi in such details because I was no more than three and a half years old when we moved to Cleveland, Ohio. It was their belief that I had adopted my parents' experiences for my own.

I had no logical proof for my memory, but my parents were wrong; it was the same diseased dirt, air, and sun that supported slavery and would infect a generation with despair and a withering sense of worthlessness. My parents were wrong; no one can convince me that I didn't feel the effects of slavery the moment I left the womb.

I remember looking out through an old tattered screen door over a barren cotton field at the break of dawn, as the sun made its way over the empty horizon and time seemed to stop, and I was paralyzed with the beauty and the simple joy and magnificence of being alive. I remembered marveling at every detail of a living, breathing world and being fixated on the individual puffs of cold morning air rising like smoke from the earth and finding their way up through the cracks of the tattered floorboards of the shack. I remember a red water pump and the potbelly stove in the center of the room and disappointment when I realized the stove was as cold as the morning air. Yes, Mississippi was as real to me as if it were yesterday.

My family arrived in Cleveland, Ohio in 1956. Pandora McCollough came into the marriage with three daughters from earlier relationships, Maedean, Lurateen, and Alcil. It was an unspoken rule that a woman didn't bring children into a marriage, so Maedean was married off before her fifteenth birthday, and Alcil was given back to her father. They both would live in Chicago during my early years. A prospective husband for Lurateen had been found in Cleveland, so my mother brought her to Cleveland as well. By the time we arrived in Cleveland, Big Willie and Pandora Drake would have added five more children: Mary Louise, Jimmie, Willie (me), Lillie Mae, and Daisy. And there always seemed to be another child on the way.

My uncle, who everyone called Uncle Bud, had secured a rooming house apartment for his brother and his growing family somewhere on the Eastside of Cleveland. The rooming house had two rooms, a shared bathroom and kitchen. I simply don't remember the car ride. Nonetheless, that morning after we arrived, my attention deficit hyperactivity disorder (ADHD) kicked in, and as usual I headed straight to the screen door of the shack to look out over the cotton fields, but everything was gone.

I remember standing in the middle of this big empty unfamiliar room in a state of inertia and trying to wrap my little brain around what had happened to my world overnight. The room was chilly. There was no potbelly stove. The only source of heat was the familiar morning sun bursting through the big bay windows in one single beam. Cabinet seats circled the length of the bay windows, so I used them to pull my little body into the window to get my bearings, using the morning sun for a compass and source of warmth for my half-naked body.

When I looked out the window, instead of finding familiar signposts my perspective was from the top of a tree, at which point my little brain became disoriented. Imagine if you will: a toddler suddenly removed from an agricultural existence and placed in an urban setting, never having his feet off the ground, and one night he goes to sleep and wakes to find himself several stories up, looking down on top of trees.

Not too many of us remember the exact moment when we said, "Hello, world," but I do. This was that moment. It wasn't the unfamiliar surroundings in and of itself that had introduced me to the world, but the indelible feeling of experiencing pain for the first time, in the way a newborn is smacked on its bottom and shocked into consciousness.

The source of that pain was the big black powerful hand of my father, who had snatched me from my window perch and establishing himself as the most feared person in my world. And as it was later explained to me many times over, I began to pound on the windowpane and just before I was about to break the window and fall to my death, my father snatched me in the nick of time and commenced to whooping my ass. My father also felt the need to give me a lesson on heights, so he opened the window and dangled me out to show me just how high I was from the ground. Just as he was dangling me, my mother got up to investigate the noise. Half asleep, she'd see her deranged country-boy husband, who apparently couldn't handle being taken off the farm, about to throw her child out of the window. With only a split second to react, Pandora went into attack mode. I was about to become the bad ass little Black boy who couldn't stop getting into shit, wandering in places I had no business being, and picking up things that didn't belong to me.

The bad-ass little boy description became people's perception of me, and I owned it. Even if I had been diagnosed with ADHD, I could hear my father saying, "Attention deficit hyperactivity disorder, my ass. All he needs is his ass whipped and he'll leave shit alone. He better find somewhere to sit his ass down." My father's sentiments would prove no different than society's, who decided the only disease I had was "little bad ass Black boy, who couldn't keep his hands off of other people's shit" syndrome.

When I was around six or seven years old, in 1959 or 1960, we moved on 78th and Hough Avenue. I remember those beautiful autumn days because my mother would sometimes walk me to Crispus Attucks Elementary School, and it would be just the two of us, with her holding my hand. I don't remember ever feeling more alive and loved as I did during that special time.

Our apartment was on the ground floor. Both my parents had found work, my mother worked at a restaurant where she did everything the manager was supposed to have done but didn't, cooks were supposed to have cooked but didn't, and dishwashers were supposed to have cleaned but didn't. My father was hired as the toxic paint man. He did everything at the job that was deemed detrimental for white employees. Both my parents were still treated as the white man's mules even though we no longer live on a sharecropper's plantation.

Lurateen, my second oldest sister, became the babysitter while my parents worked. However, not too long after we'd arrived in

Cleveland, Lurateen got pregnant, married, and moved out of the house. Her husband was a big man with a violent temper. He eventually killed a man on his job and was sentenced to one to five years in the Mansfield Reformatory. Of course, the man was Black.

Mary Louise was the next in line to inherit the babysitting and overseer's duties during those hours when my parents were passing each other like two ships in the night, going to and from their respective jobs. Usually it was my father who would give Mary Louise the daily household instructions. Once Mary received her instructions she would go right back to sleep. And as soon as Mary's head hit the pillow that was my signal to head out the front door for my early morning rollercoaster ride. Through the eyes of a little Black boy, Hough Avenue was an urban paradise. People were hustling and bustling. There were all kinds of street vendors and stores and life was inviting and magical.

One morning, just when I was easing my way out of the apartment door, I heard a noise coming from the hallway landing above and I went to investigate. I saw a lady with her head between her legs. At first, I thought she was sleeping so I slowly reached out my hand to shake her. She slowly raised her head as though it weighed a ton, smiled, and like a viper snatched me to her and began to smother me with wet, sloppy, drunk kisses. And before I knew it, she had pulled my pants down and started sucking my dick like a lollypop or popsicle. Of course, at five or six years old, I assumed the result would be for her to bite it. After a while, sanity overrode her intoxication and she stopped abruptly just when my little ass was getting used to the strange sensation. Her sweet motherly voice changed to a harsh, mean cursing voice, ordering me to get the hell out of the hallway. I ran like my pants were on fire and disappeared like a thief into the early morning hustle and bustle of Hough Avenue.

My father would buy these little toy things called sparkles for us kids. You light them with a match and twirl them around real fast and they would burst into sparkling stars in your hand. That's how my body felt every time I left our apartment by myself, sparkling stars shooting off inside of me. I never saw the lady again. It was lust, but it had nothing to do with sexual desire. The lust I was craving was an overwhelming need for excitement.

I was addicted to those butterflies in your stomach that would appear at the highest point of a rollercoaster ride, the ultimate adrenaline rush. From the time I can remember breathing, drama and the unknown certified my existence and became the definition of being alive. The thing about my young ignorance, and subsequent curiosity, it propelled me onward and always dared me to look behind the next door. I never felt influenced; I always felt as though I was the captain of the ship, or the pilot of the airplane. I always felt like I was the initiator when it came to my questionable exploration and devilish endeavors. I was the explorer and the decision maker. I was that child whose line between right and wrong was undefined.

One day my father pulled up in a brand new red and black Buick and immediately my mother and he went ballistic about the car. They argued for hours about this new ride. At the time, I didn't understand why my mother was so upset but I later learned he couldn't afford the car, understanding that just because my father was in possession of the car it didn't belong to him, because he could not afford to buy it. Country boys who were straight off the cotton fields of Mississippi were easy targets for white salesmen in the 50s and 60s, selling them cars they couldn't afford and would easily lose in repossession. It was an easy con game, and my father was being played.

Neither one of my parents had finished high school. Hell, I

don't think my father ever went to school a day in his life and if he did go, he never learned how to read and write until we had moved to Cleveland. I suppose my mother, his church, and friends helped him along the way but mostly he taught himself. My mother was much faster than my father when it came to the intentions of people good and/or bad. She knew how to survive in the high-mortality, survival of the fittest world that defined the Black man's space in a white-dominated society. Pandora McCollough Drake was what you would call a people-savvy woman. She knew how to get to the good side of those people whose bad side was their calling card. She had no choice but to be on top of her game with a family that grew annually. The family secretly named her the con woman, but we would never call her that to her face. She hated the connotations of the word because her intentions were never bad. She just had an uncanny ability to get whatever she needed, even though her resources were very limited. She wasn't a greedy woman; she would give you the clothes off her back. I suppose people sensed that about her so they would always feel comfortable with her humble request, whatever it might have been.

She had lived in Chicago before moving back down south on her "got to find me a good country-boy husband" search mission. Living in Chi-town for several years she had seen it all. Nonetheless, I came to learn that everybody is a mark, and everybody can be played; Pandora and Big Willie were no different. My mother explained to my father just how things were going to play out once he failed to make one car payment. She said the car dealer would take the car back, perhaps in the middle of the night when he was asleep. It wasn't the realization that he had been played and was going to lose his pretty shinny car. What I saw in my father's blank eyes as he sat across the table listening to my mother and not saying a word, was resolve. He took a long drag from his cigarette before putting it out, and got up from the table.

Several weeks would pass before that resolve I had seen on my father's face would manifest itself. He had just given Mary Louise the daily instructions. I was lying in bed fully dressed, waiting to hear the door close behind him, poised and ready to do my usual and leave the house. However, rather than the normal sound of the door closing behind him I heard a loud bang and him shouting "MOTHER FUCKER!" I jumped out of bed to see what was going on as did the rest of my siblings. My father cussing was a signal that somebody was about to get their ass torn into pieces and usually there wasn't going to be any room for discussion; at that point, he wanted your blood. I was the first to the highly coveted middle window, which offered a view of the fifty-yard line, and all my siblings and I fought daily over the spot. Being the oldest, Mary Louise felt the spot was hers simply because of the age pecking order. Mary tried like hell to move me, but I wasn't having it, not this time. We stopped wrestling for the position when we heard my father's voice rise to the point of no return. He was arguing with a tall white, skinny, man. I pulled the curtain back further just as the white man was being body-slammed right beneath our window. The white man wrestled and threw punches for a while, but the country strong short Black man ended up on top, and the white man's face turned into a bloody unrecognizable mass of skin and bones.

Mary Louise began to cry hysterically and ran out the apartment, pulling on my father, begging and pleading for him to stop killing the man. Seeing his little girl, he eventually came to his senses. My father had to give up his pretty red and black Buick, but I never saw him smile more than I did in the weeks after he had beaten the hell out of the white man who tried to repossess his pretty car. He lost the car but gained the respect of a white man; apparently, respect from just one white man was worth a million times more to him than all the pretty red cars in the world, even if he had to beat it out of him. For as long as I could remember, my role models and mentors were thieves, robbers, rapists, and murderers, when it should have been my father.

What are the reasons and circumstances for one man to become a doctor or a lawyer and another man a criminal? I spent hours lying in my bunk wondering about that question. Why had I chosen a life of crime? The answer was much deeper than it appeared to be and seemed to hang just beyond my comprehension.

It is said that a man should take responsibility for his own actions, which I had always done even though I knew I was a fruit from a poisonous tree.

If one man was born in a privileged family where opportunity and resources were unlimited and the other man not so much, then the man with less opportunity surely would be more vulnerable to a life of crime, greater tendency towards evil deeds than if he'd been born with a silver spoon in his mouth, or simply born white instead of a descendant of Africans brought over in the hold of a slave ship.

I began thinking for days about how the African American will surely become extinct. Our demise will come from the white man's systemic denial of our access to wealth and the ironic fact that it's no longer legal to kidnap African people from their home continent.

The Federal Government should give every African American past the age of twenty-one (roughly numbering at forty million presently) a hundred thousand dollars for every ten years of being on this earth. They are, after all, direct descendants of slaves.

I knew that if my father had been a wealthy man instead of a sharecropper, and all the opportunities afforded every man was laid before me, chances are I would have not been a criminal.

But no matter how long his family had been away from the South and the unforgivable lifestyle of being a descendant of slaves, the South was always a reference point I inherited.

This recurring dream was no doubt galvanized in my mind by the folk tales of my family's Mississippi experiences and became infused into my consciousness, sitting around listening to my parents talk about their lives growing up in the South. These vivid tales allowed me to become a part of those experiences with a single heartbeat. Through this recurring dream that was made real and brought to life by the family tales allowed me to feel and endure all the circumstances that my father and his father's father had experienced before.

How much of these recurring dreams of the old shack in the middle of the barren cotton field was real or make-believe, I didn't know. But what I was certain of is that the dreams became a constant in my mind's eye, playing over and over throughout my adolescent years until it became a written fact of who I was, and the reasons for my what-if.

I often found myself wondering how my life would have been had I grown up on the cotton farm and remained a virgin to materialism and had not become addicted to the daily worshiping of the false gods of the American Dream. Who and what I would have been had I been content to live the simple life, with a roof over my head, a loving family, and enough food in my stomach to survive? Who would I have been had I grown up learning how to be subservient to and accepting of the white-dominated culture? But something inside of me knew that was not reality.

Rat Gang

We moved from 78th Street to Addison Road. But unlike most young kids whose parents moved around every few years to dodge the rent man, I was never concerned with making new friends or get involved in territorial conflicts like other kids because nothing makes the new kid more popular than to see him riding through the neighborhood in the backseat of a police patrol car.

My brother and I were bad kids. The kind of bad that when we played cowboys and Indians, if we captured you there was a good chance, we would try to hang you for real.

When it came to bad ass kids, there weren't too many boys in the neighborhood worse than us. But there was this one boy who had our entire crew shaking in our boots and pissing in our pants ... we were scared to death of Lloyd. Lloyd was one of four brothers: Happy Tooth, Edward, and Robert were the other three.

Edward, who they called Tweedy Bird, was the most celebrated of all the brothers. While Lloyd was a strong-armed bully who terrorized and shook our little delinquent Addison Road crew down daily, Tweedy Bird was the jack of all trades when it came to be committing juvenile crimes. He introduced me to criminal planning and crime strategy 101. Prior to seeing Tweedy Bird in action, my delinquent endeavors had always been spontaneous. I was an ADHD kid, so I had never planned anything, as patience wasn't a part of my DNA. Like snatching old ladies' purses, I saw it and took it. Tweedy Bird gave everybody a task, like a general giving his troops a game plan of attack. He would have us stage a fight in front of a store to create a diversion while he would take money from the cash register or slide behind the counter and take BB guns. Sometimes even a real gun. Observing Tweedy Bird, I learned patience and the importance of creating a game plan. Tweedy Bird had a Doctor Jekyll and Mr. Hyde personality, one minute he's giving you the shirt off his back and the next minute he's shooting you in the face with a BB pellet gun. I still have that pellet scar on the bridge of my nose. Half an inch to the right and I would've been known as One-eyed Willie.

I picked up a lot of my juvenile delinquencies from a lot of guys in the Hough and Wade Park neighborhood in the summer of 1962, but I learned more hanging around Tweedy Bird in one week than with anyone else. I realized early on that I was not good at taking orders from people, authority was torture for me. Telling me to go right meant let me see what the hell I can find going left. I took the opposite path of everyone. Life just didn't feel satisfying following the same path of others. It was downright boring to wake up every morning with the same soup warmed over; it was like prison.

There were two kinds of street hustlers: followers and leaders. Followers ended up being losers, and leaders ended up being winners, it was as simple as that. There was something innate and unexplainable inside of me that made me hate being that person whose significance and needs were under the control of another man's directions. It was as though my slave forefathers were talking to my spirit; rebel, rebel, against authority.

In the summer of '62, I became the lead dog in our little group of delinquents. "Follow me." "Let's do this or that." I was the instigator even if it was something as playful as jumping off garages, or delinquent as stealing soda pops from a delivery truck to snatching an old lady's purse. Whatever it was, everyone expected me to be the front man and I never disappointed. I was always one of the youngest at only nine years, but always one of the biggest kids in our little group. I enjoyed being the crash-test dummy. I was a different kind of dude. My thirst for drama and curiosity was an addiction. If life had no challenges what's the use of living? I had to see what was on the other side of the mountain. I danced to the beat of a different drummer. Going first wasn't a choice, it was a need. It was who I was. Other young boys imagine themselves being superheroes or wishes for material things that the young wish for, but not me. Imagine being the first to see the moon. The blue sky. The ocean. A mountain. A bird flying. My wish was to be first. I was cool with being first in whatever life had to offer.

Jimmie, my brother, and I were only eleven months apart. We affectionately called him Bruh. Bruh and I, until around my twelfth and his thirteenth year, had always been inseparable. I have no recollection of a world without his shadow during that time. Bruh not being by my side would have been like the sun not rising in the morning. I had to see his face every morning and I supposed he felt the same need. Indeed, his presence aided and abetted all that was inside of me.

When we moved on Addison Road, we met the twins Phil and Phillip Williams. The twins lived in the townhouse buildings that connected the courtyard on the Dellenbaugh Avenue side. The courtyard was a line of adjacent buildings that circle around Wade Park Avenue, Addison Road, Dellenbaugh to 71 Street and back to Wade Park completing the circle. The connecting buildings resembled a big yellow castle fortress. The courtyard buildings had some of the biggest rats you'd ever seen anywhere in the world. These rats were so big they had the audacity to attack you in broad daylight. During the summer months, the four of us would meet in the big courtyard by the trash dumpster to kill rats. Our goal was to chase the rats out the dumpster into the open courtyard and kill them. There weren't any pretty baseball diamond or manicured football fields for us to let off youthful exuberance, so we learned to manipulate our environment to our will. Killing rats became our Saturday morning pastime. The tenants who lived in the courtyard buildings loved the entertainment. They gathered on their back porches and watched the festivities as though they were emperors watching gladiators slay lions in a Roman sport arena. We felt important, the way children felt when their parents came to support them playing baseball or football. It was my job to get the rats out of the trash dumpster. To accomplish this task, I used a long bamboo fishing pole with nails taped around the end. The contraption allowed me to spear any rats hiding in the corners and underneath the garbage. When we'd rattle the bins, the rats would run out the dumpster and would be met with a barrage of bricks and bottles.

This one time, we had already killed several rats when I felt something at the end of my spear. It wasn't moving, so I assumed it was a dead rat I had killed. After some maneuvering, I was able to hold it against the wall of the dumpster and slowly raised it up and out the dumpster with the spear. It appeared to be a big dead rat from all the blood. But upon closer examination, and to everyone's horrible surprise, it turned out to be a still-born baby that someone had thrown into the dumpster.

After that, everyone referred to us as the Rat Gang. The infamous story about the dead baby changed every time someone told their version. However, the Rat Gang name stuck, and would be forever etched in the minds of the people in the Addison Road courtyard apartments. But the thing I remember most about that day was the police paddy wagons; I wondered why they had to bring all those big police paddy wagons for such a tiny little dead baby.

Wade Park Elementary School was a normal elementary school. What I mean by normal is guards weren't masquerading as teachers. I had never been in a classroom where the children weren't like me and the teacher's only concern wasn't whether I was sitting down and not acting a fool.

The teachers at Wade Park Elementary took pedagogy seriously. I was entering the third grade and it was the first time I remembered an effort to learn was being demanded of me. Subsequently, the teachers' concern exposed my learning disability, which I didn't understand. I just thought I was a dumb kid. No one was moving around and talking, everyone was quiet with their heads stuffed in their books, studying and focusing on their assignments. I had no clue why I couldn't keep up with the lessons, so I started to act up to mask my ignorance and began to take on the role of the class clown. The phrase, "slow learner" was bandied about, and I felt embarrassed. My self-esteem took a nosedive every second I was in school. I felt out of place. If I hadn't been in love with Miss Big Boobs who sat next to me in the third grade, I would've never gone back to school. I probably would've spent my entire mornings at Rockefeller Park or the Cleveland Museum of Art. But the thought of not seeing those big boobs greeting me in the morning at least three times a week was out of the question. She had to hold the record for the biggest boobs ever on a third grader. My mother used to say, "Boy, you're smelling yourself now, is that it?"

For the most part the teachers were all cool at Wade Park. I can't remember my third-grade teacher's name, but she was a white elderly lady. And unlike most white teachers during that time period, whose teaching methods were influenced by a racist society, my third-grade teacher would let us know there was a concerted effort to give us a subpar public education and she tried her best to level the playing field for us. She loved teaching and it showed. She wasn't pretentious. It didn't matter what color her students were. She was full of energy with an unquenchable thirst for teaching. She would always arrive early, and her car was always the last one to pull out the parking lot.

The abolition of slavery was only one hundred years old, so it was par for the course for me, a poor Black ex-sharecropper's kid, to feel low self-esteem and a measure of inferiority systemically, but I never felt that in my third-grade class. What I remember most about my third-grade teacher was the confidence she gave me. Confidence to look white people straight in the eye and lie with a straight face. I still can hear her voice, and feel her little fragile hand lifting up my chin and saying, "Up, up. Right or wrong ... don't be afraid to always hold your head up high, and look them square in the eye." She left no doubt this was her most important lesson.

This little thick-eyeglass-wearing nerdy little boy named Dan lived next door to us in the same duplex, on the corner of Melrose and Addison roads. His mother, Leslie, and stepfather, DJ, had a little store on Lexington Avenue where they ran numbers. Daniel's pockets were always full. His money drew a lot of friends, real and fake. I didn't care about his money; I liked Dan because he was just like me, he was defiant and loved to get into shit. He wasn't afraid to push the juvenile delinquent envelope just for the fun of it because he didn't have to; his parents were nigga rich. Nerdy Dan was a ten-year-old pimp. He didn't know he was a pimp and his whore didn't know she was a whore. Her name was Chassidy. But if you called her Chassidy she would kick your ass. She preferred to be called Chas. Chas was two and half years older than Dan, and at least three years older than me. She didn't stand on a corner and sell her body; she was a little hard-nosed tomboy girl who felt more comfortable wearing pants and pulling her panties off for the crew than hanging out with girls that were discovering painting their nails and talked about their pretty dresses. We were little bad-ass boys and Chas was a little bad-ass girl who dared to hang out with bad-ass boys in the hood. Looking back, we all represented the sum of our experiences.

I often wondered how Chas got to be who she had been. She did anything Dan told her to do, like "Show them your pussy," and she would drop her pants. "Give everybody some pussy," and she would let them run a train on her. Of course, she made Dan pay dearly to be the pimp. In retrospect, perhaps Dan was the youngest trick I had ever known because not once did I feel Chas wasn't in control.

After a while, Chas and I began to hang out a lot, people started calling her my girlfriend and both of us would deny it. Dan didn't accept her as his girlfriend because no one wanted to be around the nasty girl and claiming her as your girlfriend was out of the question, unless your name was Little Bud.

I was thrilled and honored to be thought of as Chassidy's boyfriend. Whenever my mother would say, "Your girlfriend" is here for you, neither one of us would dispute the assumption. Chas was a tomboy and I was daring and adventurous; we were a perfect match. Chas knew how I felt about her because when she said "Jump", I would say "How high?" She had me wrapped around her finger. I was the first little boy pussy whop without ever having had any pussy.

Every day I would ask her to give me some, but she would only give me a future promise. "I'll think about it," she would say. And every day, my reply would be, "Well, have you thought about it yet?" And she would say, "I told you, I'll think about it." I would do all sorts of challenging things young boys did to try to impress her. This one time it was riding my bike down a steep hill at Rockefeller Park. To make things even more challenging, I had replaced the original handlebars on my bike with a car steering wheel.

I crashed into a tree and was thrown several feet into the air, slamming my head on a big rock and splitting it open to the white meat. I was knocked out cold, woke up covered in blood and didn't know what the hell had happened to me. Chas took me up the hill to Mt. Zion Hospital and was credited with saving my life. All the way to the hospital I kept reminding her that I did what I said, therefore, she had to give me some pussy. I supposed she didn't want my blood on her hands or perhaps to shut me up, she promised to give me some the moment I was released from the hospital. Perhaps a week or so later, I knew it was too early for me to be leaving my house because I remembered I still had the big white turban bandage wrapped around my head. Nonetheless, I had made it clear to Dan that Chas had promised me some pussy. And for him to come get me the next time Chas was giving him some.

The day had come, and several little nasty ass boys and one little nasty girl were in the attic of an abandoned house on Cory Street. Dan was regulating the order. I was at the end of the pussy-train line waiting my turn patiently. I was nine years old and didn't have a clue what I was about to do, but that never stopped me before and I wasn't going to let it stop me now. Chas was sexually consensual and obviously experienced for her age. She knew only a few of the crew was sexually matured enough to be harmful. As for myself, I was too sexually immature to be considered at all. So, when my turn came around, she said, "You wait for next time." I reminded her of her promise. But again, she refused me, repeating, "I said next time."

I don't know how and why as young Black boys we had come to refer to sexual intercourse in such a coldhearted misogynistic way. We all deeply respected our mothers and Black women in general; it was clear to us that Black women were the reason and the backbone for everything that breathed in our world. But somehow here we were. Perhaps as some have suggested, the brutality of the system of slavery, only being several generations removed, and exacerbated by circumstances of our present oppressive environment, there had not been enough time for the generation of the little Black boys of the ghetto to build a strong foundation in morality and inner restraint. We were still being treated like animals therefore, we acted accordingly. In other words, if a baby wakes up every morning to rain, how can you expect him or her to understand blue skies?

Days or perhaps a week or so later, after being turned down once again, I decided to seek professional advice. I found my mother in the kitchen preparing my father's evening dinner. There weren't any microwave ovens back then, and if there were, we certainly couldn't have afforded one. Nevertheless, my father demanded his meals be hot when he got off work. My mother would time her culinary preparations down to the last minute to have his food steaming hot when he walked through the door. Naturally, she'd get extremely upset when someone threw her timing off. "Boy, why you in my kitchen moping around, what is wrong with you?" I said nothing; I couldn't find the words at first. She said, "Okay then, if there is nothing wrong with you, get the hell out of my kitchen so I can finish Big Willie's dinner." So, I blurted out, "Why my thang isn't like everybody else's thang?" What! She stopped her preparation, and with a furrowed brow, she gave me a once-over, and after a moment of contemplation she said, "Who's everybody? What have y'all been doing with that little girl?" Before I could fix my words, she said, "Don't you lie, boy." I said, "Nothing, I swear to God." She stared at me, looking me up down as though she was waiting for the truth to burst out of me like a pen punching a water-filled balloon.

"What do you mean your thang isn't like everyone else's thang?" I said, "My thang is little."

She replied, "Because you little, you only nine. (Or ten, whatever age I was at the time). "You keep that thang in your pants, boy, you hear me?"

Whenever there was a discrepancy about something, I would use my brother as a point of reference. "Well, Bruh is only eleven months older than me and his thang is bigger than mine."

I supposed she was relieved to find out it wasn't nothing serious, like a gender-confusing issue.

She said, "Pull the thing out, boy, and show me."

I hesitated, not from embarrassment because I wasn't afraid or embarrassed to tell or show my mother anything, but it was her tone of voice that had given me pause. So, with a little hesitation, I pulled my business out right there in the kitchen. She told me to stand up in the kitchen chair so she could get a better look at it and before I could stop her, she reached over and started bouncing my whole package in her hand like she was examining fruit in the grocery store.

She said, "So, you think it's too little for you, huh?"

I was looking down at my business in her hand, so I didn't see her grab the big butcher knife off the table that she had been cutting up the chicken and had raised above her head. "Okay, since you don't want the damn thang ..." Bam!

All I remember is seeing the knife raised above her head, and coming down, and something flying off the table in the air (a chicken wing or a leg) thinking it was my Johnson. I must have fainted or blanked out. My brain didn't connect the dots in that instant. I didn't connect or associate the pain until a beat or so later, everything was still attached. I fell backwards, clutching my business and crashing to the floor. My mother was standing over me with a menacing expression, knife still raised above her head as though she was a deranged woman.

She said, "Give it here, boy, come on let me cut it off, apparently you don't want it."

I remember scooting backward as far as I could and pulling my pants up. "I do want it!" I screamed several times.

She leaned down and pointed the knife inches from my nose. "Well, you better act like it."

One day Chas and a few of our little Rat Gang crew decided to go hiking in Rockefeller Park. Being a girl, Chas prided herself at being the lead dog among a group of bad-ass little boys. We were doing our own thing and somehow or another Chas got separated from the rest of us. We heard some talking and quietly went to investigate. To our surprise we saw several older teenage boys pulling a train on her. But this time it was against her wishes. She was already lying naked from head to toe on the nasty dirty ground, which she would never do. She was being raped. I recognized a few of the teenage boys from the neighborhood. They were tough, kick-your-ass boys. My crew was younger and didn't want any parts of these boys, so my crew took off in the other direction. Telling me as they were leaving, I'd better come too if I knew what was good for me. As always, if you tell me to turn right, I would go left … so I stayed and watched. I didn't know what to do.

After several boys were finished, I decided to slowly walk over where they were, keeping a sprinter distant, and called out to her, "Chas let's go, it's getting late." My voice startled the boys for a moment; they scrambled and froze like a deer in headlights. They regained their criminal composure once they saw where the voice had come from. They sized me up and realizing I wasn't a threat to stop them, they continued, telling me to shut the fuck up. They were a pack of dogs in heat. I moved around to get a look at her face just to make sure what I was seeing wasn't consensual. And her eyes told me what I already knew. Chas promiscuous reputation was well known in the hood and once these boys saw her in the seclusion of the park, she had no chance. I called out to them to let her up, explaining to them that her mother was looking for her. This time one of the boys waiting his turn feigned as though he was about to come after me and I moved quickly to gain a little distance. He didn't want to chase me too far and miss his turn.

I can't remember how many they were, but they were at least four or five. I remember her clothes were ripped and we had to piece them together before she could leave the park. I gave her my shirt. Nothing was ever said about the rape.

Chas played football and baseball in the street and jumped garages just like she had always done. But she never let the crew run a train on her after that, no matter what Dan tried to give her. Looking back, I think she never gave me some because she wanted me to continue being her boyfriend and respecting her.

Chas didn't have a father, her mother moved off Melrose and that was the last time I saw her.

We moved on the corner of 105th and Empire early fall of 1964, several months after my eleventh birthday. Our apartment was located right across the street from Columbia Elementary, and two blocks down from Empire High School, so it was very convenient for my parents who by now had a house full of elementary school-age children.

The front windows of the apartment faced 105th Avenue and the windows on the side faced Empire Street. The apartment was above a bar owned by some old white people, and adjacent to a row of houses on the side of Empire Street. For a kid with ADHD, 105th Avenue was like I had died and gone to street heaven. I was able to see all the happenings north and south on 105th street and in the early '60s, 105th was a nightlife destination. But it was the Empire side of the apartment that I was most intrigued with. I had made friends with two girls who live in the adjacent Rowhouse the same day we moved in the apartment. Not long after I made a challenge to the girls that I can climb out my kitchen window on their roof, and they dared that I could not. Of course, I did, and they invited me into their bedroom. I told my brother about it, and the next time he joined me. I was still too young to have real sex with a girl, but that wasn't going to stop me from trying.

One night when Bruh and I were in their room, their father knocked on the door. He was halfway through the door when the girls pushed it closed, explaining to the father that they were naked. Bruh and I scrambled under the beds. Their father was a huge, mean-looking man. The father talked about their household chores not being done and staying up all night. Bruh and I were too afraid to breathe, so trying to make it out the window was out of the question. So, we remained trapped under the beds, sweating bullets until the father finally left. Bruh was a year older than me, but even so his body had matured fast for a boy his age. He had a dark shadow mustache and began to get real pussy by the age of twelve. We both knew the difference between real pussy and boning a girl. Boning was like committing petty larceny, and real pussy was like committing grand larceny. The risk of getting caught in that big man's house, in his daughters' bedroom, at one o'clock in the morning, fucking the man's daughter was way too risky for Bruh. As for me, it was never about the booty, it was all about riding the rollercoaster to the top and waiting for the butterflies to fill my stomach and plunging downward with my hands raised in the air, intoxicated with fear.

The Glenville neighborhood was ruled by the gangs, such as We Della Mores, Devil's Disciples, and Majestic Gents to name a few. Bruh and I won all our fights, so we were promptly recruited in the Jr. Devil Disciples. The Jr. Devil Disciple turf was 105th Street. A little bulldog dude named Bobby Love was the president at the time.

The most significant time for me in the gang happened in the summer of 1964, we had a "gangbang" in the Garfield playground. A lot of dudes got fucked up, somebody brought a rifle to a fistfight and a boy was killed. The cops caught the boy who fired the fatal shot. After that incident, the gangs slowly started to break up. The pressure from the police was constant. If you asked ten people who were there in the fight that day no one would be able to tell you what we were fighting about. The thing about gangs, there had to be a chain of command and as I mentioned before I had a problem with authority. I was finished with the Devil Disciples the night of the gangbang.

Violence symbolized the young Black generation in the '60s like baseball and apple pie symbolized America. I was born in a decade of violence; the Vietnam War and the Civil Rights Revolution were in full swing from 1954 to 1968. Long before Mohammad Ali uttered the words "I ain't got no quarrel with them Viet Cong" the very words had been uttered many times throughout the Black community. Cell phones, videos, and social media wouldn't be invented until another forty or fifty years, therefore the Civil Rights Revolutionary War wasn't being televised ... for real. Crime became a way of life for those of us who lived in the war zone.

The 105th Street boys that Bruh and I hung out with the most were Bobby Love, his uncle Mike Suggs, Hiawatha Little, and Otha Short and a few others. Although these dudes were just as tough as my Rat Gang friends from the Hough neighborhood, when it came to delinquent mischief, the Rat Gang had no boundaries. The dudes from Glenville parents had food in their cabinets and refrigerators. Glenville was still a working-class neighborhood when we moved there, white merchant flight was not fully completed. On the other hand, the Hough neighborhood had long been the poster child for the ghetto of Cleveland. My new Glenville friends played in organized little league baseball and football teams. Our Hough friends killed ghetto rats for sport.

Angel of 1965

It was the fall of the year of my twelfth birthday. I was slowly becoming a normal little kid on 105th street, playing baseball for Fat Tim Father's Little League Washington Senators in the summer, and Pee Wee football for Fairfax Recreation Center, the Tidmores in the winter. I never would forget my one and only football coach, a big barrel-chested, serious man we called Mr. Edward.

I liked baseball but I was in love with football and couldn't wait to get on the grid-iron. Indeed, I was becoming a normal little boy. However, my boyish becoming would end suddenly one evening after a hard Pee Wee football practice.

I remember being tired, hungry as a bear and dragging myself home. During these lean years food in my house was first come, first served when both my parents had to work. There were eight mouths to feed at this time and if I messed around, which I often did, there wouldn't be a crumb anywhere.

I was considered a big kid for a twelve-year-old, but I was never a greedy kid. Given the choice of eating or staying outside all day playing football, I would choose football every time. When I began to engage in organized sports my activities became more scheduled, so after football or baseball practice, I would come straight home for dinner.

I had no time to waste. I bolted to the kitchen and made a straight line to the refrigerator, stove, and then the cabinets. I found nothing. "Who ate all the damn food?" I shouted to no one in particular. Mary Louise came into the kitchen and announced in her take-charge voice what I had already known, "If you would've brought your butt home like you were told, you would've had some food. So, blame yourself." I was not in the mood to hear her big mouth sarcasm. I was twelve years old and Mary Louise was fourteen. I sized her up. I still wasn't ready to try her yet even though I was certain the ass whipping she used to put on me was over. Nevertheless, the ass-whipping was still fresh on my mind. She was a girl, but it didn't matter. I never fought just because I thought I could win, for me the most important thing was the fight in the dog. I never wanted so much as a busted lip if it was avoidable. I didn't believe in winning at all cost, I believed in winning at no cost. Mary still had too much fight in her for me. "Shut up!" I said. "You're not my mother." She fired back, "Make me, black ass nigga, if you think you bad …!" Mary was my father's lightest-skinned child, and she never missed an opportunity to remind us of that fact.

We had a brief standoff, so I kept on searching and throwing pots and pans around just to antagonize her, knowing she had to clean up after me. I knew my efforts weren't going to produce any food. As I said my mama was working again. This time it was at the Woman's Hospital laundry room. She gave Mary Louise strict instructions what time to prepare and serve the meal, but most importantly it was Mary Louise's job to make sure all the kids got fed. "It's not my job to watch your food, you should've come home like you were told and you would've had some food."

She knew she was dead wrong for allowing the rest of the kids to eat my portion. I wanted to punch her in her big mouth, but instead I feigned the punch, she flinched but quickly regained her composure and jumped into her boxing stance.

"Try it boy," she said. "And I'll beat all the black off of you. You think you tough, try it with me ..."

Mary Louise had a lot of fight in her, but she knew the same as I knew the days of kicking little brother's ass had come to an end a few years back. I decided to go out and hustle up something to eat so I changed out of my football uniform. I had to hurry because a city-wide curfew had been imposed. Mostly the curfew was for Black folks. The city was a time bomb. The Civil Rights Movement, el-Hajj Malik el-Shabazz, better known as Malcolm X, had gotten killed; the Vietnam War, Black Nationalism, and Carl B. Stokes setting the stage for his run at becoming the first Black mayor formed the backdrop that me and my band of juveniles danced around this particular night, in the late fall of 1965. I couldn't articulate all the fuss going on around me. All I knew was that it was a matter of Black or white and on this night, it would come to bear. The white-owned stores that were being shut down and, in some cases, flat out abandoned, were being looted every night.

My parents kept a roof over our head and food in our stomachs. There was no reason for me to steal anything. I may have been hungry, but I never felt starvation. Normally I would've stolen a pack of baloney or junk food, but things weren't normal anymore. My Pee Wee football team had had a contact practice and that ended up sapping what little nourishment I had had that day. I could've waited on my mother to come home and she would have solved the food problem, but something was drawing me down a familiar path and I was helpless to do anything about it. As for my parents, the civil rights narrative was another way of saying Black folks finally had enough of the white man's bullshit. But my mother and father wanted nothing to do with the chaos in the streets. They were all for a better way of life and trusted in the teachings of Dr. King. But they weren't about to march and let the white people spit in their faces, hit them upside the head with billy sticks, and let dogs bite them. They were from Mississippi and had had enough of that bullshit for a lifetime. What people did or didn't do in protest was of no concern of theirs.

I had been under strict instructions to come straight home from football practices. But if my parents told me to do one thing, I would do the other.

As I was about to hit the streets, Mary Louise jumped in front of the door, standing with her arms akimbo. "And where do you think you going, boy?"

Her posture suggested that I would have to physically remove her from in front of the door. I told her it was none of her damn business and for her to get the hell away from the door. She said if I left, she would tell Daddy. Threatening to tell my father was the ultimate threat in our household.

I'd had enough of Mary Louise's bullshit and time was of the essence, so I decided to use my hold card. She had been having sex with this dude named David Dunkins. Bruh and I had watched them, screwing in my parents' bed several times.

"And if you do," I said. "I'm going to tell Daddy that Bruh and I saw you giving that boy David some pussy in his bed."

Mary Louise Drake almost passed out. I thought for a moment she literally forgot how to breathe. She stumbled and reached out to the wall to balance herself. Her facial expression was a manifestation of fear and horror: her eyes were like those big bulging eyes on the Black person in the movies who suddenly comes face to face with the monster. There was no more for me to say. I gently pushed her aside, opened the door and left.

We couldn't afford a lot of household conveniences but when both parents worked, occasionally they would get a telephone in the house. Therefore, as I was leaving, I shouted back over my shoulder, "When Mama calls home, tell her I am sleeping." I didn't get a reply, so I figured Mary hadn't found out how to breathe yet.

Glenville was changing me. I had fallen in love with being a kid and playing team sports. But there was something missing, sports did satisfy my addiction for drama, and when the urge hit me, I would walk all the way over to my old Hough neighborhood to hook up with the Rat Gang for some juvenile mischief.

As I was leaving I ran into a little dude who lived in the apartment a few doors down, named LP, whose mother was a whore. LP was one I remember hanging out with that was younger than me. I took joy in trying to corrupt his mind with delinquency but, turns out his mind was already delinquent therefore he was always game for anything I would throw at him. LP's mother was never home so he basically did what the fuck he wanted to do.

Everyone had a neighborhood name. It was a rite of passage when your peers discarded your government name and gave you your hood name. Bobby Love, the president of Jr Devil Disciples had given me the hood name "Sleepy". Bobby used to stop by to pick me up every morning to go to school and would literally have to pull me out of the bed, so he started calling me Sleepy Head, which was eventually shortened to Sleepy. Personality-wise, the hood name Sleepy was the total opposite of who I was, because little did Bobby know that when he was tucked in his warm bed at night, I would be roaming the streets, wide awake.

It was dark, around 9 PM by the time me and LP knocked on the twins Phillip and Phil's door on Dellenbaugh Avenue. On our way over, LP and I had noticed that the windows of Kaufman's hardware store on 105th Street had been broken and boarded up with plywood. When the twins asked me what's up, I told them the plan was to break into the hardware store on 105th Street and take some bikes, BB guns and money.

I lied with escalating hyperbole, explaining to them that I had seen the hardware store owner hide money in the store on many occasions, not to mention the BB guns and bikes. The reality was that the hardware store had been abandoned. After a boy name Carlton was added to our little band of thieves, we decided five were enough to get the job done.

Every time the crew asked me about the hardware store, I would embellish more and more. Carlton and Phil were beginning to doubt my story but once we started drinking the fifth of Wild Irish Rose wine, my story became more and more believable to everyone, including myself. By the time my Rat Gang arrived in front of Kaufman hardware store on 105th Street it was around midnight. The courage of the wine had worn off and the gang could see the place for what it was: an abandoned store. A symbol of the white Jewish merchants' mass exodus from the Eastside of Cleveland.

It took some convincing for me to be able to get the Rat Gang's courage back up to the point where they would give me a hand in removing the plywood and subsequently enter the abandoned hardware store with me.

The hardware store was next to an apartment building separated by a narrow alleyway. It was decided LP would stand watch outside while the rest of us went inside. Inside, the store was pitch-black. We couldn't see two inches in front of us, so we just grabbed everything we stumbled into that wasn't nailed down. We didn't think about all the noise we had made removing the plywood and now stumbling around inside the store. The front door had a deadbolt so we couldn't open it from the inside, therefore we had to bring the stuff to the window and have LP transfer it to the alley.

After several trips, LP informed us that a nosey lady had looked out her apartment window and saw him bringing stuff in the alley. He said she didn't say anything, so we kept at it for what seemed about half an hour, until we heard LP's high-pitched scream, "Police!" The gang hit the alley and scampered like roaches when the lights are turned on. I realized the cops had the place surrounded so I quickly searched and found a hiding place in an abandoned garage and scrambled behind an old dusty dresser, breathing hard and shaking like a pair of craps. The cops had caught everyone but Carl and me. LP was the only one who saw me run inside the garage. And it didn't take him long to turn into a canary bloodhound, singing and sniffing me out for the cops.

I could hear the one cop ask him, "Is this the garage?"

And I heard his whimpering sniffling voice answered, "Yes."

But it wasn't LP's voice that raised the hair on the back of my neck, it was the cop's voice. Instincts told me to fear that voice. This wasn't your routine "catch a Black boy and take him to the juvenile detention home" cop's voice. This voice was the sound of death. I'd made a mistake by hiding in the garage, and now I didn't have a choice. I knew that if the cops entered the dark garage with no witnesses, he would surely kill me. My only chance of making it out of the garage alive would be to run for my life.

I was hiding on the side of the old dresser. I heard the garage door slam open with a loud bang. I hadn't noticed it before it was as though it suddenly appeared out of nowhere a light shining through a small opening in the back of the garage.

"Anybody in here?" the death voice called out.

I got myself into a racing stance, there was no time to think. I ran toward the light. That was the last thing I remembered before everything went dark.

Subsequently, the Cleveland newspaper carried the story, although buried it in the back pages. The story read:

YOUNG SUSPECT IN BURGLARY IS
SHOT IN BACK BY POLICEMAN

A 13-year-old burglary suspect who ran when ordered to stop was shot in the back and seriously wounded early today by a policeman.

The boy, Willie Drake, of 10427 Empire Ave. was in Mt. Sinai with pellet wounds in the head, neck and back. He was believed involved in the burglary of the Kaufman Hardware Store at 1140 E. 105th St. He was shot by Patrolman John Kincaid shortly before 3 a.m. as the boy ran from an empty garage at 10407 South Blvd. Kincaid yelled twice at him to stop and fired his shotgun twice at the fleeing boy.

Kincaid, 26 and two years a policeman, was visibly shaken when he described the shooting. "In a case like this we have no way of knowing whether the fugitive is a man or a boy, is armed or not. We know that if he is armed, he can take a shot at the officer holding the flashlight," the policeman said. "These boys were aware they were committing a crime."

He said his first shot missed and the second dropped the boy. He said the range was about 25 feet. The prosecutor ruled the shooting was justifiable.

The boy, of slender build and 5 feet and 4 inches tall, was in fair condition in the hospital today. His parents Willie and Pandora Drake were at the hospital with him.

Drake, 35, a spray painter and Mrs. Drake both were at work last night. Mrs. Drake is employed in the laundry at Woman's Hospital. Drake said: "I could understand if a policeman would shoot a boy in the legs, but why did a grown man have to shoot a boy in the back?"

The Drakes have seven other children, aged 5 to 14. The oldest, Mary Louise, oversaw the children last night. She said the boy Willie left about 7 p.m. saying he was going to spend the night with a friend.

Police arrested four boys, including 13-year-old twins, in connection with the attempted burglary of the hardware store and sought a fifth youth. One of the arrested boys was 11.

Police were called by a neighbor who saw the boys carrying goods out of the store and stacking it in front of her home at 1134 E. 105th St.

The boys scattered when the police cruiser arrived. One was caught running on South Blvd. Two were found hiding in grass nearby.

Patrolman Kincaid and Edward Commines, searching the area, spotted the boy Willie hiding in the garage. He ran through a gap in the rear wall and the shooting followed.

One boy was arrested at home. The fifth boy being sought is 12.

Young Suspect in Burglary
Is Shot in Back by Policeman

A 13-year-old burglary suspect who ran when ordered to stop was shot in the back and seriously wounded early today by a policeman.

The boy, Willie Drake, of 10427 Empire Ave., was in Mt. Sinai Hospital with pellet wounds in the head, neck and back. He was believed involved in the burglary of the Kaufman Hardware Store at 1140 E. 105th St.

He was shot by Patrolman John Kincaid shortly before 3 a. m. as the boy ran from an empty garage at 10407 South Blvd. Kincaid yelled twice at him to stop, and fired his shotgun twice at the fleeing boy.

Kincaid, 26, and two years a policeman, was visibly shaken when he described the shooting.

"IN A CASE LIKE THIS we have no way of knowing whether the fugitive is a man or a boy, is armed or not. We know that if he is armed he can take a shot at the officer holding the flashlight," the policeman said.

"These boys were well aware they were committing a crime."

He said his first shot missed and the second dropped the boy. He said the

Turn to Page A 4, Column 6

Young Burglary Suspect
Is Shot By Policeman

(Continued from Page One)

range was about 25 feet. The prosecutor ruled the shooting was justifiable.

The boy, of slender build and 5 feet 4 inches tall, was in fair condition in the hospital today. His parents, Willie and Pandora Drake, were at the hospital with him.

DRAKE, 35, A SPRAY PAINTER, and Mrs. Drake both were at work last night. Mrs. Drake is employed in the laundry at Woman's Hospital. Drake said:

"I c o u l d understand if a policeman would shoot a boy in the legs, but why did a grown man have to shoot a boy in the back?"

The Drakes have seven children, aged 5 to 14. The oldest, Mary Louise, was in charge of the children last night. She said Willie left about 7 p. m. saying he was going to spend the night with a friend.

Police arrested four boys, including 13-

year-old twins, in connection with the attempted burglary of the hardware store and sought a fifth youth. One of the arrested boys was 11.

KINCAID

Police were called by a neighbor who saw the boys carrying goods out of the store and stacking it in front of her home at 1134 E. 105th St.

The boys scattered when the police cruiser arrived. One was caught running on South Blvd. Two were found hiding in grass nearby.

Patrolmen Kincaid and Edward Cummins, searching the area, spotted Willie hiding in the garage. He ran through a gap in the rear wall and the shooting followed.

One boy was arrested at home.

The fifth boy being sought is 12.

I was in the hospital for three weeks; my mother said I must have had an angel following me around because it was truly a miracle that I was alive. My court trial was held two months later. The judge knew I wasn't healthy enough for any kind of incarceration, so I was put on juvenile probation. When it was all said and done the juvenile court sided with the Cleveland newspaper article, stating that under the circumstances, the patrolman was justified in trying to kill me; age and the color of my skin had nothing to do with it, the boy was committing a crime.

I never felt like it was personal. I was Black and that's what happened to Black people. Therefore, like every Black person in America, I just accepted racial circumstances to be the norm, like death and taxes.

The Cleveland newspaper lied about my age, making me thirteen years old instead of twelve, figuring perhaps the public would be able to stomach a cop shooting a teenager more than they would a twelve-year-old, but it wouldn't have made any difference if I were six years old.

I was still only twelve years old, but I felt much older and wiser. I still was too young to believe in or conceptualize my mortality. I had changed, the world around me had changed. I felt out of place going to school with people whose worlds seemed to be much smaller and simpler than the world I knew. So, I stopped going to school, and my truancy ended up breaking my probation.

For the first time in my life I started staying away from home. My parent's words had lost all meaning, so I begin living with my older sister Maedean and running the streets. The medical attention I had received was the kind that poor people were given; my bullet wounds were not completely healed before I had to relinquish the hospital bed to a paying customer. The juvenile authorities finally caught up with me for not going to school and sentenced me to a year at Hudson Farm. The timely incarceration would save my life.

I knew guys who would have stars tattooed under their eyes every time they were sentenced. I never understood the stardom of incarceration. I never understood how things like being shot and nearly losing your life were considered a badge of honor. I hated pain and loved freedom the way a person loved air. The pursuit of infamy was never because of peer pressure; death was inconceivable to me only because life seemed to be an infinite experience.

Hudson Farm was the first stop and the first attempt to rehabilitate me. The boys they sent to Hudson were mostly from the Cuyahoga County court system. I remember the orientation instructor telling us that one of Hudson Farm's famous alumni was Bob Hope, and I remember thinking who gives a fuck about Bob Hope. What, were we supposed to be thankful to get punished and locked up by the same damn people who did it to Bob Hope? Fuck Bob Hope.

My parents had lost me to the streets of Cleveland when I was around eight years old. My mother used to say, "I'd rather you be locked up than somewhere dead in the streets." My mother always got what she prayed for. Hudson Farm turned out to be one of the most enjoyable and rewarding experiences of my young life. If it hadn't been for Hudson Farm, I probably would have ended up like what my mother said, somewhere dead in the streets; instead I ended up with a roof over my head, three hot meals, and a warm bed to recover from my wounds. What more could my mother have asked for her child?

To go down in hood infamy is every young thug's dream and I had become a living legend at the age of twelve. Getting shot by the cops certified my young gangster status among my peers simply because not many live to claim their badge. Every time the story was being told about me being shot it grew and grew. I became bigger than life to my young thug peers at Hudson.

Whenever I had my shirt off, my back would draw stares and small crowds wanting to hear about all the bullet marks in my back. At the end of my explanation, I was often told, "Man you supposed to be dead." Or I had to be strong and tough to be able to have survived. This reaction would come from a naïve group who believed all the pellet marks on my back represented a machine gun or separate handgun blast rather than pellets from one shotgun blast.

I never thought about it in terms of me having a certain amount of toughness or narrowly escaping death. Death was not on my radar. I felt the invincibility of youth the way most low-income children felt who went outside to play. I only knew one way to live. On the other hand, I knew I was pushing the envelope, and walked the thin line between being courageous and being a damn fool, that was my choice. But being Black and living dangerously wasn't a choice; it was a way of life, and who I had been all my life.

I took risk other young boys wouldn't imagine ever taking; walking the tight rope was a part of me. Without risk life was boring, it was simply who I was. I should have run away and joined a circus.

In the hood, if your reputation didn't precede you, you didn't exist and if you didn't exist you didn't stand a chance in juvenile lockups.

Hudson Farm turned out to be a Cuyahoga County detention home reunion. I knew just about everybody. When the new boys arrived all the boys lined up in front of their respective cottages to get a look at the new arrivals.

My name was the only name being called out. "Sleepy, what's happening, my man? You need anything?"

"Sleepy, you cool?"

"Sleep, what cottage they are putting you in?"

It felt like I was home. It was highly unusual for me not to see a familiar face when I arrived at any lock-up. I had been a veteran of juvenile detention homes, but I never could get over the nervous feelings when I first arrived at a new facility. Hudson Farm was no different but hearing all the warm greetings put me at ease. The new boys who had arrived with me would notice my popularity and would begin to stick to me like glue. Hudson Farm was on a hill in rural Hudson, Ohio, an "Andy of Mayberry" town on Route 8, south of Cleveland.

If I remember correctly, there were four cottages and each cottage had a maximum of twenty-five boys. For whatever reason, I was assigned to the Washington cottage. The Washington cottage parents were the Kings, an elderly white couple. Mr. King was a chain-smoking, making him grumpy, humpbacked, barrel-chested, mean-ass old man who didn't take any shit from anybody, including the administrative staff. And if Mr. King had to tell a boy something twice, he would swing on the boy for making him repeat what he had said. However, you had to be slow as hell to get hit with one of his slow-ass haymakers. His punches weren't quick at all but every so often he would catch a boy upside the head. On the other hand, Mrs. King was as sweet as can be. She was passive and played the good cop role. The couple was the spitting image of the TV show, All in the Family.

Mr. King had a no-excuse policy for cottage duties. No one could leave the cottage until everyone had finished their job. The cottage was run with military precision; every boy had a job in the cottage and at the very least went to school. Boys like me, with ADHD or who just had a lot of energy to burn, had jobs outside the cottage. I worked on the farm. Every month there was a surprise cottage inspection and the cleanest cottage not only would get to take home the trophy, there would also be an additional prize awarded, such as perhaps allowing the winning cottage to stay up at night. If a cottage won for three months straight, there would be something like tickets to the Hudson Theater. Hudson Farm was always trying to instill manners, morality, and culture into the downtrodden little Black uncivilized boys from the ghettos of Cleveland. The school was heavy in the direction of vocational; we learned how to use our hands in metal and woodshops. I loved the challenge of making something out of a block of wood or a piece of metal, transforming something otherwise useless into something useful.

My most enjoyable time at Hudson Farm was spent as a farm hand. My job was basically feeding the cows and chickens. I did just about everything a farm hand would have to do on a fully functioning farm. What I loved most were those early Saturday mornings when the grass was still wet with the morning dew and the air was redolent with the pungent smell of the animals, listening to their different sounds calling out for food in an animal symphony.

Railroad would get transferred out a few months after I had arrived. He was one of the oldest boys at Hudson Farm by far in 1966, the year I had arrived, perhaps seventeen. Railroad was a bona fide booty bandit. We had known each other during a brief encounter on the streets but mostly by reputation. I had gone to elementary school with his younger brother, Skip. The first time I had dealings with Railroad I was with this older guy named Al. At the time Al and I had just stolen a pitbull puppy and were walking down Hough on our way to Al's house with the puppy. I think I was around nine or ten years old at the time. We happened to run into Railroad mugging a man in broad daylight. The man was pissy drunk but still had enough fight in him to make it difficult for one boy to take his wallet. Railroad asked, or I should say demanded that Al and I help him relieve the man of his wallet, so we did. The drunken man was stumbling and throwing punches in the air, but his efforts were never a threat of harm to us. We were able to duck and dodge his attempts to hit us with ease.

I held the puppy for the most part while Al and Road played "hit the drunken man." When the drunken man turned to face Railroad, Al came behind him and cold-cocked him. When the man turned to face Al, Railroad would cold-cock him. They went back and forth until the man was knocked out cold. I took the man's wallet when he finally stumbled and staggered to the ground.

Anyone who showed a sign of weakness coming into the juvenile system in the '60s became a target for older boys like Railroad. In juvenile lockups in the '60s, you had to be able to fight and you had to have a reputation for being a crazy motherfucker, or veterans of the system like Railroad would make you their girl. I never remember hearing someone calling a boy "gay." Back then gays were called punks or fuck boys.

Technically I was still a virgin when I arrived at Hudson farm. I can't remember the exact month I arrived, but I was thirteen. I wasn't born in a hospital; I was born at home and delivered by a midwife. So, I had never been circumcised. I can't tell you why, but it was too painful for me to jack-off quickly and time was of the essence when jacking off.

Jacking off was the teenage boys' rite of passage. Not being able to jack off at thirteen made me feel like I was stuck in a child's body. Jacking off required a swift rapid-fire up-and-down motion, which for me was too painful because my penis' foreskin was tightly attached to the head. Black dudes called it "jacking off" and white dudes called it "jerking off." No matter what you called it the big fish stories were all the same that was being told in the shower. And I could lie with the best of them. If a boy said, "Mr. King almost caught me. I jacked off three times last night." I would respond with a story like, "Man, that's nothing, I jacked off five times."

You couldn't be dilly-dallying with your pecker all night the way I would have to do because you'd get busted by Mr. King making his rounds. You went to the hole for jacking off but getting busted wasn't as serious as it was embarrassing. Unless they caught you jacking off in the proximity to a white woman. So, you had to be quick.

I remember the exact words the big fat stinking Hudson Farm nurse said when I was being examined by the Hudson Farm's resident doctor and them discovering I hadn't been circumcised, "Damn heathen."

The thing about openly racist people, their words don't have any sting. Therefore, my only concern was finding out "What the fuck was not being circumcised meant?" When I found out I was floored. I wasn't as concerned about the pain, as I was with them reducing the size of my already limited meat. I wasn't about to let them cut a piece of my dick off. I told them I refuse, and the fat bitch threw me in the hole.

The cook whose job it was to feed the boys in the hole heard me crying and asked why I was in the hole. I told her I refused to let them cut my thang. She finally figured out what I meant, and it was hard for her to suppress her mirth. Once she seemed to have gotten herself together and composed herself, she proceeded to explain the Christian belief surrounding the ritual, stating circumcision was nothing more than a sacrifice of "sinful human enjoyment" but her meaning got lost in translation. And I thought she meant I was being punished for jacking off. Once again, she couldn't stop laughing, it was hilarious to her. They released me from the hole and my mother came down and reassured me everything would be alright and signed the medical papers for the operation.

The male foreskin, or prepuce, is supposed to be the principal location of erogenous sensation for males. Removing the prepuce was supposed to have substantially reduced my erogenous sensation but like everything else, it was the opposite for me. The first week it was painful to even urinate but by the second week with the stitches still in, I started what amounted to the slowest jack-off session in the history of jacking off. In the end, the pain was well worth it, *halleluiah! Halleluiah!*

I couldn't keep my hands off my new toy. I was constantly having wet dreams and wondering what it would feel like with a girl. Surely, they knew what would happen when they locked young boys up at the threshold and height of their puberty, with raging testosterone and the absence of the opposite sex. Surely, they knew lust and temptation would constantly challenge the sexual morality of the alpha male against the weaker males. How could they not know?

We all had to take showers together like a herd of cattle. The boys who were passive and afraid would face the shower walls or look at the floor like ostriches with their heads in the ground, intimidated by alpha males who couldn't keep their hands off their newly discovered manhood.

I didn't feel any physical desires for boys. My mind was a desert in that regard. But sometimes my dick would have a mind of its own, and created a mirage or illusion, and when that happened a boy's mouth became a girl's mouth.

There were more boys who would turn themselves into girls, than boys getting raped and forced to be girls. The first thing everybody wanted to know when two boys were caught in a sex act was which boy was doing the giving and which boy was receiving? The unspoken rule was that only the boy who was receiving would be labeled a homosexual, a "punk" and/or "fuck boy."

The administrative authorities never disputed that sexual release was not a normal human function but choosing to be the girl in a sex act, in most cases, was believed to be a personal choice. Therefore, the boy who had chosen to be the girl was punished and ostracized the most. Being openly gay wasn't accepted back in the day.

I learned much later throughout my extensive experience with incarceration, the human animal when caged will act like an animal caged. Depravity consumed him in most cases. I had maintained a clean institutional record at Hudson and became eligible for a home furlough. The furlough was for twenty-four hours; I'd leave for Cleveland Friday evening and would have to return to Hudson Farm Saturday evening. My furlough plans were set up to go over my sister's house. I had just turned fourteen.

Maedean had moved to Cleveland from Chicago because she had stabbed her husband and his girlfriend. It wasn't that she couldn't fight, she'd just rather cut you than waste energy fighting with you. Maedean was a no-bull-shit woman, always politically incorrect, and didn't care whose feelings got hurt. I was thinking the reason Maedean wanted me to come over her house was for me to be able to drink some beer and smoke cigarettes, away from the watchful eyes of my parents. I had no idea she had hooked me up with some pussy. My mother was in on the plan as well. As it turned out, both had concerns about my sexual development, worrying about me becoming gender confused ... liking boys instead of girls, some crazy shit.

So, they had plotted and strategized to make sure I knew what it felt like to be with a woman, before I had to go back to Hudson Farm. "Keep that thang in your pants, boy, you hear what I am saying? I mean it." My mother would always remind me in a whisper at the end of our visits and out of earshot of my father the moment he had left the dining table. I think she found it a bit comforting to know I was all boy and my dick would be looking for expression, if anything. Nonetheless, aggressive or passive, it was still homosexuality in the eyes of my sister, mother, and society at large.

When my mother and I arrived at the house, Maedean and several of her friends were sitting around the kitchen table drinking and playing cards, with Cheshire Cat looks all around. They made me feel like a Thanksgiving turkey. I sensed something was up, and it didn't take long before Maedean confirmed my suspicions by physically manhandling me into her bedroom. The bedroom had a red light in the night lamp. Her bed was made up nice and neat, and sitting at the head of the bed facing the wall was a tall, skinny, short-haired Black chick, smoking a cigarette. It didn't register; I thought she was just another friend of my sister.

When she turned to face me, I noticed she was younger than my sister but much older than me. Her face was pleasant, and she was dressed up neatly. I felt my sister's heavy hand in the small of my back, shoving me past the threshold. Then it hit me, the reason she was there.

I had thought about this moment many nights all the wet

dreams but now that it was happening, I had no clue as to what I was supposed to say or do. I just stood there with my mouth open.

Maedean told the young lady in a demanding tone of voice, "Here he is, now you know what we talked about so don't be messing around."

The words sent nervous shockwaves throughout my entire body. The young woman put out her cigarette, kicked off her shoes, and began to undress. I was still frozen stiff, with my mouth open.

"What's the hell wrong with you, boy, you don't like pussy? You're punking with them boys in that place."

Maedean never had time for beating around the bush, she went straight to the point. When I returned to Hudson from my furlough, I began to itch uncontrollably around my crotch area.

The Washington cottage was put on quarantine locked down due to crabs. I suspected the young woman gave me the crabs. Crabs! What the fuck was that? It left me traumatized and that erased any memory of how it felt to have sex for the first time. Three other boys had come back from their furloughs as well, so it was never established which one of us had been the crab carrier.

I got my final release from Hudson around the summer of 1967. A month or so before I was released, I'd learned how to hot-wire cars from a little white boy who worked in the car shop. I don't remember his name, but this little dude stole a cottage parents' car and took the Andy of Mayberry, Hudson, Ohio police force on a wild chase that ended back up at Hudson Farm. Everybody enjoyed the "Smoky and the Bandit" show and I made it my business to get to know him personally.

The first car I stole was my father's car. My father was a

member of this gospel singer group called the Swanny Nightingales. His group would go on weekend singing engagements and this one time he left, around two in the morning when everyone was fast asleep, I took his keys. I crashed into several parked cars a few streets over, and when I got out and ran, the car was still rolling and running. My mother knew that I had taken the car when the cops knocked on the door looking for my father and told her his car was crashed several blocks over, but she also knew if she'd told him what I did he would have beat me within an inch of my life. Her words not mine.

A month or two later, I stole a blue and white convertible Mustang that I hotwired using a hanger on the solenoid switch. I knew how to steal a car, but I still didn't have a clue how to drive one. But I was determined to learn. I don't remember where I stole the car; all I remember is driving up and down 105th street from St. Clair to Superior, and the car jerking. The clothes hanger solenoid switch connection wasn't good, and it was making the car start and stop. The car finally cut off in front of the Masonic Temple near Garfield Avenue. My hot-wire connection had come loose. I got out, raised the hood, and began tightening up my hotwire when I heard a voice say, "Hey, boy, where'd you get that car from?"

Sitting on the steps of the Masonic Temple were two girls who had witnessed me struggling with the car. They knew this beautiful car didn't belong to my little raggedy ass, so they started fucking with me, yelling, "Hey, boy, that car isn't yours, where'd you steal that car from?" "Is that the police I see coming?"

They were having a ball seeing me sweat and laughing uncontrollably. In order to quiet them down, I dared them to join me in the stolen car for a joy ride. They accepted my challenge without any hesitation and began calling one another names and wrestling for the front seat. The Mustang had bucket seats and neither one was going to get in the back. So, before the cops pulled up on us, I told them they could drive, and I'd get in the back seat.

The loud-mouthed girls' names were Blondell Robertson and Brenda Bell. It was decided that Blondell would drive first and then Brenda. I felt like a player with two girls fighting over me. The fact they were fighting over the car seat was irrelevant.

We rode the Mustang until it ran out of gas. Blondell ended up driving the whole time, while Brenda ended up sitting in the backseat with me, talking the whole time. Everything she said was right and witty to me. Everything I said was right and witty to her. It was clear Brenda and I was falling for each other.

We ended up walking Blondell home first. We talked and laughed, pushed and playfully punched each other. The way two young people's bodies seemed to have the need to do. By the time we reached her door, Brenda and I were in love.

Brenda lived with her mother and two older brothers. Her mother had a male name, Jimmie, the same as my brother's. Her brothers were Sunny and Ray. Ray would be the only family member who wouldn't exploit my affections for Brenda. I became Miss Jimmie Bell's gofer, going to the store and fetching whatever she wanted at her beck and call, and buying her beer with my last dollars. As for Sonny, I was his lame; he'd cheat me every chance he got, playing dice or cards, taking my hard-earned hustling money. Eventually, Brenda would put an end to their exploitation.

You can have sex many times but the first time you have sex might not be the first time you experience the pleasure of it. I experienced sex for the first time with Brenda. She didn't smell like cheap wine and cigarettes; she smelled like flowers, a summer breeze, candy, and excitement. I remember thinking I can do this every day of my life and wonder why people wasted time doing anything else.

Before Brenda, I thought sex was the pleasure of the body. Now, with her as my girlfriend, sex turned out to be the pleasure of the mind and body. I was crazy in love with her, had deep thoughts about her. I became soft for her. Dedicated and committed to her. Emotional about her.

Looking back, I was fourteen going on fifteen. My love was the kind of love that was in the moment and limited to what was then the present. My love was young love, cold and selfish. It was a new love, a confused love … and painful love.

I didn't know that true love would take time, patience, and commitment. I had neither. I didn't know I had to live first to be able to love in the present. Ultimately, I was thankful for Brenda's pussy, whipping me in the summer of 1968 and making that year unforgettable.

A Matter of Black & White

The family moved from 105th street to 115th street off St. Clair in 1966. I was released from Hudson Farm in the latter part of 1967. I began living at both my sisters Maedean and Mary Louise's respective homes on Lynn Drive. When one of them would get fed up with me, I would go down the street and stay a month or two at the other one's apartment. In November of that same year, Carl B. Stokes was sworn in as the fifty-first Mayor of Cleveland and the first Black mayor of a major city. Martin Luther King, Jr. was assassinated the following April 4, in the spring of 1968. I remember believing when it first was being reported, as did a lot of my young street life thug peers, that the death of Martin Luther King Jr. was all a hoax being perpetrated by the white fake news. Until the following day, I walked in my house thinking there was a party, and no one thought to let me know about it. My aunt Bea or someone was crying. My mother was explaining to everyone in the room that her brother was with Martin Luther King Jr. when he was shot and killed. At first, I remember thinking my uncle was killed. I was surprised to find out my uncle, Marrell McCollough, was the cop. He was a CIA agent, but my mother wanted to keep her explanation simple, for simple people.

My uncle was the man kneeling over Dr. King in the iconic

photo as the Civil Rights martyr lay dying on the hotel balcony, with Reverend Jesse Jackson, Andrew Young, and others pointing in the direction of where the assassin had fired. I only saw my Uncle Marrell only once or twice and made a mental note to stay as far away from him as possible, after all, he was a cop and I a criminal.

The young Black folk in the community was being pressured to choose a side. Black nationalism, Black separatist Muslim, or the non-violent pacifism concepts of Martin Luther King Jr. who, like Malcolm X, had been assassinated. There was no middle ground for young Black people. Not taking a side left them vulnerable to the wrath of the radical groups and organizations that were all vying for the mental and political control of the Black community. I was living a thug's life, and all I wanted was to be left the fuck alone. I wasn't a sheep or a martyr. I didn't care who you were or what group you were representing, my motto remained the same: fuck authority, white or Black. Surviving was all that mattered to me but if someone were to ask me to define what survival for me meant I would have not been able to tell them. I was fifteen, and undefined myself.

Even the new Black mayor, Carl Stokes, couldn't keep the city under control. The Black community had enough of the white racist-controlled Cleveland police force, and it all boiled over on the evening of July 23, 1968. The mayor had been in bed with the city's Black Nationalists who were very instrumental in getting the Black votes out that had got him elected. The Black Nationalists had total disdain and no trust whatsoever for the white Cleveland police and the Justice Department. Therefore, the Nationalists appointed themselves judge, jury, and part-time executioner for the Black community.

On July 23, 1968, the Black Nationalists and the Cleveland

police department had a failure to communicate and before the smoked cleared seven people were dead, including three cops. Johnny, a distant cousin on my mother's side of the family, and one of the original members of our Rat Gang, became a member of the Black Nationalists, and was infamously known as Little Armed. My cousin and several other young Nationalist soldiers were convicted for their part in what became known as the "Glenville Shootout" but the man who was held responsible for giving the orders, Fred Armed Evens, was found guilty of the deaths.

Civil rights at its core, to me, was about economic disparities. Therefore, when the Glenville riots erupted, we went directly for the high-priced items in the neighborhood, jewelry stores, pawn-shops, and furniture stores. However, I took more than econom-ic pleasure in looting these types of business for the simple reason these were the types of business that preyed on Black people. They were the types of business that charged usury interest, and when your parents died the loan debt was passed down gener-ations.

I had done a lot of juvenile delinquent damage in the span of six or seven months I had been home from Hudson Farm. I was enjoying my ability to steal cars this time, such as a '62 Buick. It had to be around the days and weeks before the summer break because school was still in session. But I remember it being a beautiful summer day. Whenever I would steal a car, I had to show it off, so I would hit the main streets: 105th, Superior, St. Clair, etc. As soon as I turned the corner on 105th with my nov-ice driving ass, a black and white patrol car pulled right up be-hind me. I saw them in my rearview mirror and casually turned down the next side street. Perhaps I never put on my turn signal, but it did not matter; at fifteen, my head was barely above the seat. The cops hit the corner with me, and I floored the big Buick. I flew down the street and hit the corner of Parkwood with the patrol car right on my ass. I turned the corner and bailed with the car still rolling, bounced up without a scratch and hit a backyard. I looked back over my shoulder at the two white cops and I began to pat myself on the back a bit prematurely for my brilliant escape, taunting and laughing at the white cops.

My self-assurance was short-lived. The one cop took it personally, as he bailed out of the patrol car after me. The chase was on. I had not counted on the cop being young and in better shape than I was. Up until that point all the patrol cops I had encountered were fat or out-of-shape dudes who got tired after running two blocks. But this was a rookie white cop in shape and full of spunk. Again, I couldn't have been no more than fifteen. I was not the fastest guy, but I was an athlete and was confident I would be able to shake the cop because this was my hood and the cop was not familiar with the short cuts. When the cop struggled over the first fence my confidence grew even more and I started talking a little trash.

"Man, you cannot catch me," I shouted over my shoulder. Before I could get the words out of my mouth his first shot hit a tree next to my ear and I realized I had made the same mistake as when the cop shot me in 1965. I had chosen an ideal place to be killed, in a secluded backyard where no one would be a witness to his attempted murder. The over-grown foliage in the backyards gave the cop plenty of cover from the public eye. How could I be so stupid? I belonged to a rare fraternity that experienced firsthand that, nine times out of ten, if there were no witnesses, a white cop would shoot a Black man in the back.

It was déjà vu — his second shot hit the fence I dove over, his third and fourth shots were so close only God knows why I am still alive. The young cop wanted desperately to bag him a little nigga trophy. I learned from an early age that our skin color separates us. And I realized there was too much water under the bridge for things to change or be forgotten in just one hundred years. I didn't waste energy on things out of my control. I accepted the way the white man thought and treated me because I knew that my father, if I were to tell him, would not be able do anything about it. White privilege and prejudice weren't things I thought about daily; it was like the air I had to breathe to stay alive, and it would always remain American as apple pie, baseball, and capitalism. I took white people's position of authority and control of the American universe to be the world they had inherited, the same way I had took the Black man's struggles to try and wrestle equality from his vice ... laborious and futile. So, I rebelled; I became a criminal. I wasn't trying to inherit that Sisyphean shit. Life was too short.

My criminality, I suppose, was born of that innate understanding that if I could not defeat him, the white man, I had no other choice but to learn his wicked ways. However, I cannot remember ever having any deep-seated thoughts of revenge against white people. One would think I would have been an easy recruit for Black hate groups because white cops had tried to kill me many times. White people never were a threat to me, as mostly all they wanted from me was that I recognize their privilege, the same way I recognized the white cops' privilege to kill me.

Up until the 70s, white cops were mostly the Black man's natural enemy. If you were a white police officer, you were taught to kill Black men. I can testify to that fact. More Black men have been killed for petty crimes on American soil than they had been over several wars in faraway lands.

Growing up, my teachers both white and Black made a conscious effort to bury Black history as deep as they could, as ignorance was truly bliss for us little Black kids entering America's public-school system. Slavery was a dirty word that people never uttered aloud. The fairy-tale stories did not have a slave back story. The parents of Alice In Wonderland, Little Bo Peep, and Jack and Jill were pure and innocent and loved Black people. Alice's parents would not think twice if Alice would have grown up and married a Black man ... and lived happily ever after.

When the '60s rolled in with Black consciousness, my generation began to understand and recognize that our Black heritage was not something to be ashamed of, and we let white people know it was cool to be "Black and proud." My generation had the audacity to challenge racism, and I was down with that.

The chase between the cop and me had started on Parkwood Avenue. I hit the backyards, heading east and coming out on Len Drive Avenue. I ran down to the elementary school and circled back around, heading west in the same direction I had come, back toward Parkwood Avenue to lose the cop. But this cop was relentless. The words "black-ass nigger" started off sounding like frustration, but each time the sinister words rolled off the cop's lips, there was no mistaking he meant death. The young cop seemed to become more motivated as the chase intensified. By the time I got back to Parkwood, I was losing steam and started looking for a hiding place. Kids were all around, going to and from in the vicinity of the junior high and elementary schools. I dashed under a porch with the mad cop hot on my trail. I somewhat felt relieved having reached Parkwood and out of the deadly cover of the backyards.

"Bring your ass out from under there, right now," he managed to say while trying to catch his breath. I do not remember my reply, if there was any. I probably was too tired and scared to reply. I do remember hearing the sirens, and the crowd of people who had gathered talking and shouting. The only reason I came from under the porch was due to a Black lady saying, "Come out from under my porch, boy, nobody going to hurt you."

A police officer grabbed a hold of my arm and roughly pulled me out from under the porch and hauled my little ass off to one of the many waiting patrol cars. But this was a different cop. I looked around for Clint Eastwood and he was in the backseat of a patrol car next to me. I thought nothing of it until a white shirt police captain removed him from the backseat of the neighboring patrol car and then I saw he was handcuffed the same as me. I was confused, until I heard the white hat cops talking to the crowd of loquacious Black ladies that had gathered around the police car, pointing at the crazy cop. I was released from juvenile detention back to my parents' custody and was given a date to appear in court, which I was not able to keep.

My father and uncle had gone back down south to rescue their baby brother from Mississippi, closing the final chapter of the sharecropping Drakes' legacy. Unfortunately, not long after he was here, Uncle Thomas was wrongly accused of trying to pick the pocket of a guy in a bar and the guy ended up killing him. The guy hit Uncle Thomas over the head with a big stick. When Uncle Thomas got to the hospital, he went into a coma and two white doctors approached my father and his brother for their little brother's organs, at which point my father and uncle tried to put the two white doctors in a coma.

My uncle died a few weeks later. My grandmother was devastated, as was the whole family. My grandmother demanded that her baby boy's body be brought back to Mississippi to be buried.

In 1967 nothing had changed; everything was just as I remembered; my grandmother still lived in the shack in the middle of the barren cotton field. However, I had no memory of the white man's rules of the southern land, how Black folk could not eat or drink out of the same place as white folks or look a white woman in the eye.

Bruh and I left my grandmother's hot and cramped two-room place with all the relatives and went into the one-horse-town looking for a hamburger. We discovered a nice little cool restaurant with big breezy fans, red-and-white checkered tablecloths, and shiny soda fountains. A perfect place to have a burger and a cold Coke on a hot summer day. We were sitting at the counter enjoying the breeze, waiting for the pretty white girl to come and take our order. I remember exactly what I was wearing that day. I had on a gray suit and some green penny loafer alligators' shoes. I do not remember what Bruh was wearing but we were player sharp. Suddenly it dawned on us that we had been waiting for the girl to take our orders for over half an hour. So, we began to raise our voice in protest when my father burst through the door and grabbed us in a bear hug to his chest as though we were five- and six-year-olds.

At first, my brother and I did not know what to make of my father's unusual behavior until we followed his eyes to the faces of the angry-looking white men who had gathered at the tables behind us. My father began to apologize while dragging us toward the door, speaking to no one how we were raised in the north and did not understand how things were done down in Mississippi. I never saw my father scared of shit, until then. Seeing my father scared took being scared to another level for me. Twelve years had passed since Emmett Till was lynched after being accused of offending a white woman. The men in the back were undeniably the Klan, or just as dangerous as the men who murdered Emmett Till. My father told us later the only reason the white men didn't beat the hell out of us was they weren't sure we weren't undercover FBI agents because of the way we were dressed. They told my father, like one of those old cowboy movies, that they didn't want to see our black asses after sundown. It was a long time before Bruh, and I would cross the Mason Dixon line again.

Several weeks later, with nothing to do, I convinced my thug crew to break into the ward office of a young city councilman named George Forbes on the corner of 115th and St. Clair. We ended up taking a couple of his IBM typewriters. The councilman's office was across the street from a Black Nationalist hangout called Hulls Restaurant. Two Nationalist peons saw us break the councilman's window and threatened to tell, which I am sure they ended up doing. They considered us renegades since we refused any Black Nationalist affiliation and were therefore considered parasites to the Black community. George Forbes wasn't your run-of-the-mill councilman as he had a street reputation and mentality. He was never without his gun and didn't hesitate to use it.

Everybody had warned me not to fuck with Forbes, but I didn't listen. Without thinking, I had stashed the hot IBM typewriters in my parents' garage right before the break of dawn and around the time my father would be coming home from work. I suddenly realized my father would see the typewriters in the garage, so I had to move them before he got home. I didn't have time for a well-thought-out plan, so I decided to move the typewriters across the street in a neighbor's backyard. I knew it would be risky to leave them out in the open, but I would rather lose the typewriters than risk my father's wrath. I had moved two of the typewriters and just as I was running across the street with the last one, a car came speeding down the street and slammed on the brakes just before turning me into roadkill.

I couldn't react. I was literally a deer in headlights caught red-handed, and of all people, the driver turned out to be George Forbes. The councilman leapt out of his car with his gun drawn and arrested me. The Cleveland newspaper would later write, "Councilman takes matter of cleaning up crime in Ward 10 in his own hands" or words to that effect. With several juvenile fugitive courts issuing warrants out for my arrest, the law eventually caught up with me and sent my little bad ass to Boys' Industrial School (BIS) in the fall of 1969. There were institutional levels of juvenile delinquency in Ohio. Hudson Farm was usually reserved for first-time juvenile offenders. BIS was for second timers. There was yet another juvenile institution called Tico Juvenile Correctional, but it was more of a holding place reserved for juveniles in the year of their eighteenth birthday.

Boys' Industrial School was my first introduction to juvenile incarcerated punishment, as opposed to rehabilitation. In BIS, you opened your mouth when you were told to speak. You moved when you were told to move. The average stay at BIS, which was affectively known as the HILL, was only six months. Punishment and pain are a swifter deterrent for most young boys, but not for me. I was released in 1969 and didn't skip a beat. I started going strong with breaking and entering with dudes much older and very experienced in breaking into buildings. Sometimes the job would be as complicated as using the building's construction blueprint to determine how to climb through the HVAC system duct work, or as simple as breaking the front windows in a smash-and-grab.

This time, we were doing a simple smash-and-grab to a high-end man's clothing store. I rounded up several St Clair dudes to hit the store with me. Leslie Perkins (whom we called Jap) and I had checked out the store a few days earlier and while we were casing it, we would turn clothing hangers in one direction so that it would be easier for us to grab a lot of items at once. Everybody would be assigned to a different clothing item. The plan was for Jap and me to grab the suits. White Charlie and Bruh were going after the coats.

The police station was down the street, so we had to get in and out in five minutes tops. We pulled up and I cut the locks on the gate with cable cutters I'd stolen off an Illuminating Company truck. I had an arsenal of tools for breaking into shit. I even had a concrete saw and welding torches. The minute I finished cutting the locks, Jap was busting the store-front glass and jumping through the window. The glass was half an inch thick; the shit can kill you if a piece falls on you. I'd learned my lesson from a similar smash-and-grab sting, where I almost ended up like the dude in the movie Ghost; a piece of glass came down and missed hitting me on the top of my head, instead hitting me in the thigh, missing an artery by a centimeter. So, I waited for a couple of beats to make sure no remaining glass was about to fall. Just as I was about to hit the bend in the store, Jap came flying back around and past me.

It didn't register with me that he was empty-handed. The overnight security guard had leveled the shotgun barrel on Jap's fleeing backside. Two shots exploded back to back, one hit Jap square in the right side of his ass and ripped it off. I was watching this shit while sliding on the marble floor tile directly toward the shooter. I couldn't stop my momentum; all of this was happening in a split-second in slow motion, it seemed. Dude thought I was about to attack him; he didn't realize I couldn't fucking stop sliding toward him. Apparently, it was a double-barreled or some gun with just two shots because he panicked, dropping his shells on the floor trying to reload.

By now I was so close to him I could smell his sweat. He took a round-house swing at me with the butt of the shotgun. I dodged the blow and fell into a rack of clothing; regained my footing, and ran back the way I came. Just as I cleared the store front window, a shot-gun blast rang out. I saw Jap still lying in a big puddle of blood moaning in pain.

I met Jap not long after my family had moved on 105th. One morning, both of us just happened to be stealing from the same store across the street from my apartment. We both were creeping. I just wanted to steal some candy, but Jap was there to hit the till. Till-tapping was another way of saying it, stealing money from the cash register. I forgot about stealing candy and watched him do his thing. When he was done, he threw me a few dollars and said, "Now, buy you some candy."

I followed him like a little stray puppy, creeping and Till-tapping. We became close friends, but now I had no other choice but to leave him bleeding in the gutter. He understood. Jap requested that I come visit him in the hospital. At first, I thought he had requested me because he had some break-out scheme up his sleeve, but I later discovered he just want me to help him get some pussy from his girlfriend Judy Bird. And wanted me to come with her and watch out for them whatever it took for him to fuck her, being that he was handcuffed to the bed and half his left ass cheek was gone. As it turned out, the nurses and doctors, as well as the guard was stationed outside the room didn't mind. I helped Judy hold up her ass in the air above him and they were able to get off. If you were to ask any man what their last request would be before they are shipped off to prison, its pussy, without a doubt.

Jap's near-death made me realize it was time for me to consider keeping the next gun I ran across. I had stolen a lot of guns but never considered keeping one. My hustling was all about finesse and I didn't see the need to carry a heater, until now.

I came across an old rusty "owl head" .32 caliber and hid it in my parents' basement. My father was never without a handgun and hunting rifles in the house, so I felt comfortable holding a gun but had never fired one until I fired the "owl head." The rusty old gun misfired several times and when it did manage to fire it felt like it had exploded in my hand. The bullets were so old you could barely read the label. I got the oil my father used to clean his shotgun and pistol and went to work on the old rusty gun, but no amount of cleaning could save it. The gun never fired again.

Breaking and entering was my main hustle at the time so it didn't take me long to come up with another gun. This time the gun was a brand new .38 snub-nosed revolver still in the box. I remember like it was yesterday because it was the first time I had taken money, jewelry, and a fur coat out of a house. Prior to that, I had taken only guns, TVs, and stereos.

As always, the first place I went to off my hot stuff was the poolrooms on 105th Street. I'd been going in poolrooms since I was around twelve. Normally, young hustlers under the age of eighteen weren't allowed to go into poolrooms, but hot items were good for pool room customer business. Everybody was always looking for action. The Players poolrooms on the corner of 105th and Superior was the first poolrooms I would stop at, but the rack man was a shitty motherfucker who always tried to get my stuff for nothing. And this time I knew my stuff was good, so I took it down to Riley's. All the old hustlers and pool sharks knew me in the two main poolrooms on 105th street, Players and Riley's.

Word travels fast when you sell good shit for pennies on the dollars. Most of the time, I would just drop my hot stuff off to the rack man and come back for my paper a few hours later. All the poolroom rack men loved to see me coming because they knew I didn't have any clue as to how much the items I had stolen had been worth, so their mark-up was like taking candy from a baby. They could throw me a couple of dollars and I wouldn't say a word. This time the rack man informed me that an old gangster who had just gotten out of the penitentiary named Fred Stedman was interested in buying my whole sting and wanted to have a word with me. My antennas were up because normally I never knew who the rack man had sold the stuff to, or how much he sold it for.

As it turned out, Fred was a dark-skinned man with impeccable taste in clothes; he had on a black raw silk suit, a soft cashmere straight button sweater and black tie-up alligator shoes with a shine so deep you would think the shoes were made of patent leather. He told me if his girl liked the stuff, he would buy everything from me. He wanted to meet me because he wanted me to be able to come straight to him whenever I had stuff to sell. At first, I was a bit leery but the more I looked at the old player I realize this was a man who didn't play games.

I got all my stuff from Riley's rack man and left with Fred. His girl was at his store on Wade Park Avenue. I can't remember the car he was driving but it was an old bucket. As he was driving, he asked to see my gun. How he knew I was packing was beyond me but then again what else would you expect from a gangster? I took it out and gave it to him without hesitation. He pulled out his gun from his shoulder holster and gave it to me in a show of mutual trust. His gun was a .38 snub on a .45 revolver frame. The gun was heavy. At this point, I didn't have a bit of experience with guns, but I knew this was a special piece of hardware.

84

The gun wasn't new, but you could easily tell the gun had been taken care of and respected by its owner.

Fred noticed my heightened fascination. He said, "You like that, huh?" I could only reply with a nod. My gun was nothing compared to this work of art. Before he handed my gun back, he took a bullet out of the six-shot revolver and spent the empty bullet-hold to the firing pin. I had no clue what he was doing. He then handed it to back to me. He went on to explain that I should never carry a revolver with the firing pin on a bullet. I replied with, "But that only leaves me with five shots." He gave me an incredulous look and said, "If you have to fire more than five shots, what are you doing?" I asked him what I should do with the extra bullet. He looked at me. "Keep it. You might need it one day."

The old gangster bought everything I had. Once we got through with our business, he took me to his store basement and gave me my first shooting lesson. He let me shoot his gun first. The gun didn't move when I fired it, unlike my gun, which almost jumped out of my little hand. He told me to get a bigger caliber gun, suggesting I get a .45 caliber since I was learning how to use a gun for the very first time. Fred said the reason the army issues .45 caliber automatics was that a .45 caliber is heavy and the heavier the gun the more control you have over accuracy. The worst thing you can do in this game, he said, is kill somebody when all you had to do is shoot them. He handed me his gun to make his point.

I was seventeen when I picked up the heat to hustle with, but fortunate to have met Fred Stedman, who knew the game. Fred had been a mob strong-arm man for the Eastside numbers racket. He didn't know it, but he taught me more in a week than I would have learned in a lifetime about the heat.

The first time he took me in a policy clearing house, my jaw dropped. I'd never seen that much money before. I was sure there was more money in this old house than it had been in the neighborhood bank. I saw a couple old dudes with guns, but to me they didn't represent nearly enough security. Everybody seemed to be too nonchalant with all that money around. What I didn't know at the time was that this money belonged to the mob and whoever tried or succeeded in robbing the place wouldn't live to spend a dime.

I hung out with Fred for about a month or so. Every morning he would take me by a different clearing house on the Eastside. Fred was hoping to make the point that he was open for business. However, Fred's business had gone the way of the stagecoach and dinosaurs. Illegal lotteries were coming to an end around the early 1970s and the mob was in the process of closing and moving all their gambling operation money into legal casinos. What was left of the mob's Black numbers booking territories was being split up among Black politicians and creditable entrepreneurs in the community, entities like the Virgil Brown Money Exchange.

At some point we all become a dinosaur. What I would learn over my years of incarceration after having traveled the same beaten path of the old gangster is that the world doesn't stop for anybody. If a person goes to jail for a year or even six months, shit changes drastically and by the time that person learns how to deal with the change, shit has changed again. The person finds himself constantly chasing change and being behind the eight ball of life.

Milky-man's Baby

My Glenville crew was mostly boys with a certain finesse. When they saw that I was on some gangster shit, they drifted away from me. They wanted nothing to do with me. Committing a crime with a gun and the possibility of doing hard time wasn't part of the script for them.

But I was champing at the bit to move into my new vocation. A street hustler settles into his vocation around the age of sixteen: a thief, pickpocket, pimp, con-man, armed robber, a hitman. I gravitated to the gun game because it brought instant gratification. I had no patience. Not only was the reward immediate but it seemed to offer me the maximum thrill of a rollercoaster ride.

The first place I ever robbed was a bar. I put together a four-man crew. As always, I had hyped the sting up and sold it as a rags-to-riches once-in-a-lifetime chance for whoever had the nerve to join me in the caper. Robbing the bar, I told them, would set us straight for the entire year. However, by the time we got in front of the bar everyone had bailed on me except this one little half-white-looking dude. I had been seeing dude around the neighborhood. He was hard not to notice because of his unique looks. Dude had a lot of European mixed in him, but his Blackness was dominant. He could even be mistaken for Hispanic or one of those dark-skinned Italian dudes who were a descendant of Hannibal. But his appearance aside, when he spoke, you knew he was Black, he sounded like the blackest nigga alive.

Whenever I would run across him, he had a black eye or some battle bruise on his face that manifested his conflict with the world in which he moved and lived. Add to that, Mike constantly had to prove his blackness. He was different. I liked different. I liked the underdog. I like going right when everyone else was turning left. I took a liking to the street fighter.

I was ready to cancel the robbery sting, but dude produced a sawed-off shotgun. And like so many people who first encountered this baby-faced soft-looking dude, I too misjudged him off the rip.

The sawed-off told me dude had balls, but I still wasn't convinced he and I would be able to pull it off by ourselves. I thought to myself he just didn't look intimidating enough. Hopefully, the sawed-off shotgun would be able to command order and make up for his soft features. On the other hand, looking down the barrel of a sawed-off shotgun, often, made people go blind.

Mike jumped on top of the bar and shouted in a voice much blacker and bigger than he looked, "Don't anyone move, and everybody empty your motherfucking pockets on the damn bar."

Dude had that kind of hair that Grand-mama called, "That good kind of hair, that middle ground hair between a Black person and a white person's hair. The kind of hair you could style either way, like a white dude or a Black dude."

Mike's complexion wasn't high yellow as they say in the Black neighborhood when describing a light-skinned Black person whose parents were mixed, white and Black. His complexion was more like the complexion of a Hispanic person. And Mike wasn't a big dude, as he only stood five eight or nine at best. When we met, he was wearing his hair in a big wild afro that seemed to have a mind of its own. I would remind him every so often that he missed his calling and should have gone to Hollywood and became an actor. But he would give me a look as though my suggestion was just another backhanded compliment that he had learned to accept.

We bolted from the bar with a couple of hundreds. I had an empty feeling in my gut after the robbery. Most of the men that were in the bar wore blue work uniforms like my father wore; these were hardworking people. It would be the first and last time I would rob a legitimate establishment.

Mike told me when he was a kid this old Asian lady started calling him "Milky-man's Baby." He said, had he realized what the old bitch was implying, he would have beat the old bitch's ass.

Intriguing was the best word to describe my relationship with Mike. He was different and had a lot of levels but what mattered the most was the fact he was game like me. I hadn't met a dude in the Glenville neighborhood who was game for hustling with a gun, but this dude had the heart of a lion. Although you could not tell it by looking at him.

We started hanging out frequently. All the girls thought he was "cute." Girls who had never said a word to me were suddenly my friend, and where there were girls, or "chicks" as we called them, there was drama. "Chick drama" followed Mike like a big dark rain cloud, and I found myself anxious to see when, where, and on whom the cloud would burst.

Sometimes, Bruh would join us, but Mike and Bruh would end up clashing over something and I would have to step between them. It was always a challenge between them because

Bruh was dark-skinned and Mike was light-skinned. Light-skinned niggas always tried to prove to black-skinned niggas they weren't soft, while black-skinned niggas always tried to prove to light-skinned niggas that they were soft.

All and all, Mike never really allowed anyone to get a good look inside of him, so I kept my distance. He walked around with a chip on his shoulder as big as a log, yet he had no choice. He was different. The way he looked was different. The way people looked at him was different. The way people approached him was different. So, I figured he had no choice but to react differently. I asked Mike point-blank, "What the hell nationality are you? Your daddy white or what?" He realized there was no malice in my words, so he smiled and said, "How the fuck I know. I think the motherfucker is Indian or Italian." He didn't have any hang-ups about his heritage, clearly it didn't matter to him what his bloodline was because he was confident in his Blackness. He owned it, and would invite you to challenge his Blackness, at your own risk.

He didn't give a fuck what others thought about him. I was cool with that, if he could hold his own, and there was no doubt he could. I imagined that he had learned at an early age that his lighter complexion didn't define who he was inside. And that he knew and felt just as Black as the rest of the Black children who stared at him whenever he entered a new classroom or moved to a new street. He learned early on to manipulate people's misperceptions of him to his advantage, in love or war. I would watch people sizing him up. And when that happened, I would watch the joy in his eyes after seeing the surprise on people's faces the moment he had thrown the gauntlet down to defend his Black mantle, emphatically ready to prove he wasn't who they had thought he was.

The day had come when he figured he had to prove his toughness to me. We got into a beef over a pool game in Riley's poolroom. He had no clue that I had ADHD. Hell, I didn't even know it at the time. I had no patience when it came to games, cards, checker, chess, pool, anything that required patience and sequential details. I would suck at it.

Like your normal ADHD-afflicted person, I would do anything to get the activity to move along faster, even if it meant losing. Therefore, I was marked to lose when it came to games of chance. I felt resentment about it when I conceive that people thought I was slow, when I knew I was moving faster than they were.

Sequential steps and inertia irritated the hell out of someone with ADHD and create a painful discomfort. The game or endeavor is usually aborted regardless of the benefits or cost.

ADHD was once described to me as a person with a brand-new Ferrari living in a town with speed limits no higher than 25mph. The person saw all the signs, and understood the consequences of speeding, but they couldn't help but to challenge the powerful car with a heavy foot on the accelerator.

I knew Mike, or anyone for that matter, was going to win any game of chance we would play. In a sense, we were no different, always having to prove ourselves. For Mike, it was his Blackness, and for me, it was mental.

I could not articulate these feelings at the time they were happening. I just thought I was impatient. I didn't know any other way to feel.

Like Mike, who had used people's perception about his physical capacity to his advantage, I had to learn to use people's perceptions about my mental capacity to my benefit. The only way you gain experience in something is to gain experience. Mike fought often, growing up looking like a white boy in a Black boy's world. He lived in a constant state of competition and rivalry. He kept a black eye. But his black eyes were mere advertisements to let people know he was a fighter. I can't remember my exact words, perhaps it had been something like, "Nigger you going to give me my money back." To which he said something like, "We can fight."

I remember his nonchalant, gentlemanly duel approach to us fighting gave me pause, and my anger was replaced with curiosity, cautiousness, and perhaps a subtle fear of the unknown; the way a predator is confronted with a strange animal. On the surface, the animal seemed vulnerable and defenseless, but something tells you to be cautious, take your time and figure out where his threat might come from.

My blood pressure had subsided from that boiling point level where I was about to get physical with him. I supposed Mike took my apprehensiveness for a measure of victory, but I didn't care. I still felt a measure of physical superiority but at the same time I had no doubt it would be a hard-fought scuffle in the alley, and I had not planned for that kind of fight, not at all. So, I pumped the brakes on my emotions and swallowed my pride. I took a picture of the situation and I realized his confidence had stemmed from sizing me up after seeing a love tap fight between my brother and me, and he figured he would be able to take either one of us in a fight. Confidence is a weapon, even if it's misplaced. He had underestimated the fight in us, not realizing we fought ten times harder than we did when the opponent was not a brother. It didn't matter again, the fight still would end up being hard-fought because of his confidence. It wouldn't have mattered if I had whupped his ass; his victory was in the fighting, not whether he won or lost.

I was impressed with how his mind worked. There was a part of me that did not want to lose his friendship. He reminded me of this Irish boy I fought in the detention home. The reason I knew dude was Irish was because when I called him a honkie, he replied by saying he was Irish, not a honkie, "nigga." I thought, what the fuck is the difference?

Everybody said I had won the fight but it sure as hell did not feel like it to me, the Irish dude wouldn't quit. I remember people asking the guard to come over and stop the fight between us. Back then the guards waited until inmates stopped a fight themselves. I promised myself never again would I underestimate someone's ability to fight by the color of their skin. Not that I thought Mike was white, just his willingness to fight at the drop of a dime and his light skin reminded me of the Irish dude.

Like Mike, I remember thinking the little white boy would be just another scared white boy. I thought my threat would be enough to scare Milky-man Baby and he would just hand over my money. But no, this little red nigger was standing in a fighting stance, looking like that hard-fighting motherfucking Irish dude.

At this point in my life, I had decided to let Smith & Wesson handle most of my disputes, especially those where victory was questionable. So, I used some lame excuse to talk my way out of fighting and gave Mike a way out as well. For me, competition for pride was a worthless booty; no thrill of victory had ever measured up to the agony of defeat for me. I did not live for rivalry and winning at all cost was an oxymoron that had zero chance of happening with me. Winning was all that ever mattered, with no cost.

But more than my uncertainty of a physical victory, I was totally intrigued by the way this dude's brain was wired. He was calculating, and thoughtful. I was spontaneous. He was patient, and I was quick and decisive, always in a hurry. We were both like two thieves on the look out for something that we did not have. He was solid, and it was easy to see he had been limited only by his own choices, not his abilities. He wore his flaw on his sleeve, his hair-trigger temper that reminded you of the gangster characters played by actor James Cagney in those old black-and-white movies. If I wasn't into creating my own drama, I would not have minded sitting with a bag of popcorn and watching the "Life and Times of the "Milky-man Baby."

All our girls in the neighborhood couldn't wait to give the Black boy with the good hair and mixed features some pussy. Black and proud wasn't all the way in for young Black girls ... the lighter you were, the prettier you were to them. Mike did not turn down too many girlfriends or wives who wanted to give their pussy away. We all had our share of pussy drama, but it seemed pussy drama was always following Mike around. You would hear stories about him getting caught fucking somebody's wife or girlfriend and him ending up having to fight or shoot his way out of the pussy jam. For the most part, he did not seem to be going after chicks, but it was the other way around.

Anyway, one day, my childhood friend June Morgan, and I were walking with Mike down 105th street when we ran into a chick Mike had been sneaking around and doing. Chick's name was Debra or something. Suddenly, Mike and this girl Debra got deep into a pussy drama argument. It was the classic "she said, he said," and so on and so forth, until out of nowhere the girl pulled out a .22 caliber pistol from her purse, spun and shot Mike point-blank, dead center in his mouth.

She had shoved the gun right in his face as if she were throwing a punch, and it stunned the shit out of me. It was surreal and I could not believe what I had just witnessed.

After we got ourselves together, we halfheartedly lunged at the girl, but nobody was packing a gun, so when she said, "Sleepy, don't make me have to shoot you, too." I stopped in my tracks and threw my hands in the air and said, "Okay, okay." June reacted the same, we both gave the girl all the space she needed to make her quick exit. We immediately turned our attention to our friend who was losing his balance, gagging and bleeding from his mouth profusely. The fact that he was still standing and conscious was a miracle. June and I were able to flag a passing car. It was more of a hijacking than getting the driver's consent, but nevertheless we needed to get Mike to the hospital.

We did not know where the bullet hit him, his head was lolling backwards, and his eyes were closed. He did not look too good … so I told him to open his motherfucking eyes and don't be looking like he was going to fucking die on me. "Do not worry. I am not going to die until I kill that bitch," he said. We dropped him off at the hospital.

As it turned out, the small caliber bullet had lodged in his gums and the doctors removed it successfully. His only concern was his looks and inability to keep his two front teeth. He would survive.

That summer, Mike and I started robbing numbers drop-off spots and drug dealers. Fred, the old numbers gangster, had taught me that sometimes the threat of your gun is all you would need to rob someone. As our reputation grew throughout the city, so did our extortion and protection services.

We took an Eldorado from a young guy whose mother was a big-time whore named Mary Ruffin. It was a big deal to us. Mary's pimp, a dude named Sweet Pie, had hired some muscle to get the car back by any means necessary.

Now, a childhood friend of ours named Ron was shot in his

leg that same summer. Ron escaped to the roof top. He was shot with a .22 caliber, the bullet going past right through his leg. They found Ron on the roof top, where he had bled out from a single shot in the leg. The bullet had severed a main artery.

The hitmen they hired to get the Caddy back from us ambushed Mike as he was walking out of the poolroom. They pumped three bullets in him and left him on the curb to die. Mike had been shot four times that summer and was able to cheat death. Mike was favored.

The Heater

I was leery when it came to trusting people with a gun in their hand when knocking off a sting unless it was my brother or Mike.

Mike could be hot headed, but he was a professional with a gun in his hand. In the gun business, you had to be fully aware of controlling your emotions because you held life and death in your hands, with only a split second to decide. Losing control of your emotions could turn a simple robbery into a murder, with all the consequences that follow.

I had confidence in Mike because his biggest and most uncontrollable emotion was courage. We both agreed to keep our gun business strictly about the paper. I would test Mike just to see how committed he was to the craft and challenge him in a target shooting contest. "Two shots, the closest one to the 'O' in the stop sign would win." "One shot, and the first one shoots out the streetlight wins." We challenged each other to the draw, pulling our guns with speed the way cowboys did in those old Western movies. We became confident in our abilities to be faster and more accurate than our opponent in any situation. We never shot anyone by accident. We were professionals and respected the game. The power of the heater was addictive to us. And it became an unwritten code of ours to not rob legitimate businesses unless the business was used as a front for something illegal.

I was tripping, as they say, and justified robbing as a modern-day Robin Hood, who purged the neighborhood of the numbers bookies and drug dealers who were preying on the innocent hardworking people in the neighborhood.

What difference does it make, whether you are a doctor who saved lives or a criminal? We all feel the need at some point to justify the reasons we do the things we do or did. To have lived or live, is to have purpose, no matter how delusional or insane you were or are.

A disagreement ensued up at Riley's poolroom. The guy who had been in the middle of the argument came back with his crew and Mike found himself smack in the middle of a gun battle. They told me the gun battle lasted a good ten minutes, with bullets flying everywhere. When the dust cleared, one of the guys lay dead on the ground. His gun was still in his hand. Mike was sent along with several of our cohorts to Mansfield Reformatory on a manslaughter rap.

When one of our dudes got killed or went to jail, we never were concerned about perhaps we could be next. We were young and invincible; we were stupid.

Our stick-up-men reputation was growing. That very summer, my brother, June Morgan, and I were ambushed coming out of Prince House, a place where we'd usually hang out. The Robertson brother controlled a lot of illegal actions on 105th Street. Whenever we wanted to sell the drugs or jewelry we had taken in a robbery, Prince would act as our fence. Prince was the oldest of the brothers, Shorty, Bird, and Randolph. Whoever ordered the hit did their homework because they had us dead to rights, they knew we would be high as hell after we left the Prince spot. At the time, we drove a '66 blue-on-blue Buick Electra 225.

Bruh had nodded off in the back seat and had never come up

stairs. June Morgan loved the Robertson brothers and Prince was his favorite so June would always stop through just to holla. We were not in the house for a long time. I was driving, and as soon as we got in the car, which was a four-door, suddenly we were flanked by two hit men, who materialized out of the darkness on both sides of the front car doors, carrying automatic carbines. The front door windows and windshield glass disappeared in a hail of gun fire. Only the grace of God kept us alive. All three of us were strapped. My gun of choice was the snub-nosed .38. I cannot remember what June was packing at the time, but it did not matter because our guns were useless. The only thing we could do was duck and pray. However, my brother Bruh carried two .45 autos. I used to think he was being a bit dramatic, until that moment.

Fortunately for us the hit man did not see Bruh in the back-seat, because his nod had turned into a full-fledgedlay-down-in-the-backseat. Long story short, Bruh rose and got both hit men from on top of us, his two guns blazing. Nothing gets order faster than the sound of a .45 cal. Moments after the hitmen had left, June and I still could not move. Perhaps we had gone into shock. Nevertheless, Bruh had bolted from the backseat and continued shooting." "If you niggers aren't dead, you'll better get the hell out of that car, now!"

It could have been any number of dope boys or numbers bookie people who were responsible for ordering the hit. I never found out but the rumor circulating throughout the hood that summer was that several drug boys had anteed up together to send a message.

With my partner doing a stretch, I became a solo robbery act but eventually hooked up with a few Hough cats named Skip King, Lorenzo Conway, and Wayne Talbert from St. Clair to knock off a dope house.

The sting was simple. I had set up the play with an order to purchase three ounces of heroin. Conway did not have a gun, so I had to get him one. Skip King was never without his heater, and Wayne would play the role of the junkie drug tester. Wayne Talbert was a boss hustler. Wayne was dragging, nevertheless he was thirsty to play the role because he had caught a gorilla-size heroin habit.

I ended up getting a 380 Beretta from my sister Maedean's boyfriend. Conway did not want to use the 380 so I gave him my .38 snub and I took the unfamiliar Beretta 380. I would learn that if a guy did not have his own gun for a robbery sting, he did not need to be there.

We arrived at the house and I immediately told the shake-down door man that everybody with me is packing heat except my drug tester, and that our guns could not be compromised. This was not an unusual demand, as it kept everything real when you were being upfront about protecting your cash and your personal safety. These dope boys were professional. They made a few security adjustments in the house and told us it was cool for us to come in packing our heaters if everybody kept their hands in plain view. We agreed and they let us in.

I had put together a Michigan bankroll: two hundred dollars were made to look like at least ten thousand dollars. The door man led the four of us to a nice-size dining room with a big table in the center of the room. On top of the table was approximately a pound of China White. I could not believe my good fortune. I could hardly restrain myself from upping pipe right then and there, but my instinct told me to search for the security adjustments that the doorman had mentioned. A man with a carbine rifle with what had to be a sixty-round clip attached was standing in the bedroom door off to the side. He wanted us to know he was there. My crew was situated on one side of the table and the dope boys on the other side. The heroin was advertised to take a strong six-cut.

Wayne was enjoying his role. I could not tell whether he was drooling at the mouth for real or fake when he suggested he wanted to straight-line a McDonald's spoon of the dope with just a three-cut. Still playing the dope fiend, it was Wayne's belief that the drugs boys were hyping their drugs. To play it safe, I suggested he snort a three-cut. If he overdosed, I was thinking, everything would be fucked up. Sticking to his role, bragging about the quality and quantity of dope he had had before, trying unsuccessfully to convince me he would be able to handle main lining a three-cut, Wayne finally snapped back to the task at hand. I looked around the table at my crew and they were sweating bullets and shaking like drug store craps. Whenever I was able to make eye contact with one of them, he would shake off the play, suggesting that it was too risky, their eyes begging for me not to try anything. In my mind I was thinking these fake ass gangsters, pissing in their damn pants.

There is a thin line between confidence and courage, and stupidity. I was determined to cross that line that day, and no one would be able to stop me otherwise. I rationalized the only way to pull it off would be to grab the main guy as a hostage and force the peons to put down their weapons. Grabbing the hostage would be the hard part since he was on the opposite side of the table. The conversation was light and tense. Good for us that Wayne had a gift of gab and was able to cut through some of the thick tension in the room. The main dude was packing what is known as a 38-lemon squeezer tucked in the waistband of his tightly knit pants. I took note that he was right-handed.

My plan was to tie up his gun hand with another introduction handshake. "What's your name again?" as I extended my hand across the table to him. As soon as he made contact, I pulled him across the table and use my left hand to dip for my heater and pressed the gun flush to his temple all in one motion. "Don't no-body fucking blink," I said calmly. The move took everyone by surprise, including my shaky ass crew. "Don't anyone fucking move!" I repeated. The sniper in the bedroom came all the way out shaking and pointing the carbine rifle back and forth from me to my crew, who began to duck and scramble, expecting shots to be fired soon. "Everybody just relax," I said. The carbine guy began hyperventilating, asking the dude who I had hostage what he wanted him to do. I answered the question for him, "Drop that fucking rifle, now! Or your friend loses his motherfucking brains." The carbine dude decided his best option was to retreat back to the cover of the bedroom, repeatedly asking his partners what should he do, nervously training the menacing rifle sights back and forth in the direction of me and my crew, who by the way were still at the table with raised arms and their hands trying to touch the ceiling, begging carbine dude to take it easy and not to shoot them, giving me a sure sign of who they thought was in control of the situation.

Wayne left no doubt who he thought was in control as he drove headfirst out the living room window as soon as I grabbed the dude. Shit was tight but there was not any need to panic. I was clear Wayne had disagreed.

I was never nervous during a sting because my actions were always quicker than my emotional evaluation. In other words, I never had time to feel nervousness.

The standoff seemed like it had gone on for an hour when in fact it was only a few seconds. You could hear everybody's nerv-ous breathing. Skip moonwalked toward Wayne's self-made exit.

Conway, shaking so hard from the threats from the guys with carbine, dropped his heater on the floor but regained some sense of self-preservation and dove on the floor to retrieve it. The drug dealer at the far end of the table put his heater to Conway's temple the same way I had done his partner. Everybody is shouting, pleading, and making threats but no one is complying with anyone's demands. Aside from the two hostages, no one had a clear shot in the crowded room. I came around the table and got tight to the body of my human shield and danced with him cheek to cheek to the living room, threatening him to let my hand go before I blow his brains all over this fucking house!

No shots were fired at this point. Everyone seemed to be aware that as soon as the first shot was fired death would surely follow. It was the first Mexican standoff I had ever been a part of, and hoped would never again. I was sure my hostage could see the fear in my eyes, just as sure as I could smell the fear seeping from his body. The cold steel pressed to his temple must have finally persuaded him to relax his grip on my hand as he continued to say in a nervous tone of voice, "Okay, take it easy. Alright, man, take it easy ... you can have the dope." The second he released my hand I pulled his gun out of his waistband and he bolted for the kitchen covering the back of his head waiting to hear the sound of my gun ... and the feel of the bullet splitting his dome open.

I was too concerned for my own safety ducking in the nick of time from several carbine bullets whispering a fraction of an inch past my ear. I dove on the floor returning fire in the direction of the bedroom. Dude for some reason decided not to put a bullet in Conway's ear but instead shot him in the abdomen and hip and dashed for the cover of the bedroom with his partners. Conway fell to the floor screaming like a scared cat pleading not to be killed. It was total mayhem in the house. Never raising my head, I fired in the direction of the bedroom and immediately felt the return heat of the carbine bullets whizzing through the paper-thin dry walls that separated the living room from the dining room, and the first bedroom. If I rose, I would surely be hit by one of them bullets. I fired again to let them know that life and death was a two-way street.

I remember seeing those tight gun battles in movies and TV shows where four or five guys were in an apartment or house gun battle, bullets ripping through the walls and nobody gets hit, and thought to myself, that was some bullshit, nobody can survive with all that lead going through those paper-thin walls. Well, I am a living witness that probability will not determine when it is your time to die or live, trust me. I had a friend named Dennis who got hit five times and three or more of the bullets were head shots: he walked out of the hospital. When it is your time to go, God will let you know. I felt a bullet bounce off my head like a flat rock skimming across a still pond. Another man dies, another man lives ... their purpose is simply not the same. I kept them honest with return fire, but I only had two bullets left. I emptied the automatic. I thought about Fred the old gangster and was thankful there had been a full round of bullets in the revolver I had taken from the dope man.

The silence was broken when Conway started begging for his life again. I was bleeding profusely from my head, running down my face. I did not think I was fatally shot but the blood was a reminder that I only had a few more seconds to control my own destiny. The carbine sniper was growing more confident with every shot. But I was keeping his ass locked down as well. I figured they were firing their weapons while lying on the floor because most of the bullets were in the middle or high on the walls. But it was still too risky for me to make a dash for the living room window where Wayne had made his escape. The window was in clear view of the bedroom's line of fire.

"Okay, let my dude go," I said, "and I'll come out." There was no reply, but I heard mumbling and whispers. I shouted, "The police are coming, we all are going to jail. Don't think for one minute your neighbors didn't call the police after hearing all this gun-fire!"

That got their attention. "Okay, throw your gun out and come out with your hands up." I said we probably got five minutes before this street will be full of cops. They knew I was telling the truth. It was the early '70s and gun fire was still common in the hood, but we had been firing for at least five minutes, which was a long time for a gun fight. Silence. "Just let me get my partner and we're out of here. I am coming out, but if you kill us just remember my two dudes who left are going to tell the cops who killed us."

I came out with one hand up and kept the other hand on the 380 Beretta; my survival instinct just would not let me drop the gun. The carbine guy suddenly found some balls and told me to drop my gun in a voice I did not hear before. So, I dropped my gun. They took a few minutes before throwing us out the back door. We looked and felt like two pigs who had been lucky enough to escape from the slaughterhouse, covered in blood. I managed to carry Conway about three houses from where we were. I heard the cop's sirens in the distance and laid him on the ground and told him to tell the cops somebody shot and robbed him. His wounds were not life threatening; he was going to survive but he was in a lot of pain.

I told myself it was time for me to chill out and stop dancing with death.

Values and Principles

Brenda and I had a baby girl and named her Elisha. A beautiful, big-eyed bundle of joy born on July 7, 1970. Like most young Black people who brought a child into this world before they were even financially stable adults, we fucked up. We knew nothing about being parents. Hell, we knew nothing about ourselves. Brenda had a mental health problem and battled depression daily. Some days I would have to literally stop her from pulling her hair out. As for myself, well I had a behavioral disorder called attention-deficit hyperactivity. We both decided to self-medicate ourselves, dropping out of school and succumbing to the evil lure of the street life.

We loved our baby girl more than two young people who made a mistake and brought a child into a world could ever love anything. We told ourselves we wanted a child, but we were ignorant of parenthood, we knew nothing about the challenges of being parents. I was still a child myself, and Brenda, she was overwhelmed.

Responsibility, hell, I doubt if I could spell the word at the time. My commitment to fatherhood was a function of my economic stability at any given time. Sacrifice to me was another name for punishment. I thought life was a function of how much fun you could squeeze into a twenty-four-hour day.

My father was always tired; all he did was sleep and work. His life seemed hard, like punishment. I was determined to go in the opposite direction. I was not about to become a hamster on the white man's treadmill. I became a parent like my father, but I remained who I had always been: a man-child who kept doing stupid, irresponsible things and relying on all the adults in the room to take care of my mistakes.

Practicing safe sex was not a conversation a young thug like me was trying to have. My daughter Elisha was barely past her first birthday before I would meet Denise and she would become pregnant with my son Lamar. By then I was eighteen, but nothing would change. I neither had the time nor the mental space for the drama that two baby mamas brought to me.

My children were a blessing. I loved being a father, but fatherhood was a mistake. Baby mamas were a mistake. So, I kept doing what irresponsible young thugs did. Which was nothing. I had no patience for drama. I wanted everything instant, including my relationship and the loves of my life.

The streets demanded that I be a different kind of man, with a different kind of understanding, values, and principles about women. Every woman or girlfriend I met would not be virtuous. And I struggled with that fact. I was like every young person who falls in love for the very first time, becoming a fool for love. But I would soon find out that it takes a fool to learn that love don't love nobody. Love was selfish and personal, so I stopped being a fool. I had become a man and like all men, I was hypocritical when it came to a relationship with women. It made no difference if I had the moral mentality of a caveman. I demanded a virtuous woman, and since that was impossible, I had to treat all of them likewise.

I had to face the fact that it was a different script than what my father had used … his script would not play right in the world I had chosen. I had to force myself to stop being emotionally invested in the women in my life. Often you can tell what type a man a boy will become by the girlfriends he chose and the girlfriends that choose him.

She was a booster, which is another name for thief. The best apparel boosters were always the fat girls. Apparel boosters did not grow on trees, but a young street player was always turning out a young fat girl who was dying for emotional attention.

Margie was different. She was self-made and a rare find. I met Margie through Blondell, my brother's girl. Blondell and Brenda, my baby's mama, was not on speaking terms. They had fallen out with each other as they would often do. Brenda and Blondell were gangster hood chicks who specialized in the Murphy. There was nothing Brenda and Blondell wouldn't do to trick a lame out of his paper. They were the original ride-and-die chicks in the hood.

Brenda was not good at boosting. She was more comfortable using her womanly persuasive nature to get her advantage. On the other hand, Blondell was more of an in-your-face roughhouse chick and was better than an average booster. Introducing me to Margie was Blondell's way of getting back at Brenda.

Margie was thick but pleasing to the eyes. Her curves were well-proportioned to the rest of her body. She did not have fat ankles or a triple chin. Her ass was big and round. She had a pretty face, nice legs, and natural long hair. She was fine for a big chick and she knew it. She displayed no semblance of lack of self-esteem.

And she was a bitch most of the time, had a fucked-up personality and a mean streak. She threw her weight around and bullied her little crew of whores and talked fly to dudes. I always had a thing for brash women like Margie. I suppose I like the fact that they usually would be game for just about any hustle.

Blondell and Margie were trying to sell a car full of men's suits at the poolroom and I was like a hound dog picking up the scent of a fox. I was no different than any other young hustler, fresh threads was everything to us, and knocking off a booster who would be able to make that happen: game on.

Even though the competition between dudes was furious for a good thief, dudes were not trying to fuck with Margie because the big bitch had a nasty attitude and would let dudes know off the rip that she was not down with giving her shit to a nigga. I knew it was her intention to knock me off, but she wanted to play by her rules. I was a challenge to her. Blondell had told her who I was, so I was the ideal example to show her crew how the game really was supposed to be played.

Margie knew her talents were in high demand and she used it to her advantage. During our cat-and-mouse chase she asked me flat out, "Why should I give a nigger my money and steal for him? Do I look stupid?" She went on to say if I could answer that question, she would gladly give me all her money. Of course, I had nothing to clap back with. I was not that dude with suave witty lines at the ready that would make girls drop their pants. It was rare that I would engage a chick in a cat-and-mouse game, as I didn't have the patience. Plus, I was a bit chauvinistic when it came to women. As the son of a sharecropper who kept his woman barefoot and pregnant, I had that "do as I say, woman, and no-back-talk" mentality.

I could not answer the question and she knew it. She was full of herself. She wore a perm and threw back her hair out of her face like a white girl. I remember thinking her hair must be a wig only to discover that it was not. She had big boobs, a big round ass, and a small waist. She hung around whores and thieves but had a condescending air toward them. "Stupid bitches" were words she used often. She let everyone know that it was her belief that bitches were stupid for giving their hard-earned money to a pimp or player.

During our cat and mouse, we would often meet at a bar. She would have had several drinks. I would be razor sharp and she would show me off to her whore and booster friends. I was snorting heroin, but Margie used cocaine which was considered a "big time" drug back in the day. I would end up staying the night at her place. I played this dog-chase-the-cat game with her for weeks. She was waiting on me to turn in my player card and be her boyfriend, and I was content on playing the waiting game in hopes that she would see the light and become my boosting whore.

Then one day, the question was answered for me by an old childhood friend. Margie and I were sitting in the Brougham Lounge. She had had a few drinks and was giving her crew a few choice words. There was this one little Twiggy-looking whore that hung around Margie that she was overly protective of. Perhaps she and the little whore had a lesbian love affair or whatever. Anyway, in walks Tweedy Bird fresh out the joint. I had not seen him in years and no one in the bar knew who he was, or if they had heard of him no one had recognized him with the fresh penitentiary look.

Tweedy Bird had his sights on Margie's little friend the moment he walked in the bar. I called him over and offered to buy him a drink and after I gave him the "get down for what you know" sign, he immediately started putting game down on Margie's little friend. It was clear the little chick was looking for action. She was nice, high yellow complexion with a boy's haircut. She was advertising, wearing a sizzler mini skirt that came with the matching panties that had become fashionable that summer for the bad girls.

Margie began ear hustling and running her big mouth, dipping and whore blocking, playing the mother hen role, and parked her big ass all in Tweedy Bird's business. After a while Margie began to speak for her friend and telling Tweedy Bird what the little whore did and did not want to hear. Tweedy Bird asked me if Margie and her little friend were my whore and of course Margie took offense to being called my whore. She began talking about how she was not one of these stupid bitches who give a nigger her money, etc.

It was then I decided to sit back and watch the drama unfold. I assured Bird she was not with me and tried again to head off the train wreck that Margie was heading into, but she would not calm down. Once Tweedy Bird was assured that the little chick was not with me, Margie's ass-kicking was a foregone conclusion.

The barmaid told us to take our shit outside the bar. Bird's only objective was to knock off the little independent whore, and from where I stood the little chick was giving him signals, so the player tried one last time to sidestep Margie with his words directed explicitly at her friend. The last straw was when Margie stepped between them, and physically bumped Tweedy Bird.

Long story short, he went Sugar Ray Leonard on the big-mouthed bitch, formally known as Margie. He beat her big ass good and slow, purposely carrying her in the first five minutes of the one-sided fight and enjoying every minute of his work, breaking her ribs and her jaw in the process.

When Margie realized her mouth had signed a check that her ass could not cash, it was too late. Her eyes searched the crowd for someone to help her; our eyes locked, and in that moment she knew I had answered her question. That was the last thing she would remember prior to her lights being turned off. I scraped the big pissy bitch off the curb and took her to the hospital where she would remain for weeks. Ironically, when she did leave, her big mouth was wired shut. The only thing she could eat was humble pie and she had to suck that through a straw.

The day I picked her up from the hospital I bought her a dozen roses. We never made an official announcement that she was my booster, but the money she started giving me was much more than what it had been. No doubt about it the ass whupping changed things and humbled her street game, but it did not break her feisty spirits. She flat-out told me that if she had to steal and give me money, we could not be together. I admired her for her will; as mentioned, I really liked strong-minded chicks. Margie was strong. But eventually, she ended up leaving the game for the comforting arms of the church. I never saw or heard from her again.

Patience

I never like waiting on other people to give me anything. I had no patience, always a restless soul. I wanted everything now not an hour from now, or tomorrow, but right now. The hell with delayed gratification. So once again I had to pick up an old friend and ride with him, Mr. Smith & Wesson.

I started knocking off small drug dealers and numbers bookies drop spots. During this period, I became a lone wolf. I had lost confidence in everyone but myself. I never liked robbing with my brother because it compromised my ability to do my job. I worried about his health and I suppose he felt the same way as I did. Perhaps in the back of our minds both of us did not want our parents to lose a son to a bullet or a life on death row. When and if I needed another gun for a job, I would round up some young thugs in the hood that were trying to make a name for themselves. Young up-and-coming stick-up dudes would do anything for a chance to go on a sting with me. But getting the right young dudes was not easy.

I needed dudes who would be willing to take orders ... and do exactly as I said without deviation, because my life would depend on it. And above all, they had to be able to keep their mouths shut.

I had mapped out the strategy for a dope sting. I drilled my little crew for a week on the details like an army sergeant and demanded they followed my orders to the letter or else they couldn't be a part of my sting. I'd promised myself never again would I attempt a stick-up without everyone knowing exactly what their role would be. Again, I always had to be in control of the situation, which meant everyone did what I instructed them to do without hesitation.

For this sting I needed two guys, but it turned out it was hard finding anyone who wanted to fuck with this dope spot. Everyone I tried to recruit wanted no part of the sting because they feared the big Black fire-breathing nigga who owned the enterprise. I didn't care how big and tough anyone was supposed to be, because my Smith & Wesson made every man a midget once I had the drop.

I'd been casing this big Black dude's dope spot that was disguised as a shoeshine stand business for months. The shoeshine stand was in the front parlor and he did his dope business in the back room. There was never anyone getting a shine and sitting around playing checkers or chess like there would be in a normal shoe-shine business. The place was quiet, which meant everybody in the hood knew what was being sold in the place of business.

On the day while I was casing the joint, I played like I was this guy with a hot date desperately in need of someone to clean my shoes off. I was wearing a white suit with little red, blue, and orange specks in the fabric. My shoe was blue and white. I was razor sharp. I had purposely put a black smidge on my white shoes.

When I opened the door a bell at the top of the door began to ring, signaling to the big black monster in the back parlor that someone had entered his spot. He stuck his big black face through the curtain to see who had entered his establishment. I nodded and went and sat down in the shoeshine chair. After several minutes passed by without anyone coming out from the back, I began to put on the impatient customer act, shouting, "What do a nigga have to do to get some damn service out here, damn!"

Big Black was a heroin dealer. He sold the best Mexican Mud outside of Chicago and didn't sell anything under an ounce. Moreover, he rarely sold his product to anyone living in Cleveland. Every car I had seen in front of his fake shoe joint had out-of-state license plates. Therefore, it wasn't close as to which customer was more important for him to wait on. Finally, he got tired of my five-dollar mouth and stormed from the back parlor and decided to put an end to the "fake shoeshine business owner, customer always right" charade.

"Get the fuck out of here, motherfucker."

I played dumb, looking around as though he was talking to someone else in the room. "Who me? I didn't mean any harm. All I want is for someone to wipe the dirt off," I said as I lifted my shoe to his face. He smacked my shoe out of his face. At this point smoke is coming out of dude's nose. "I tell you what, I'll wipe off the black smidge, just give me a clean rag."

The two dudes who had been doing business with him in the back parlor found this exchange humorous, which served to make him that much more agitated. Big Black was an ugly motherfucker. He was the dude who never had a chance with the pretty girl until he got some money. I represented that player who would never give him that chance.

Big Black smacked my feet out of his face. "Motherfucker, if I have to tell you one more motherfucking time to get the fuck out here, you'll wish you never came in here."

I scrambled off the shoeshine stand as though I was scared

stiff and left in a flash. You never wanted to make a sting personal, but I couldn't wait to see Big Black's ugly motherfucking face at the end of my Smith & Wesson.

That following Saturday, I ran across two young thugs my age at the poolroom who had no clue about his spot and infamous Big Black reputation, so they were more than game for a dope house robbery sting. My instructions to them were simple: one of them was to hold the doorbell and the other would get the money and drugs after I got the drop.

When we arrived at the fake shoeshine business, there were several cars out front, all with out-of-state plates. The bell above the door was literally a doorbell. I had placed a couple of bread crates for my dude to stand on to be able to reach the doorbell above the door. He did, and we eased through without making a sound.

Big Black was a big ugly dude, mad at the world for his ugliness. And all his life he had used his physical stature to take his ugliness out on people he had met throughout the drug game. He had a gun, but he never felt he needed a gun to protect himself in a physical confrontation, so he rarely carried it on his person. He knew his looks and reputation intimidated people so I imagined he felt that would be enough to keep static from coming his way.

I decided to use that confidence to get the drop of him. I had heard that Big Black was moving anywhere from ten to twenty thousand dollars of heroin a day, and his only security was a cow bell at the top of his shoeshine parlor door.

Nobody thinks they are that tough, I thought. But apparently, he did. This Big Black nigga had read his own "tough guy" press clipping.

My robbery strategy was simple: walk right in and rob him in broad day light. We each had on a pair of desert boots. Creepers, which are soft-bottomed spongy sole shoes, which didn't make any noise. As instructed, one of my dudes held the bell over the door. I wasted no time making a bee line to the back room, with gun drawn, both hands on the handle grip ready to fire. When I eased through the curtain it took them a moment before anyone noticed I was even in the back room, holding an ugly .45 caliber. Big Black had his back to me, running his mouth and preparing a package for one of his customers. The stunned expression on his audience's faces let him know something was wrong behind him. He turned to see me smiling with the ugly gun.

Robbing a bank or some other legitimate establishment is much different than robbing a dope establishment or a numbers policy house where there is likely to be a gun drawn from the get-go. And the thing you don't want to do is come in shouting like the movie guys do in a bank robbery scene.

In a dope or policy house robbery, the first thing you want to do is take a deep breath and calm your nerves to make sure your gun hand is steady; that's the most important thing. You can't panic, you got to realize and have confidence that the drop rules the moment. You got to have an extraordinary level of confidence in your ability with a heater. If you don't have the confidence, rather than a stickup man, you become a dead stickup man or a dope house killer.

After the botched robbery attempt with the Hough boys I had lost a measure of confidence. Now, if a guy had a gun in his hand and I had the drop, I wasn't sure how I would react. But I was ready to get back up on the horse. To get that edge back, I trained like I had never trained before. I wanted to be the best. When Big Black turned to face me, I said, "The first one who moves will be the first one dead." I let them know all I wanted was the money and drugs, not a lot of dead bodies. And the sooner he made that happen, the sooner we'd be on our merry way.

It immediately registered with Big Black who I was, and he knew any resistance on his part after what he had said to me wouldn't be a wise move. So, he nodded his head in the direction of the dope on the table. After I made everybody empty their pockets and disrobe down to their underwear, I sent my dude to retrieve the three and a half ounces of heroin. Perhaps there were more drugs and money to be had but I couldn't take the chance. I wanted to be in and out in ten minutes flat. I took what was in sight and left.

I followed that robbery up with a poker game stick-up. We had an inside set-up man. The inside connects said it was a high stakes poker game and there would be no less than three stacks on the table at any given time. In 1970 dollars, three grand was a nice sting. I took the same little dudes I had with me that knocked off Big Black. The inside man's job was to leave the back door open and for his efforts we would split the take even with him.

Splitting the take evenly with the inside setup man would have not been a problem, but we barely got five hundred from the game. So, my crew decided not to give the lying mother-fucker shit. There is no room for false information in the stick-up game and our set-up man lied. Lying about the particulars of a sting could literally get someone killed.

The dudes in the poker game we robbed lied as well. If some-one got robbed for two dollars, by the time the news hit the poolrooms and beauty shops it was ten thousand dollars. The person who was robbed always lied about how much was taken from them. But the set-up man must know how much money the sting was worth; in this case, he too had lied. The dudes we stuck up in the poker game said they all was robbed for nothing less than five hundred so when our inside man heard about the money that was supposedly taken from the game, he felt he had been crossed. He knew the money was not on the table, but he was certain it was in the players' pockets.

Weeks passed after the poker game stick-up. I was leaving Riley's Poolroom on 105th Street. It was a hot summer day. I had begun to strap up every day because it just was not safe to go outside without my heater anymore. I was gaining an infamous dope house robbing reputation and raising a lot of stink in the neighborhood. I felt naked leaving the house without my gun, the same way a person would feel without shoes on their feet. On the other hand, sometimes you can have all the fire power in the world and it won't do you a bit of good because as I said before it's all about the drop, which was the case on this particular day.

I was leaving the poolroom and talking to someone over my shoulder. Just as I crossed the threshold heading out the door to the streets, I turned back and came face to face with a double-barreled sawed-off shotgun. Pointing the gun at me was our poker game setup man.

"I told you, Sleepy, I told you I wasn't nobody's motherfucking punk. Your niggas think everybody's a motherfucking punk … "

"Hold it, hold up, wait a minute. What are you talking about? We didn't get anything from that damn game."

But dude did not want to listen to any reasoning on my part. He was full of rage and was trying to summon up the courage to pull the trigger. I began to mentally weigh my options as fast as I could. If I dipped for my gun, he would blow my head off. The dangerous man was the man who was afraid of the man he wanted to kill or was about to. Dude was afraid of me. Therefore, I knew I would be better off pushing the envelope.

"I told you, Sleepy, I was no motherfucking punk, but you didn't listen, did you, motherfucker?"

He wanted to see me beg, but my begging would only elevate his courage. "Wait, wait a minute. Hold up, hold up, motherfuck! They lied to you. We only got five hundred motherfucker dollars from that game, that's on everything I love!"

I reached in my pocket and threw what I had at his feet. The money woke him up from his murderous trance and allowed me to moonwalk farther. Just enough distance to get even with the cars parked on the curb.

A huge crowd of people had gathered. My would-be killer realized the dollar bills on the ground weren't nearly enough. He said, "I don't want that bullshit motherfucker. I am going to kill your ass, nigga!"

As I inched further backwards, I could not take my eyes from the two black holes of the double-barreled sawed-off shotgun. I kept moving backwards, and feeling for the parked cars, only to stumble off the curb between the cars to the ground. Flat on my back I waited for the inevitable. I covered my face and heard two loud gun shots. I felt no pain, assuming the shots were from the sawed-off. I opened my eyes and scurried to my feet and pulled out my gun.

To my surprise, one of the gun shots had been friendly fire coming from across the street. Somebody had shot my would-be killer in his ass, which simultaneously caused him to squeeze the trigger on the sawed-off shotgun. It took me awhile to register what was happening. The only thing that really mattered to me was that my ass was still intact.

I saw my assailant dragging his leg and a girl pulling up in a car. He hobbled to the car and they sped off. My first thought was the police had saved my ass, but that thought was erased immediately when dude called out my name. "Sleep, you cool?" That was how and when I first met G-II, a renegade Nationalist-turned-armed-robber, extortionist, drug house robber, and FBI informant.

I could care less what the streets thought of him. Dude had saved my ass big time and I was indebted. Not too many street thugs could use a gun like G-II. He meant to hit dude in his ass from at least twenty to thirty yards away ... it was broad daylight and there was a street full of witnesses, so killing him was out of the question.

G-II carried an Army issue .45 caliber automatic. The effortless way he commanded his firearm was a thing of beauty, it was as though the gun was a part of his right hand.

Dudes like G-II were products of FBI training. They were used to penetrate the Black radical movements in the 1960s and 1970s. These dudes were double agents who played both sides of the fence and did whatever it took to get the job done, with the license to do it. And when they were no longer needed, like those Vietnam vets that came home from the war only to find their service to their country was no longer needed and devoid of honor. So, they got angry and rebelled.

G-II could not unlearn what he had been trained to do. And I did not hesitate to put his skillset to use regardless of what my infamous peers thought of him. Everybody in the streets knew G-II's undercover status so when guys saw me with G-II they distanced themselves from me. I did not care about what people thought of me as this was a business decision. Dude was a professional and I was tired of bringing fake gangsters to a real gangster fight.

The eastside of Cleveland is geographically small compared to other major big cities when it comes to who was doing what in the crime scene. G-II and I outwore our welcome in the hood quickly. His bridges were on fire and mine was smoking.

That summer, my brother, G-II, me, and several members of our stickup crew were charged with a few drug-related murders. Bruh and I packed our suitcases and headed to Michigan and then on to Chicago. But his baby mama Blondell snitched on us and the fugitive taskforce knocked us two months after we had arrived.

After spending over a year in county jail we would eventually beat the murder rap. When we got out, we headed to Detroit. That would be the last time I would lay eyes on G-II. Some years later, I got the word in the joint that G-II's woman, Kathy, had put two slugs behind his ear while he slept.

Heroin

I ended up selling ten-dollar heroin caps for my uncle Lionel on the streets of Detroit and caught a gorilla-size habit. A heroin habit is like kidnappers holding you hostage inside your own body, and each time you meet their ransom demands, they ask for more money. Their price gets higher and higher and you realize the kidnappers had no intention of ever letting you go free. And like Patty Hearst, you learn to dwell in darkness and no longer cared for the light as you become one with your kidnappers.

You literally turn into a vampire that sucks the life out of your very own soul. But you long for the old you. You call out but there is no reply. You tell yourself somehow someday you will escape. You miss seeing your family, you missed looking forward to the future; you miss making new friends and being open to new things, new challenges, a new start, a new world.

You realize no one is coming to save you, ever. You would have to turn on the lights yourself, and when you do, to your surprise, you find yourself surrounded by a room full of mirrors. And you discover that your kidnappers had departed. It had been years since you had a chance to see yourself in a mirror, so you move closer to get a better look. You notice something very peculiar; something is different about your appearance. I moved closer to the mirror to get a better look, something was sticking out of the top of my head. It was horn.

The first time I used heroin, I began to grow horns and the more I used it or would be around the hideous diabolical drug, the larger my horns grew. Some people call it a monkey that very rapidly turns into a gorilla. I call it what it had been all along; a devil, whose only purpose was to kidnap your soul.

Brenda, my baby's mama, introduced me to the drug. We got fucked up on the bathroom floor. I would learn more about heroin in two weeks in Detroit than I had ever before. The street name for heroin was dog food. The name was right on point because it turned you into a doggish self-serving motherfucker, who did not give a fuck about anybody, not even yourself.

I was making far more money selling ten-dollar heroin caps than my brother made working at Ford. However, it was Bruh's job and his good credit that was the reason he was able to drive off the lot with a brand-new Caddy sedan de Ville. After a couple of months, while sitting and talking about how life was too precious to be wasting your prime years in the white man's factories, Bruh and his friend Pretty Smithy got up from the lunch table, and walked off the job, and never returned.

Turns out, a gold Caddy sedan de Ville and a black nigga with a gold tooth was a magnet for white women looking to be pimped. Bruh was very obliging; he had turned in his job at Ford Motors to become a Motor City pimp. However, he would soon find out that a pimp with only one or two whores is like the man who owned a mom-and-pop corner candy store, and always dreaming of owning a large grocery chain.

Having one or two whores drives pimps crazy. Whores without competition are wives, girlfriends, and baby mama drama. Imagine having two wives, girlfriends, or baby mamas under one roof. It has been my observation having been around pimps and myself a hustler all my life trying to live off one or two whores' asses, you either end up a drug addict or a mental case.

When the pimping goes south, it goes all the way south. Therefore, it was no surprise when Bruh lost both his whores, became a Motor City junkie and the car note was past due on the Caddy. I had paid as many car notes as Bruh, so I considered the Caddy just as much mine as his, so we both were thirstier than two junkyard dogs in August.

The plan was to drop everything we were doing and devote all our time exclusively to the heater. We imported some of our stickup crew from Cleveland, Pretty Smithy the co worker who had quit his Ford Motors' job the day Bruh had would become our intel on the Detroit dope house scene.

The difference between the drug house stickup in Michigan and the ones in Ohio was that everything was more abundant, including the level of fire-power. But it never was about trying to match the fire-power in a dope house sting. Professional robbery was all about the art of the drop and in which case it didn't make any difference if you took a knife, to a gun-fight.

We went on a wild, wild West stick-up rampage throughout Detroit. Somewhere down the road the drugs we were taking became just as important to us, if not more, than the money. I had long abandoned those romantic, idealistic thoughts that allowed my consciousness to justify my addiction, telling myself it was about the paper and not the drugs, and that I was doing a service to society by robbing drug dealers and numbers houses. My self-serving justification no longer carried water. I had lost all humanity; heroin replaced the blood flowing through my veins like a self-pleasuring orgasm that elevated my sociopathic behavior to new highs.

Bruh and I had gotten used to the horns that had sprouted from our heads, and that was who we would become from that period on. Motor City drugs were on a whole different level than Cleveland drugs.

I had met this young woman and she told me her cousin sold a little heroin and a lot of weed. We did not know this at the time, but this cousin had figured out a way to extract the THC from the weed plant and sold the derivative in a white powder that hit like cocaine. We agreed that I would be the driver because of my connection with the girl.

I dropped Bruh and Lester off in the front of the building. The game plan was for Bruh and Lester to use my girlfriend's name to gain entry. As soon as I found a parking spot and started walking toward the building, I heard gun-shots. The building had about eight apartments and it seemed like every window was throwing led out of it.

Bruh and Lester were pinned down inside the hallway. Had I not provided cover they would have been sitting ducks. I sent the would-be snipers scurrying back inside their windows.

Bruh was the last one to clear the building, and as we were running back to the car, he told me he thought he got hit. I asked where. He said in his head. Mind you, he never stopped running. Surely, I must have heard him wrong; he could not have said he was shot in the head. I took a quick glance over and did not see any blood anywhere and his gait was not that of a man who have just been shot in his dome.

"Where?" I asked just to make sure I heard him right.

"My head."

Bruh and Lester had each a shopping bag full of drugs. We jumped in the car and sped off. Bruh reiterated that he had been shot in the head and was getting a bit irritated that no one was taking him seriously.

There wasn't any blood streaming down his face. We all felt that he had to be mistaken because what he was saying was impossible, for a person to get shot in the head and still be conscious, if not dying.

Nonetheless, Bruh was adamant that he had been shot in his head. I could not see his dome from the type of hair style he was wearing. It was what they called the "perm look," best known from the character in the Super Fly movie. So, I reached over as I drove and began feeling around in the top of his head and sure enough his head was bleeding a little. I told him "I think you got grazed." He said, "No way! Uh uh man, I feel something up there."

We got to our apartment and headed straight to the bathroom where the light was much brighter and sure enough a bullet had penetrated his skull and was stuck in the top of his head. I could not believe my eyes. I got some rubbing alcohol and a small kitchen knife and dug out what turned out to be a .32 caliber bullet in the top of his dome. Shit was unbelievable.

To make things worse, we all thought the THC was cocaine but realized it was not. However, Bruh was convinced it was cocaine and kept snorting, sliding into a psychedelic bad trip. Everybody kept saying, as a figure of speech, people who get shot in the head were supposed to die. Tripping on the THC, Bruh thought he was dead. He tripped for over a two- or three-week span. I was scared he would ever regain his mental capacity again. All he did all day was set around the apartment with a blank look, he was a no-show for anything. Lester had gone back to Cleveland. Detroit and self-acclaimed Pretty Smithy kept bugging me to get in on the robbery action. He had a sting. The way

Pretty Smithy described it, the sting was a piece of cake. All we would have to do was knock on the door and they would let us in. The dope house was not in Detroit but in Flint and was supposed to have the best bag in Flint.

We arrived at the spot with no problem. Knocks on the door and dude opened it. Pretty Smithy shot dude point blank. I was behind the action, so I did not see the reason why Smithy felt the need to waste him from the jump. In that split second, I was thankful Smithy did not hesitate. I was thinking the guy must have tried to pull a gun or something.

The bullet hit the dude high in the right shoulder. Dude hit the floor, thrashing around, holding his shoulder and kicking his feet like he was riding a bike, screaming at the top of his lungs.

I let Smithy finish handling dude. I immediately stepped past Smithy, locked and loaded, scanning the room and ready to fire. Leaping off the coach with their hands in the air doing jumping jacks were a young man and woman neither one had a weapon both screaming like little girls watching a horror movie scene. The room was in total chaos. I was trying to calm the girl and her dude down, asking them where the money and drugs were and trying to reassure them, under the circumstance, that nobody was going to get hurt if they cooperated. After a few minutes they realized dude on the floor was not about to die. Smithy and I finally were able to get everybody calmed down and under control.

We had to move fast because chances were someone in the apartments next door had heard the gun-shots. Lucky for us gun fire was not unusual, so no one in the building was in a hurry to call the cops; we had time. We ended up getting a couple of bands and a little over an ounce of heroin and moved out.

I asked Smithy, "Where is the gun that you took off dude?"

"What gun?" he replied.

Turned out, Pretty Smithy shot the guy for no reason. I would learn later this was the first time Pretty Smithy ever fired a gun in a sting, and of course he had never been on a stick-up in his life. He shot dude because he thought that was what he was supposed to do.

We drove back to Detroit and I let Smithy know under no circumstances do you shot an unarmed man. Furthermore, I reminded him that a dead man would not be able to tell us where the drugs and money were hidden. He gave me this blank stare as if to say "I do not have a clue what you are talking about." On the other hand, I would rather have Smithy firing his gun in that split second than not. This was correctable, not firing his gun was not. I had learned from old gangsters like Fred Stedman that knowing how to handle a gun meant you practiced firing the weapon. And firing your weapons should be comfortable, like the comfort a prize fighter has in his ability to throw his signature punch, on time and on target. Knowing how to handle a gun is understanding that you are holding life and death in the palm of your hand and being able to manage a split second like it is an eternity.

Handling a gun, for me, meant I would be comfortable with my decision, in that split-second to become judge, jury, and executioner. I had no problem managing that split-second like it was an eternity. ADHD made me weird, the faster things got the more in control I became. Sometimes it was not about race when a white cop shoots and kills a Black man. The cop just did not know how to handle that split-second.

But it was not only the cops who could not handle that split-second. I had witnessed many criminals sitting on a prison bunk crying like a baby because they were not able to handle that split-second. In the end you become a murderer, legally or illegally, if you cannot handle that split second.

We had set Michigan on fire. And to make thing worse, I had to baby sit my brother. I could not let him out of my sight. Bruh never did anything halfway and never took short cuts. If you told my brother all he needed was a half of a McDonald's spoon of heroin for him to get high, he would shoot a whole McDonald's spoon. Bruh over-dosed on drugs and took bullets the way people caught a common cold and gain weight. We packed up and left Detroit and arrived back in Cleveland as seasoned stick-up men, with a dealer's heroin habits. Pretty Smithy came back with us. Turned out, Pretty Smithy was banging my sister Mary and he could not tear himself away, he was thoroughly pussy whipped. Mary got pregnant and their little playhouse situation became a real house situation. Smithy thought he would be able to support a heroin habit and raise a family, as a stickup man. But he found out that shit did not work.

Every morning, Smithy knocked on my door like he was still punching the clock at Ford Motors. His habit had turned into a three-ton gorilla and bills were piling up on him. My sister Mary demanded support notwithstanding his heroin addiction. The pressure would eventually make Smithy thirstier than a yard dog and make him rob spots we had knocked off over and over. He was careless but he did not care.

I was adamant about not robbing legitimate establishments and the same spot twice. But like a dope fiend he would storm out of my house and would go by himself. And in the end would leave a trail of petty robbery jobs throughout the neighborhood.

The Ohio lottery was steamrolling in and my policy house stickup opportunities were beginning to dry up. The big money gangsters who had controlling interest in the numbers racket were making their transition out of the business and closing most of their small Black neighborhood policy houses. All that was left were penny-and-dime small policy books that hardly had five hundred dollars on hand, and nine times out of ten I had knocked the spot off before.

I retired from robbing the bookies and set my sights strictly on dope boys. A detective who was on the take for the numbers racket one day pulled up on me looking like a white insurance man and told me in no uncertain terms that if I didn't stop robbing the policy houses and numbers runners on 105th Street I was going to jail. I was not concerned with the threat but unbeknownst to me, Pretty Smithy had been going back and robbing the same spots we had robbed repeatedly. They did not have a make on Smithy because he was from Detroit. True to his word, the insurance-looking detective hauled my ass in and charged me with over fifteen counts of robbery.

I would end up pleading guilty and being sentenced to Mansfield Reformatory. During this time, my lawyer told me the state had passed legislation to do away with Ohio Reformatory time. And if I prolonged my case, I would be given life in the Ohio Penitentiary for men. So, I grabbed the deal and took my punishment.

When I got to Mansfield, I received a hero's welcome. Mike, Otha, Little Man, Railroad, Curly, to name a few, were all there. It was a thug reunion.

All in all, Mansfield was a blur. Perhaps because the bit was under ten years. Nevertheless, the physical memory of Mansfield would stay with me for the rest of my life. Mansfield was the classic penitentiary. You were in rare air if you did more than five years in the Ohio Reformatory in Mansfield because one year in Mansfield was equivalent to three years of punishment anywhere else. Because of using the physicality of incarceration as punishment and deterrent for crime, there was no joint in America that exemplified punishment more than the Mansfield Reformatory. Whenever a movie producer wanted to make a prison film, such as the classic Shawshank Redemption, Mansfield Reformatory was chosen.

The guys I committed crimes with and hung out with throughout my incarceration were usually the same guys I had known since childhood. June Morgan was one of those guys.

June and I had arrived at Mansfield around the same time. The first thing you always wanted to see when you arrived at a prison was a familiar face. June had been sentenced to Lucasville instead of the Reformatory on a sentencing mistake. After doing several months in Lucasville, June was called back to court and re-sentenced to Mansfield. We ended up being cellmates the entire three years we were there.

June said Mansfield was like a walk in the park on a beautiful summer's day compared to Lucasville. I remember thinking if there was a prison worse than this place, I sure as hell did not want to go there. The state reformatory had been nothing more than a holding spot for our inevitable transition to the Ohio Penitentiary. The powers that be and the statistics had proved that reformatory time never was a deterrent for recidivism. Therefore, it was being decided that reformatory time would be eliminated after 1973 in the state of Ohio.

I did not encounter any drama in Mansfield. I got into several scraps here and there but nothing to write home about. I had fathered two children, but truth be told I was just getting introduced to pussy; hell, I had just turned eighteen when I was sentenced.

Indeed, my pussy whipping had just started, and now I had to do without it for two and a half years. During my whole Mansfield stretch all I would be able to think about would be baby mamas' pussy. And if there was one defining moment for me in Mansfield it would be when both baby mamas, Brenda Bell and Denise Washington, wrote me "Dear John" letters that arrived on the same day, informing me their undying love for me had, in fact, died.

Nobody could convince me the two women were not in cahoots but come to find out, they were not. It was just in the cards. We and I mean both baby mamas were too young to know anything about love and commitment. In the end, I could not blame them for moving on with their lives. After all, incarceration reveals who you are to people in that snapshot of your life, and it became crystal clear to both my baby mamas who I was; a young Black man on a course that would surely crash and burn.

I got released from Mansfield sometime around the early fall of 1975. I cannot remember the exact date. Why would I? When a bird is let out of a cage nothing matters except the freedom beneath their wings. My only concern was catching up. I wanted to show the world I was back. I was only twenty-one. I was still invisible and wanted so desperately to be seen. Nothing matters but life.

The first person I looked for was Mike. He was not hard to find because he had left a trail all over the neighborhood. All I had to do was follow the question, "Why are you fucking with that dirty little red nigger?"

Given the vocation Mike was in, A BAD REPORT was a good report. Mike had changed. Mansfield changed all of us; living in a cage for three years will do that to a young Black man.

We became harder from the experiences. We did not get any wiser. We got madder. We were Romans who lived and survived in Rome. We could only assume how we looked beyond the wall of the Roman Empire because there were no mirrors and because there were mirrors, we never were able to see our true reflections.

A hustler never admitted that they are a drug addict and a lowdown dirty motherfucker. He tells himself he gets high off his drug of choice because that is what hustlers do to relax themselves after a long day of extracting cash from lames. So, in our self-proclaimed context of addiction, the fiend hustler inside of us were more respected than a junkie and was able and willing to trick ourselves that we had maintained moral control of our habits. The junkie wasn't able to do that.

When you go to prison and get released, it is like you were put in a time capsule that propelled you backwards rather than propelled you to the future. The more time you do, the further back you are in time; and you find yourself committing a crime just to buy something simple, like shit paper.

When I got released from Mansfield, I was only interested in people who could help me catch up in crime. The thing is all my life I had lived behind the eight ball.

I drilled Mike to find out who was doing the heavy lifting in the neighborhood in heroin. He gave me a few leads and I locked in on a guy name Goodnight. Mike had been stalking him but never put an entire plan together. He told me a guy named Bootsie could give me a more thorough run down on Goodnight than he could, so we headed to Bootsie's house. I knew of the dude, but I never remembered him being associated with hard criminal shit. I remembered him as a dude who hustled cars. Come to find out his car stealing got derailed by a heroin addiction and like the rest of us he sprouted horns.

Bootsie had worked for Goodnight and Goodnight had crossed Bootsie or something or the other. Anyway, Bootsie seemed to jump at the opportunity to get back at him.

Goodnight booked numbers and sold weed and heroin out of a corner store. It was the heroin that would turn out to be the cause of his demise. His store got raided by the Feds and he was convicted on a heroin trafficking charge. The judge had given him two weeks to get his business affairs in order. That only gave me a small window of a week to devise a strategy to rob him.

I knew when a boss hustler like Goodnight got ready to take a long vacation he asked the court to give him time to get his business affairs in order. All that meant was he wanted time to stock up on his inventory so that his people would be able to maintain his operation while he was doing his stretch. I was right.

Bootsie was still cool with Goodnight's son. They grew up together. The father had fallen out of favor with his son because he was fucking the son's ex-girlfriend; she was an unscrupulous gold digger named Lyn. Nonetheless, they did not let the gold digger come between what had to be done business-wise.

Bootsie was able to learn from the son that a key of heroin was in play. The son was not too thrilled that the no-good gold digger ex-girlfriend would be handling things and not him.

My plan was to grab Goodnight when he left the son's house, which he would like clockwork, leading up to his inevitable incarceration date. I bought a spotlight and Bootsie did not have a problem stealing a look-alike police Dodge Plymouth. We completed our disguise with blue windbreakers with FBI painted in big yellow letters across the back.

The key to pulling it off would be keeping the spotlight directly in his face when we pulled him over. We did, and it worked like a charm. We snatched him easily.

So far, my plan had gone off without a hitch, and after a little convincing, Goodnight told us that the money and heroin were indeed hidden at his house in East Cleveland.

Showing up at the house this late with several surprise guests was different from Goodnight's normal evening protocol, which made Lyn hesitate to open the door. But the pistol in Goodnight's ribs made him convince her everything was all right. When Lyn came to the door, she had been having a phone conversation with Goodnight's friend and notorious ex-pimp named Chuck Pew who had moved from Cleveland to Detroit and became a heroine broker.

In retrospect, perhaps Lyn stated on the other side of the door that she was on the line with Chuck, but we got distracted by her children who burst over the threshold to greet Goodnight. I never understood why supposedly drug dealers would have kids in a place where they keep hard drugs. It was one of my biggest pet peeves with drug dealers. Running the numbers and having an after-hour joint was a different script than heroin. Some of these motherfuckers believed they were upstanding businessmen offering much-needed products to the community, and truly believed their family values were second to none. They reminded me of those old Italian gangster movies where you see the gangster brutally kill several people and come home and discipline his son for not doing his chores.

I would learn later that Chuck Phew had gone half on the key of heroin. When Lyn opened the door for us, she never hung up the phone and Chuck Phew heard everything that was going on. This oversight would turn out to be our doom. The plan was for Bootsie to take Lyn and the kids to a separate room to make sure they would be out of the way. We made the kids feel like we were Daddy's friends and we were there on grown folks' business. After the kids were settled, we took Goodnight to his bedroom where we knew the money would most likely be hidden.

Two things a hustler wants in his bedroom: pussy and money. Goodnight was no different. We found his cash stashed under the floorboards in his bedroom closet. Everything was going as planned, but we made one crucial mistake.

A criminal is always on a clock when committing a crime, more so in the perpetration of a robbery. It makes no difference whether the criminal is robbing the neighborhood bank or the neighborhood drug dealer time is of the essence. To be a professional robber you had to do things in a hurry but at the same time you also had to be methodical in your approach. I was always in a rush on account of my ADHD, but Mike was always detail-oriented and methodical. We were a perfect robber match, so to speak. We complimented each other that way, but not this time.

Unbeknownst to us, Chuck Phew was still on the telephone and he overheard the robbery taking place, and rather than take a chance with his friend and his family's lives he called 911.

The fact that there were children present threw us off off. It sped us up, and we missed the methodical details; the phone was literally off the hook.

Just as we were emptying the hollow bar stool legs full of heroin, we heard the East Cleveland Police bull horn. "We have the residence surrounded, come out with your hands in the air."

We couldn't believe what we were hearing. Bootsie looked out the window and confirmed what we had heard, police had the house surrounded. We had only one option. We knew Goodnight did not want another drug charge on top of his conviction. Therefore, we decided to leverage telling the cops about the drugs in the basement for his silence.

We hid our weapons and told Goodnight that if he said anything about this being a robbery, we would direct the cop's attention to the half a key of heroin stuffed in the bar stool legs. If he kept his mouth shut, we would leave with the cops and everyone would walk away clean. He reluctantly agreed to keep quiet, we thought.

The cops cautiously came in with guns drawn at the ready. We became actors and played the roles of friends of the family. The call had come in as the police station shift was changing. Practically the whole East Cleveland police force had converged on Goodnight's house. Goodnight instantly got courage when the cops entered the room, demanding answers as to what was going on. I could see his mind weighing his options when the cop kept asking the question, "What's going on? Does anyone want to explain the 911 robbery call that came into the station?"

Silence. No one said a word. We told the cops that the 911 was someone pulling a prank.

As I was explaining this to the cops, I noticed Goodnight eyeing the big white envelop Mike had taken that was stuffed with hundred- and fifty-dollar bills from Goodnight's stash. It had to be no less than ten thousand. Goodnight could not refrain from snatching the envelope out of Mike's pocket. Mike's reflexes took over and he refused to give up the envelope. They tussled over the envelop in front of the cops. "Give me back my money, bitch motherfucker!"

Had Goodnight just given the money and not used the words "bitch motherfucker," I believe Mike would have never grabbed him by the throat. But he did not, and Mike did. Goodnight decided he would be better off with another charge.

The cops had to pry Mike's fingers from around Goodnight's neck as though his hands were a vise. For a moment, the cops seemed to enjoy seeing Mike choke the shit out the neighborhood drug dealer.

After the cops pried off Mike's hands from his throat, Goodnight said we were robbers. We claimed we were drug addicts there to get our money back from the bad heroin he sold us. The inquisition lasted about a half an hour. When it was all said and done, the cops had no warrant to search his house. In the end, the cops figured they already had Goodnight on a heroin sales charge so they did not want to mess around trying to nail him on another flimsy drug charge that would most likely get thrown out.

We were charged with multiple counts of kidnapping and robbery. The State's case against us was a slam dunk. Two ex-convicts, one with a manslaughter conviction and one with an armed robbery conviction. I had only been released from Mansfield for ninety days. I was a parole violator with a thirty-five-year-to-life parole violation hanging over my head. In the end, we all were sentenced to fifteen to thirty-five years in Lucasville. I was the only one who stood a chance of doing the whole thirty-five years, with essentially two fifteen-to-thirty-five-year convictions.

Fifteen to Thirty-Five

The Southern Ohio Correctional Facility, better known as Lucasville, was built in 1972. Lucasville was supposed to be the new model for maximum-security correction. The infamous joint supposed to have replaced the Ohio penitentiary in Columbus.

The prison is best known for the riot on Easter Sunday, 1993. When the smoke cleared from the riot, nine inmates and one corrections officer were dead. The riot was one of the longest in U.S. prison history. Now, imagine, if you will what the prison was like twenty years prior, in the first five years of its existence. When the camera was not rolling.

We were packed in like we were cargo in the hold of a slave ship. When you build a prison with a certain number of beds, you must fill the beds. And once those beds are filled, they stacked beds on top of beds, until there was funding to build another prison, and so on and so forth.

I was twenty-two when I arrived at Lucasville. The odds of me reaching my twenty-third birthday were very low. Lucasville was made up of pods, which was another name for modern day cell blocks. The new inmate arrivals were housed together. If you were a soft criminal your ass was literally auctioned out to the highest bidder before you hit population. Lucasville was primitive; you had to be a fuckin' cave man to survive.

There was not a dark spot in the entire joint. The groundhog never saw his shadow in Lucasville, but it did not matter because spring, summer, fall, and winter were the same seasons. Every inch of the place was illuminated. After two years, my eyes went bad and I needed glasses.

Like any maximum-security joint, Lucasville was run by the inmates, which basically meant the administration left the inmates to their own devices. For the most part, I was locked down sixteen hours a day. Imagine being in an environment where eight hours every day were equivalent to being on a battlefield. No man was an island in Lucasville. It did not make a difference how tough you thought you were; if you did not belong to a clique in Lucasville, nine times out ten, you were a dead man walking.

In the '70s especially, the Cleveland Cliques, were some of the strongest cliques in Lucasville. If a guy from Cleveland was killed more than likely he was a snitch, or he broke an unwritten code. There were unbreakable rules and codes in prison that a man could not allow another man to brush past against. To see another man get stabbed or beaten to death was a common occurrence. I could count on the Grim Reaper showing up more than I could the sun rising in the morning and setting in the evening. Some murders stood out and stayed with me more because of the gruesomeness in which the person was killed. It was these types of brutal killings that took me by surprise and played over and over in my mind and saturated my inner being until I grew to become like the world I was in.

Bootsie and I had arrived at Lucasville several months before Mike. Mike was still spending money on his defense and had hired a fixer lawyer to look for any possible loophole that might overturn his conviction, or at least prolonged his inevitable ride down I-71.

The sixty or so days I had been home from Mansfield did not allow me enough time to feel freedom, it felt like one continuous incarceration. And as the months faded into years, it became one continuous incarceration.

There would be members of my immediate family who did not realize I had been home between Mansfield and Lucasville. June Morgan, during my Mansfield bit, prepared me for Lucasville. I already knew that the first thing I had to do would be to put together a game plan and interview troops for my clique, so I did not waste any time. The moment I arrived I got to it.

There was this one inmate we'll call him Lil' Joe since it was obvious to everyone who met him that he had a Napoleon complex. I had known him from crossing paths with him throughout my incarcerated travels. He was doing a murder bit. He was feared and I was thinking he will make a good sergeant-of-arms for my clique. Dude was also known for having one of the coldest chess games in the joint. I had pulled up on him for some chess lessons, but we both knew it wasn't his chess game I was after. I was interested in the man, not his chess game. Plus, playing chess wasn't for me. I had no patience. I should say, never had any tolerance for delayed gratification.

To the naked eye, Lil' Joe was your ordinary everyday "normal criminal." But being a veteran in this space, I knew if there ever was a place you did not want to judge a book by its cover it would be in a maximum-security prison. Lil' Joe and I were playing a chess game, and halfway through our chess game, Lil' Joe got up. I was thinking he got to pee or something. But he calmly walked over to the barbell rack, took out a forty-five-pound weight and crushed a guy's skull while the guy was doing bench presses.

The dead guy's head split open like a watermelon and his brains splattered all over the floor like a half pound of fresh unwashed chitlins.

Now, I never saw it happen, my eyes were glued to the chess board. But right before he got up, Lil' Joe had set me up for a check-mate. Getting up was his signal that the game was over. Getting up and walking away was his show of arrogance.

But this time, Lil' Joe had other things on his mind beside the check-mate that was in front of me. There was a lot of commotion. I looked up and saw that the fitness room was clearing out fast and I saw the dude and was at a loss for words. The pawn was frozen in my hand, suspended above the chess board, and I just could not believe my eyes. I never saw Lil' Joe make the kill, but I didn't have to.

I got the hell out of there. It wasn't a long-drawn-out investigation when it came to a Lucasville prison murder in the '70s. Prosecuting crimes in hell was considered a waste of taxpayer's money. The tax-paying public in the '70s didn't care about a murderer killing another convicted murderer, in a maximum-security prison.

Several weeks or perhaps longer, the smoke had not too long cleared from the fitness room murder when another gruesome murder happened. I was standing in the mess hall breakfast lining up behind two guys having a heated dispute. I knew it had to involve the gay boy who was sheepishly moving behind the one dude. I thought nothing of it. There were any number of things in Lucasville that could get a guy killed but losing control of your dick was at the top of the list. There were only so many girls around and the price for a wife in Luc was extremely high.

"Girls" were different than fuck boys. "Girls" had hormone shots, boobs, and wore mini hot pants during recreation. "Girls" were mostly transgender.

The more restraint an inmate had in controlling his sexual desires, the better chances he would have in making it out alive. I could not have been standing no more than a couple feet in line behind these dudes when out of nowhere another guy came up like a Japanese ninja and gutted dude with a boning knife. It was the most gruesome killing I had ever witnessed. He literally cut dude's stomach out standing in line, in the middle of the prison mess hall. I jumped back as did other inmates in the proximity. If the gushing blood spattered on our clothes, that would be undisputed evidence that we were there, and therefore guilty until proven innocent.

Whenever anything happened in Lucasville the first thing the guards were instructed to do was secure the premise to keep the disturbance contained in the area, which meant locking the kitchen door and everyone inside. For a fleeting moment I thought the guy had a shot at living but as soon as he reached the threshold of the mess hall door, trying in vain to hold his guts inside, the security gate came crashing down on top of him and pinned down his body beneath the steel gate. The scene was something out of a horror movie, his torso trapped and his legs they were moving as though he was pedaling an invisible bicycle, like Curly from the Three Stooges. Slowly and more slowly he pedaled until his legs stopped moving. When it was all said and done dude was covered up with a white kitchen robe, bleeding out.

All the inmates were stripped naked and searched while the dead guy lay covered up in the blood-soaked kitchen robes. Two kitchen worker inmates were ordered to mop up all the blood that was draining from his body as though he was some roadkill. The reason for the hit I heard was that the transgender had decided to leave her previous lover for the new lover, but the previous lover was not having it. So, he paid a hit man to kill her new lover immediately.

Lil' Joe the chess master said to me weeks later, as he was setting up the chess board, "Is everything alright?"

Not looking up from the chess board, I said, "Yeah, everything is cool."

"You know it's alright to go crazy as long as you can find your way back," he said.

I was thinking once a person gets down the road as far as Lil' Joe, he was lost. No road map in the world would be able to help him find his crazy ass way back to sanity. I made a mental vow to myself to never let that happen to me.

Mike eventually arrived at his new residence. I did not have to brief Mike too much on the tenants of Rome, because we both had lived in Rome for most of our lives. We understood that there was only one way to deal with people who had not valued their own lives. As for our co-defendant, Bootsie, this was his first rodeo and fortunately for him he was able to transfer out of Lucasville to a minimum-security prison within six months after the day he and I had arrived.

There were no pretention about who we were or what we had to become in order to survive. We had to make our "damn fool certifications" known right off the rip. It was black and white, fuck with me and I am going to kill you or die trying. I was no different than anyone else. My sentiments were par for the course. Lucasville was literally a world of survival of the fittest. You had to hit first. In other words, you had to be able to control or dictate the chaos or the chaos would control you. Lucasville was the hood on steroids. Everything was magnified. In the hood, a dude might get killed for a few thousand; in Lucasville, a dude might get killed because he owed someone twenty dollars.

You had two choices. Stay in the cell for twenty-four hours a day, which was like blood in the water to sharks. Or, you could become a Roman like the rest of us. It was that simple.

The cliques that controlled the gambling, prostitution, and drugs were determined by a show of sustained power. The power had to be sustainable because it was tested every week, sometimes from day to day. The hardest thing to control or maintain was a prostitution ring because trying to control the emotions of homosexual criminals was a deadly proposition on so many levels. In Lucasville, somebody was getting fucked whether they wanted to or not. Forcefully squeezing the bitch out of a man was a sad way to make a living and a sad way for a man to be forced to live. I despise those low-life motherfuckers who endeavored in that line of work. However, Lucasville was not a place to become "Captain-help-save-your-friend's-ass." Because saving your own ass figuratively or literally was an everyday job.

There were a lot of Caitlyn Jenner transformations going on in Lucasville. It was not a big deal to hear that a guy went to sleep and woke up one morning and declared that he was now a woman. One day you could be hanging out with dude and having a typical male conversation about dude things and the next day he comes out of his cell wearing booty-hugging hot pants and makeup, talking about how he always wanted to suck your dick. Whatever sugar a guy had in his tank, it would be extracted out in Lucasville, like a hungry bear taking honey from a beehive. However, you always had to be mindful that Caitlyn Jenner was once Bruce. If dude was a convicted murderer and woke up and declared he was a girl he was still a convicted murder. In other words, sugar in his tank does not presuppose he would not kill your ass.

There were a lot of dudes in the joint who forgot this important fact and it cost them dearly. Case in point, Big Tee, who ran the prostitution ring in Lucasville. Tee was doing manslaughter, which was another way of saying a Black man took a plea deal for killing another Black person. Nonetheless, Tee was once the heavyweight boxing champion in the Ohio prison system. The big punk was notorious for a straight right hand that dropped men's pants who did not necessarily want their pants dropped. Tee liked young fresh boys. Once he spotted a young dude he liked, he'd play the passive female role and two weeks later we would see the young dude with his eyebrows arched, cherry Kool-Aid lipstick and wearing the same hot pants Tee used to catch him with.

Tee went both ways. Like I said, I despised those dudes who raped guys, but I had no sympathy for dudes who allowed their dicks to beat them out. They got what they had coming. My clique sold protection, and one of our protection services was "Ass Protection." For a monthly fee, usually sent in by a family member, we'd literally put a dude's ass under our protection. Dude's mother and/or his wife would pay a handsome monthly extortion price for us to protect their husband or son from getting fucked in the joint.

There were guys who needed protection but did not have the money to pay for booty protection but would rather be killed and/or hang themselves before they lived as someone's incarcerated bitch. The drama surrounding homosexuality was a broad net over the entire prison population. It affected you one way or the other. If you did not know how to navigate your way around the culture of homosexuality in the joint, it got you fucked up.

There was this new guy who had come into our pod, K-3. He was new so he was not up on the cell block's homosexual protocol as it related to the privileges afforded to gays throughout Lucasville cell blocks. The term "happier than a sissy in boys' town" had a lot of truth to it because gays were put on pedestals and their lover would literally die in defending their wife's or lover's honor. The wives had designated chairs and tables in the TV dayroom. These chairs and tables had elaborate artistry, painted in all kinds of bright colors. You could not set at the table or in these chairs at any time unless you were given permission to do so. "Oh, my bad I didn't know this was your seat, I am sorry" — this would not be an excuse.

No one gave the new dude the memo. He was a big dude around six feet four or five. Perhaps he had always been recognized as the certified and unchallenged bully of his world. He had to feel that way because he did not seem to be uncomfortable in his new surroundings. But in Lucasville, there was always a bigger damn fool waiting for you.

I liked dude, the short time I got to know him. If I had known about his misunderstanding beforehand, I certainly would have tried to head off the train wreck because my clique was always in need of a few good men.

The way I heard it; big dude sat in someone's wife's chair. That probably would have just got his ass beat really good. But when the new big guy told the dude's wife/punk to go set his bitch ass on the floor or words to that effect, he practically signed his death certificate. So, they jumped him and stabbed him multiple times. They say, big dude died from his wounds a week later.

I never liked watching afternoon TV, especially soap operas. My afternoon routine was going to the gym when the favorite afternoon TV show came on, The Young and Restless. But most Romeo and Juliet dramatic tales of a prison love tragedy during my time in Lucasville happened when this rich white guy was there. I can't recall exactly what his case was about, but while he was doing his time his parents suddenly died, making him the sole beneficiary of the family fortune. I think dude was doing a man-one. In the meantime, while doing his time this rich dude fell in love with one of the most notorious Black guys in Lucasville, whom we called Boo Boo Banks.

Now, Boo Boo was one of those crazy motherfuckers who always stayed in deep Lucasville drama, constantly connected to murders, stabbing, rapes, etc. We knew Boo Boo loved him some gay boys, but we had no clue he went both ways until one day Boo Boo decided to come out of his cell like Caitlyn Jenner. But get this, he made an official announcement that he would only be sucking white dicks, because black dicks made him sick. This motherfucker was crazy black dicks made him sick. Really?

Nevertheless, Boo Boo's rich lover who was now a multimillionaire was able to buy his freedom on a legal technicality or he paid for his shock parole. Whatever the case may have been, dude got out shortly after his parents died.

Apparently, this rich white dude was madly in love with Boo Boo because after giving thousands to unscrupulous lawyers who lied about being able to get Boo Boo released, the white dude had had enough and used his money to try to break Boo Boo out of Lucasville.

He would bribe several prison guards. The guns were planted inside the prison hospital transport van. Boo Boo and several inmates were being taken to their hospital appointments in Columbus. The plan was for Boo Boo to hijack the van on the way to the hospital appointment. In the end, two inmates got killed and a guard was critically wounded in the failed escape attempt.

Lucasville was all the prison in real life and in the movies, you ever saw, but on steroids. Trust me, it was a different animal in the '70s.

The only time I saw a gun in Lucasville was when the white supremacist Aryan Brotherhood had it on the yard. This was July 4th, 1976 or perhaps, 77. How insane was that a gun in prison. I thought it was a shank at first. I questioned whether it was functional. Having a gun was the ultimate show of force and power for the white supremacist Aryan Brotherhood. The Black Nationalist had been pushing their weight around and the White supremacist Aryan Brotherhood wanted to make a statement, I suppose. The racist Klan guards would give these Aryan Brotherhood dudes whatever they wanted or needed to level the playing field against the Black Nationalists, Muslims, and cliques, simply because the Aryans and white cliques were the minority in just about any joint in America. It wasn't a secret that the penitentiaries were built for Black and brown people, so we totally outnumbered the whites.

The Aryans having a gun did not change the odds, but it sure as hell kept Black power from total domination. Fred Ahmed Evans' sentence had been reversed to life in prison, but he had contracted cancer. Nonetheless, his lieutenants never lost control of Lucasville and they were recognized as the undisputed leader of all the Black cliques throughout the Ohio penal system and ten times more dangerous until his death.

For the most part, cliques were limited to designated cell blocks. Our clique controlled K-3. As I mentioned we were locked up about sixteen hours out of twenty-four and that was pure mental torture. When my cell door opened, I had to move. I played basketball, football, and baseball, anything that allowed me to escape the stillness of my body. If, and when I did play cards and chess, my challenge was not to defeat my opponent across the board, my challenge was directed at the opponent in my head. Imagine the mental torture of someone with ADHD being confined.

With the nation's overcrowded prison system, around the end of the '70s, under political pressure from the Feds, the State of Ohio was ordered to take back control of Lucasville from the inmates or else the federal government would cut off the funding.

The death toll had gotten too high for the politicians to go on ignoring the situation. Mike and I had planned to apply for minimum security status as soon as it was made available to us. We were under no illusion about being able to stay alive in Lucasville for fifteen years. For us to acquire minimum-security status, and subsequent transfer out of Lucasville we needed to first be free and clear for a year of any prison bad conduct write-ups and have a high school diploma or GED. I had a problem with authority and could not stay clear of prison conduct write-ups. I had dropped out of school in the tenth grade and was reading at a third-grade level.

Mike had steered clear of write-ups for a year and had enough high school credits to take his GED. He too was granted minimum security status around 1978. When he left, I was not too sure that I would ever see him again. Before the Feds stepped in, if you wanted to go to school or get a job in Lucasville you had to go through an inmate or clique who controlled the certified placement. Simply put, document certifications for criminals inside a maximum-security prison were handled by inmates, not paid prison staff. Again, it was considered a waste of taxpayer money to have paid staff handling the education concerns of robbers, rapists, and murderers. If it wasn't about maximum security, it was of no concern to the prison administration.

However, nothing was free. Registering for school, a job, clothes, shoes, drugs, cigarettes, living quarters, bed linen, laundry, telephone calls, sex, you name it you would have to pay for it just like you would have done in the free world. However, the Feds put an end to the inmate's enterprising control. Case in point, Skinny Brown, one of our crew members from St Clair, got killed, shanked to death in a poker game. Prior to his death he had requested a move to another cell block. The case worker answered his move request six months after he was dead.

Skinny's request and reply were returned to Skinny's cellmate who read the case worker's response to us in the dayroom. "Mr. Brown, your request is denied."

When the Feds took over Lucasville, they said all inmates had to enroll in some type of school or training program, or get a job. The catch-all words were rehabilitation programming and social integration, which was the politically correct way of saying, "Stop allowing the animals to run the farm." What reason would I have for working a prison job for 10 cents an hour or $6 to $12 dollars a month?

I informed the prison authorities to tell the Feds they could kiss my Black ass because my judge didn't sentence me to fifteen to thirty-five years of hard labor. The administration countered that I would have to lock down for twenty-four hours. I refused, as did the rest of my clique. The shit hit the fan. We literally threw shit on any guard who came to our cell block with that bullshit order. Inmates who wanted to abide by the New Federal Directive were ordered to come out of the cell blocks. Most cell blocks gave some type of resistance. Our cell block, K-3, gave the most resistance. The news media had been informed, and the Feds were watching, so the racist prison guards couldn't just kill us. The guards had on body armor and fought behind plexiglass riot shields. In the end, we were no match for all the riot weapons and gear they had at their disposal. The turning point was the fire hoses and tear gas. We surrendered.

I was thrown into administrative isolation for a couple of years along with several of the so-called ring leaders. As it turned out, administrative isolation (AI) was the best thing that could have happened to me because it allowed me to be able to relax my mind. I had been in a constant state of motion mentally and physically for my entire life. Now there were no threats, no demands, no rush. My clock was turned off. Solitary confinement for me turned out to be like the tale about the rabbit, the fox, and the briar patch. It was where I needed to be. My one and only cell mate in AI was a con man who had played his way into AI because he had feared the young crazy fools like myself. But as my presence testified, there was no escaping the young crazy fools in Lucasville.

I was around twenty-four or twenty-five years old when I was sent to AI, but my maturity was that of a teenager. But time and age were not important in Lucasville, everybody was considered the same age. Among the living, you woke up alive, that's all the age that mattered. I was like any other young dude who had spent more time behind bars than in freedom. I was ignorant and illiterate, about life, but more importantly I didn't have a clue who the fuck I was.

My AI cellmate was the total opposite. He was an older man with knowledge and wisdom. The only thing we had in common was the space we were forced to share; dude was on another level mentally. I must have sounded to him like a little child who was constantly moving and asking the same questions repeatedly. He tried everything to get me to shut my ADHD trap;

he would pull out his chessboard and murder me in chess daily. And by the time I left AI, he had taught me every card game and card trick known to man. And even though he carried me in whatever game it was we played, nevertheless they didn't last but a few minutes. And I would be right back annoying him, running off at the mouth and torturing his ears with hyperbolic and irreverent chatter.

One day several books he had ordered arrived from the prison library. He was always reading a book or writing letters, so books arriving were a normal occurrence. He signed for the books and threw them at the foot of my bunk. I looked at him, and he had this cat-that-ate-the-bird smile plastered across his face.

"What is this?" I asked.

He said, "Oh, you can read, can't you?"

A bit offended, I assured him that I could. But the truth of the matter was I barely read at a third-grade level. The books were an unabridged War and Peace by Leo Tolstoy, Atlas Shrugged by Ayn Rand, and Victor Hugo's Les Misérables.

I decided to read War and Peace first and struggled for the better part of two full months to finish the book though I read it daily. My attention span was the same as a hummingbird and I would be forced to put the book down. These books would be the first books I had ever attempted to read other than the urban fiction books of Donald Goines and Iceberg Slim that barely would have two hundred pages. I had to go through this invisible ADHD wall. But when I had successfully emerged on the other side victorious, there was not a better feeling. When I finished the novels, it felt as though I had gained a measure of freedom. I discovered the bars had only denied my movement. I could escape through the pages of books, for a moment at a time, to freedom.

I became hooked and riding an intellectual high that would continue to soar higher and higher with every novel and book. I read poetry, philosophy, discovered my Black culture. Reading opened my eyes up to a world that I never knew existed. And for the first time in my life I understood the power of the written word. I was anxious to put my newfound intellect to the test.

My cellmate wrote letters obsessively and when the mail came, he received mailbags of letters. Again, the administration did not care about the money schemes inmates were doing if it didn't breach security. The prison administration didn't try to protect the bleeding-heart sympathizers who wrote prisoners in a maximum-security prison. I asked what was going on. He told me he was a minister at several churches and the letters were from members of his congregations. But as time wore on, he brought grasshopper into his confidence and opened the door to his mail fraud game. He said all these people were lonely and needed someone to talk to just like us. So, he wrote them letters.

I cut to the chase and asked him straight up, "How much money are they sending you?" He had so much mail that on occasion the mail room would overlook money orders, checks, and nude photos and they would slip through. He showed me a five-hundred-dollar money order and read letters to me showing how people had sent money to his bank account. I was hooked. He gave me over fifty pen pals and directed me to several small news publications and magazines where people were desperate for pen pals. I had no clue what I was supposed to say to these people. The old con man told me to be honest and just tell them about my situation, how I ended up in Lucasville and why I was put in administrative isolation. "Just tell them you needed somebody to talk with."

I was not confident that telling the truth would be the right approach, but I was wrong. Turned out, most of the people I wrote and received letters were from people living in the western part of the country; liberal-minded, mostly Christians who understood the fallibility of man.

A great number of my pen pals were gays but mostly older white women with a lot of free time on their hands. It did not take long before the money started rolling in on my commissary books. My account went from zero to over a thousand dollars in no time.

Meanwhile, Mike had written me about how sweet he had it in the minimum-security joint he had got transferred to called Marion Correctional. He wanted me to do everything I could to get my security status lowered so I would be able to transfer.

Part of the Feds' institutional transformation directive for Lucasville was to hire social workers, ABE and GED teachers, open the library to the general population and hire minority prison guards. To put this in perspective, the last ABE teacher (a male) who had worked at Lucasville at the time had gotten gang-graped. The new warden came in and offered everybody amnesty if they agreed to abide by the new administration rules and regulation. I agreed and signed up for Adult Basic Education classes.

I wrote a kite (a missive), to the social worker and asked them what it would take for me to lower my security status and transfer to Marion. The prison social worker spelled it out for me: I would have to enroll in school and get my ABE certificate first and pass the GED test. I accomplished both tasks in less than one hundred and twenty days. The GED test was administered only once a year. I owed it all to the old con man for planting the seed of knowledge inside of me. It was the first time I remembered thanking someone for giving me something that I could not put into words.

When I arrived at Marion, it was as though I had died and

gone to prison heaven. Marion administration was mostly run by women.

Mike had worked his hand to a point where anything that was conceivable money, drugs, etc. he had access to it. Mike had knocked off this fat social worker and she was truly paying him by her pounds. Anything he asked her for she would bring it in under her giant dress and stuffed in her humongous boobs. She would have to search for a pint of liquor in her boobs, that's how big her shit was.

I was impressed with my partner's ability to bind his environment to his will. Mike trusted my counsel as I did his, which for both of us was the most important thing we could have given to one another: unconditional trust in a place where self-preservation was the rule. Without that voice constantly in your ear, checking you about the decisions you were making or not making in a place where the wrong decisions may be your last decisions such a voice was invaluable.

Minimum security meant inmates had more freedom of movement within the prison. Mike had used the same script in Marion as we did in Lucasville, the only thing different was instead of a cell block, we operated out of a dorm. If you didn't abide by our rules and regulations, you moved out of Five dorm or suffered the consequences.

Shortly after I was settled in at Marion, I received the tragic news that my baby mama, Brenda, had been killed trying to "cross Dead Man's Curve, a stretch of freeway in Cleveland whose name spoke for itself. But I knew that was not the true story as to what really happened. Not that a truck did not kill her, but it was apparent to me that Brenda figured staying in the car was just as dangerous as it would be for her to cross dead man's curve.

Brenda's death made me think about the distance that living was from death. How short and precious life and freedom was. I cannot remember ever thinking about my own mortality until Brenda died. I suppose I thought life was forever. When you are young, forever is forever, and once forever was over with, you die. But no young person conceives their mortality. I wanted to see my children. Suddenly, I felt the importance of fatherhood. I had not seen my children in years and being able to touch and talk with them I believed would fill the empty hole that I suddenly recognized had grown bigger in the center of my heart.

The strange thing about prison is that life is paused. Feelings and emotions are paused. When you get out prison, you picked up at the same emotional place you were the moment you got sent away, and if you allowed the inertia of your physical incarceration to affect your mental growth, you are that same person.

I told myself that Brenda and I never had ended our relationship. And we had this unspoken agreement that regardless of time and distance, she would always be my woman, until death do us part. Now she was gone. I started asking my sisters to introduce me to some of their friends who they think would not mind being pen pals with me. I was tired of telling lies to old lonely white women fantasizing about black dick, and selling them fake emotions like a drug dealer selling heroin to addicts. I desperately wanted to tell the truth about my feelings.

My sisters put my lonely-hearts pen pal ad out and I got a response from a hairstylist name Jennifer and a pregnant lady name Selisa Rita Tell. Both women were friends of one of my sisters. Jennifer was self-centered and felt the need to promote, embellish, and flat out lie about herself. But I did not care. Jennifer was a beautiful Black woman. She was the manifestation of the essence of ebony in terms of her appearance. I was a man going on ten years of incarceration, so I welcomed her lies. I was desperate for attention. Anyway, I had long understood that lies were the truth behind bars, and the truth was lies behind bars.

Selisa Rita Tell was pregnant with her second child and both babies' fathers were men that never loved her, and she was a woman who had never loved. So, right off the rip I was her prisoner, her captured audience with no other choice but to listen to her admonishing of the male species. She poured her heart out to me about the shortcomings of the Black man. And here I was, the man who decided to go to church and the preacher's sermon felt as though it was directed at me, having fathered two children of my own.

The definition of a dead-beat dad: I was only eighteen when I was sentenced to Mansfield and twenty-two when I arrived at Lucasville. By time I was transferred to Marion Correctional I was an incarcerated thirty-one-year-old, emotionally deprived and ignorant to the essence of a woman. Label a deadbeat dad, and like many young Black "boys" it would take incarceration for me to be able to reach maturity, manhood, in a world whose success seemed to depend on my deceased manhood. Selisa Tell's voice, someone I had never met in person, would be the first time I would hear as a woman's voice, making me realize my shortcomings toward becoming a Black man. Mike had gotten into boxing. If there ever was a sport that fit the personality of a person, boxing was that for Mike. It was him against the world, his opponent. No one controlled the bout but him. I always got the feeling it wasn't about winning or losing with Mike, as much as it was about the challenge.

By time I had arrived at Marion Correctional Mike had won the light middleweight title. I visualized all his opponents

Mike

judging the book by its cover and making the mistake that so many before had made about who they thought him to be, and when they discovered they were wrong, they didn't have a plan B. Bruh arrived at Marion on a reduced robbery sentence. My cousin June arrived perhaps six months after. Pinky, Rick, Mike, and me all had sons by the Washington sisters and that was just a fraction of the connection and control we wielded in Marion Correctional Five Dorm.

I had not heard from Bruh in the seven or eight years I had been down. I knew heroin was the jealous bitch that had refused to allow my brother time for corresponding. But it was like no time had passed between us. I was still ecstatic to see him, notwithstanding the circumstances.

Given the circumstances, Mike had replaced my brother over the past decade as the person I could count on and vice versa. I suppose Bruh felt some kind of way about somebody else occupying his brotherly space so there was always this unspoken tension between them the moment he had arrived, plus the fact Bruh was black-skinned while Mike was light-skinned. Two alpha males ho had always been at odds with one another.

As I later found out, Bruh, too, had gotten into street boxing. He had had a few professional bouts under his belt as a club fighter, so when he arrived at Marion, Bruh was anxious to test his skills against the very best prison fighters.

Bruh was on a mission to gain as much experience as he could because his fighting window was closing, given his age. For him it was now or never.

I understood where Bruh was coming from, but I was concerned about his health. There are no shortcuts to becoming a successful fighter. Bruh sparred with guys out of his weight class but it did not matter, and he would lose just as much as he would win.

Mike and Bruh got into a serious argument after sparring in the boxing room. Mike felt that Bruh was going too hard in their sparring match. A real fight between them was imminent. The only thing for me to do was make the fight off limits to the dorm. I did not want anybody running off their mouth about what happen on the streets or in the joint. The fight would be a private affair; no one would be allowed to watch the fight. A few inmates started to challenge my authority and ability to tell the whole dorm what they would and could watch, but they realized my threats weren't given lightly and decided it would be wise not to challenge my authority. The fight was in the shower away from the eyes of the dorm. Bruh went in first and the moment he turned to face Mike he paused as though he was waiting on the referee to signal the start of the bout. But that split second pause was all Mike needed. I forgot exactly what he hit Bruh with I am thinking it was a hook because that was Mike's signature punch. Nonetheless, the punch landed right on the button. Bruh staggered and rocked back but never lost complete balance. My brotherly reflex made me jump to Bruh's defense, but I stopped short. Caught in non-man's-land, there was nothing I could do.

I was amazed Bruh was still standing considering the force of the bare knuckle shot directly on his chin. There was no doubt a man with a lesser chin would have been knocked out cold. Mike knew he had thrown his best shot as well. Bruh grabbed Mike to clear his head. From that point on the fight became a wrestling match. After they rolled around on the shower room floor a few minutes I broke them apart. The correction officer was due to make his schedule rounds in the dorm and I did not want them to get thrown in the whole for fighting.

I was upset at Mike for throwing the first punch. It was a fight, not a boxing match, but after all Mike and I been through

Marion Correctional upon my arrival, early eighties.
Second from left Willie "Sleepy" Drake and crew

Mike had earned my restraint in that moment. This would be the one and only exception, and the last time I would allow somebody to hit my brother without feeling the full force of my wrath immediately. Nothing a man respect more than witnessing first-hand another man's mettle on the battlefield. The fight built a mutual respect between Bruh and Mike. They grew closer, damn near inseparable. I slept much better at night.

We ran Five Dorm with an iron fist. But we all had gotten older. We were no longer the twenty-year-old thugs willing to risk it all for self-defined principles. After a few uneventful years, the Federal Government got around to implementing the Security and Rehabilitation directive order at Marion. The criminologist experts', goal was to make Ohio incarceration experience as humane as possible, but to do so was impossible. In the following months, our Five Dorm clique would be broken up. Bruh went out back to Marion's Honor Farm. I was transferred to Chillicothe Correctional down in the southeast part of the state and Mike was transferred to Lima in the western part of the state.

Pain & Suffering

Chillicothe Correctional had been a federal prison back in day and converted into a state penitentiary. It was by far the best state joint I had ever been locked up in. Right before I was transferred, I had obtained my Associate of Applied Business degree from Marion Technical College, and had my credits transferred over to the Ohio University General Studies degree program. Chillicothe was one of a few prison institutions that had a distance learning bachelor's degree program at the time.

The overall prison atmosphere was laid back. The joint was mostly made up of old-timers doing life-bits, pedophiles, and new wave sex-change homosexual. There also were a lot of public servants such as judges and policemen who got caught with their hands in the cookie jar. It was the only Ohio State joint with a stand-along movie theater, a tennis court, putt-putt course, and the best hooch I ever tasted in prison. However, Chilly was still a state prison although the atmosphere had that laidback federal vibe. The guards were laid back, if the problem wasn't physical or a breach in security the administration waited for the inmates to bust themselves. In other words, the environment did not occupy all my time. Moreover, I did not have Mike and my brother's backs to worry about daily, so most of my brain power and energy was transferred to the pursuit of knowledge.

I was beginning to see the light at the end of the tunnel and believing in the real possibility of freedom. Everything was going along well. I felt a sense of hope for the future that I'd never felt before. Then one day it all came crashing down, and just like that, hope became an illusion.

I was informed that my father had terminal cancer and wasn't expected to live past ninety days. Apparently, my family had known for some time, but it was decided not to tell me until the very end. The prison administration gave me a choice to either go to my father's funeral or visit his bed side in the hospital. Obviously, I chose the latter. When I got to the hospital several of my sisters were there. My mother was dealing with health issues and complications from diabetes and she had not been feeling well herself. However, the strange thing about my visit, to this day I can't remember anyone being in the room but me and my father.

I never knew my father as a man; I only knew him as a boy, although I was thirty-three years old. My personal relationship with my father, as was everything else in my life, was stunted by all the years of my imprisonment. I never got to really know him and that would always be one of my biggest regrets and losses in my life.

When I was first transferred to Lucasville, my father and mother would come down to visit me quite often. They understood the importance of making sure the infamous prison authorities knew I had family support. Occasionally my father would pop in by himself, during which time we would make awkward small talk. I would ask how everyone was doing by name and he would say they were doing well and after that our monotone question-and-answer session would come to an end. The conversation would just hang in the air until the half hour visit was up.

This was how we started out when I came to see him lying on his death bed. I don't remember what I said but I remember being short of breath and hardly able to speak. I felt as though I was in a rush, realizing this would be the last conversation I would have with the man who was my father.

My father had three sons, Jimmie (Bruh), myself, and my youngest brother Lamar. Bruh the oldest, was his spitting image. However, my mother would remind me that it was I who had more of his traits. As I think back, perhaps she was right because we clashed. Nonetheless, this would be the last conversation I would ever have with my father, and determined to go beyond my comfort zone, I asked him how he felt, knowing that he was dying. I can't tell you why I asked him that question. I suppose I thought his answer would somehow reveal who he was to me. The question took him by surprise. He paused, one of my sisters adjusted his pillow so that he could look me in eye, and I realized I had never looked him in the eye as a boy. I knew him by the sound of his voice and not by the features of his face. He said, "I feel alright because I have faith in my Lord and Savior." Or words to that effect. "I gave my life over to my Lord and Savior Jesus Christ and it's in His hands."

I remember thinking and feeling he had to keep talking, there must be more for him to say. My spiritual ignorance at the time didn't allow me to understand the meaning and magnitude of the last words he would ever say to me. I thought his answer was too short and didn't quite cover all the frustrations and disappointments he surely must be feeling about his life that was cut short. How could he be so calm when he knew his life would soon be over? I don't know what I wanted to hear from my father. Defeat, regret, outpouring of emotions; certainly not the resolve that I heard in his voice.

I remember probing him to say something more. There had to be more he wanted to say. He must have something else he wanted to say to me. We couldn't just let our conversation end like it had always ended, but it did.

As I was riding back to the prison, I stared at my hands shackled to the seat of the van, thinking about my father. I'd promised my father many times that I would be a better son and each time I had failed him. I remember a cool chill coming over me, realizing I would never get another chance to prove it. My mother passed away six months later from a broken heart, wrongfully diagnosed as diabetic complications. My mother's heart had been ripped out of her chest. She could've survived without a leg, which she had lost to the diabetic debilitating disease, but not without a heart. She figured there was nothing more to live for and I was thankful that her pain and suffering was over.

The prison authorities allowed me to visit her body at the funeral home and once again I didn't see anyone there but my mother lying in the casket in a room full of people that I am certain was filled with friends and family.

I went back to the parole board and they gave me ninety more days. I had stopped going to school even though I only needed one more semester to obtain my bachelor of General Studies degree. My parents' deaths devastated me. There were days that I literally couldn't move, so I didn't come out of my cell. And on the days that I would venture out I ran the yard until I was told to lock down. I had gotten a one man cell for the first time in what now was going into my eleventh year. Perhaps getting word that the storm inside of me was about to erupt, one day the warden of the prison paid me a personal visit to my cell.

The warden was a young man and he hadn't been on the job long. He sat on one end of my bunk and offered his deepest condolence for losing both my parents in a span of nine months. He knew the parole board had given me another ninety-day flop but told me he was confident I would make parole the next time I see the board. He said, in so many words, that the Parole Board was just testing me to see how I would react after all that had happened, and he was there, he said, to encourage me not to fail the test.

I most certainly would have failed the test had not the warden showed up that day. Because I couldn't find any reason for me to give a fuck anymore. It was the first time the thought had occurred to me that right before the dawn is the darkest part of the night.

As a kid growing up, I used to fight my brother and sisters and often I would find myself wishing that I was the only child so that I would have more stuff and more attention from my parents. I remember asking my mother why she had so many children and she would say something like, "Boy, one day, you going to be thankful for all your brothers and sisters."

My sisters Lillie and Zanita arrived to take me home from the released intake-outtake center, a place where they sent inmates coming in and out of the prison system. They pulled up in a brand-new triple black 560 Mercedes Benz. The car was impressive but not as impressive as the prison gate rising to my freedom had been. And my mother was right, this day I was thankful beyond words for all my sisters and brothers. I climbed into the backseat and off we went, north up I-71. Several miles into the drive I noticed a small package wedged between the back armrests. The package was folded into a paper football. The game I played behind the teacher's back when I got bored in the classroom, thumping the folded paper football through the make-believe field goal post of the student sitting next me. I unfolded the paper and discovered a white powdery substance. I kept the discovery to myself for the time being, thinking it was heroin. As we drove and made small talk about my long-awaited freedom and how it felt to be free and what food I desired etc., I began to feel a bit paranoid. I decided to get the illegal controlled substance off my person, passing it to my sister Zanita riding in the front passenger seat. At first, they both played coy. Eventually, Lillie went on to tell me her husband controlled the cocaine supply from St. Clair to Superior. She did seem to care about the package of cocaine in the back seat of his car. She was upset that he had become lax and careless. The cocaine brought to light what a guy I had met in the prison release facility was trying to tell me. His name was Luthor. Dude knew my sister and was close friends with her husband and he was being released two weeks before me. Luthor was finishing up a two-year sentence for cocaine procession. He told me that my sister's husband, who went by the street name Freddy Foxx, was the man I needed to see if I was looking to get on. I had no clue what dude meant by, "Get on" until my sister Lillie's explanation about the cocaine I had found in her husband car.

One thing was for certain: I had no intention of trying to sell cocaine. But robbing cocaine sellers, taking it ... that, I had not decided yet.

Lillie told me the package was sixteen grams of cocaine. Back in the day, sixteen grams of cocaine had been too expensive for the average joe to afford daily. Cocaine in general was reserved for the affluent. Foxx had cornered the market at least in the Glenville neighborhood on cocaine when he introduced sixteen-gram packaging. His strategy was to make a larger amount of cocaine more practical and affordable for everyone. Foxx was to be the Henry Ford of cocaine ... mass production at an affordable price.

1987

I had done time and been released from juvenile institutions and Mansfield Reformatory but when I was released from prison in 1987 after spending a decade behind bars, I experienced a different kind of freedom.

It was decided that I move into my deceased parents' house in Garfield Heights. My nephew Jabs and baby sister Sharon were still living in the house at the time and I wasn't going to disrupt people's living arrangements. Therefore, I decided as soon as I got some money for an apartment and any family member wanted to take responsibility of the house they were welcome to do so.

I was in my early thirties, but I could count on one hand the women I had sex with at that point in my life. On the street I was never a pussy hound. Pussy was like air to me; I just thought it would be something that would always be there, until one day it wasn't.

After doing a decade I was desperate to make up for lost time. I promise myself I was not about to turn pussy down ever again. Young, old, fat, shiny, pretty, ugly, white, Black, Hispanic, Asian, whatever. If her pussy were willing, my dick would be obliging. My nephew Jabs and his conniving buster friend had made some arrangements with a white chick and her dude to provide me with some pussy. Apparently, these two freaky young dudes were curious to see what it looked like, when a man who had not had sex in over a decade gets his first piece of pussy. I could have charged admission because they were on some thirsty freaky peep show shit. All I wanted was some pussy. The whole neighborhood could have squeezed in the bedroom for all I cared. Come in and grab a seat, have a bag of popcorn and a cold beer and watch me fuck this bitch.

I didn't have time for no romancing as I needed my nuts out of the sand immediately. The next day I tracked down Jennifer, my hairstylist pen pal. After a day or so of romancing we got into a hot, lustful relationship. After the sex it was obvious that we had nothing in common, and our personalities clashed. She was bitchy and I was chauvinistic. I was a free man in a free world and pussy now was a dime a dozen ... the bitchy bitch was not worth my time and I did not care to be around her another minute.

The first days and weeks I was home I tried as hard as I could not to walk up to women on the streets and just ask them point blank for some pussy. "Hello, my name is Willie. Can I have some of your pussy, please?" But one day I could not restrain the urge, kind of. So, I approached this elderly lady whom I'd met at the grocery store on 131th and Miles. She had two little girls with her, and I found out later they were her granddaughters. They were leaving the store with too many bags to carry. I offered to help. When I say elderly lady, at the time I thought she was in her late fifties or perhaps sixties. But in retrospect she might have been younger. I assumed she was older because she had a head full of grey hair but now that I think about, she probably was no more than ten years older than me at best because her face didn't have age lines. I never asked about her age. Let's just say she was of the age when a woman owns her gray and overall mature appearance. I flirted with her off the rip. I told her how beautiful she looked and how pretty the dress she had on was. My compliments caught her off-guard a bit. But she was a woman used to being complimented. She was confident, accepting, and flattered all at the same time. And if I didn't know any better, which I most certainly did, I would have thought her, "Well, thank you, Casanova" was patronizing. She probed to check whether my flirting had any real teeth.

She said, "It's not every day a woman runs into a gentleman, you got to watch it out here, people are crazy."

I said, "I know what you mean." My eyes told her my context was authentic and my lust was real. Reassured, she immediately gave her consent for me to undress her with my eyes, putting her bag down in the trunk of the car, bending and tooting her ass with a prolonged pause, and turning to face me, arms akimbo. We stared at each other and what was understood didn't have to be voiced. We smiled. A beat or two of silence followed as we concentrated on putting the remaining grocery bags in the car. I knew she was taking a moment to consider her options. The ball was in her court, so to speak. She was that woman I had fantasized about that I would on occasion see walking with a group through the prison on prison business. All the inmates would line the hall undressing the women with unapologetic lustful eyes. I wanted so badly to stop and tell her how beautiful she was, or how nice her dress was, or how nice her perfume smelled, that had announced her intoxicating femininity and would linger on the premises long after she had left. What I would have given for an opportunity just to touch one of these women soft hands ... and hear her voice in confidence.

I'd promised myself that, whenever I was released from prison, I would seize any opportunity to tell that certain type of woman just how I felt.

My fantasy had manifested. She had two little girls with her who had been ear hustling the whole time. She sternly ordered the girls to get inside her small car. I told her I didn't want her money and undressed her again with my eyes. I told her the only thing I wanted was her phone number, if she wouldn't mind giving it to me. She stopped putting the bags in the car in mid action and looked me up and down. She gave me a fake appalled look and asked, "How old are you?" I had that penitentiary glow on my face and looked younger than my thirty-four years would indicate, I supposed. I told her I was thirty-five and her tone changed, and we began the cat and mouse game. She asked why I didn't have a wife or a girlfriend, and I told her I had just been released from prison last week. She froze and again leaned back with that stretching of the neck and raised-eyebrow look. She asked me what I did to get locked up and my hesitation caused her to stop organizing the groceries in the little hatchback and turn to face me as though she was expecting to find a monster in place of the man she had been talking with.

I said I robbed a drug dealer. She repeated, "A drug dealer?" I went on to explain the particulars of my case as fast as I could: robbing Goodnight and the fact children were in the house, but she still couldn't wrap her head around the fact I was given ten years for robbing a drug dealer.

By now her two granddaughters were getting restless, calling their grandma. Her apprehension about me was being replaced with indecision. She and I knew this might be her only chance. Her groceries were all packed in the car. "Thank you," she said and ordered her granddaughter to retrieve her purse off the seat. Again, I told her I was cool. "Well, it was nice talking with you."

"I am curious," she said, "what did you do in there in all those years?" I told her I went to school and worked out just about every day. It was her turn to undress me with her eyes. She couldn't hide her excitement and reach out and touched my shoulder. "Ooh, you are strong," she said, biting her bottom lip.

I was reminded of a cat watching a canary. By now we were in the parking lot for a good fifteen or twenty minutes. We were just standing in the parking lot, not saying a word, nodding our heads and smiling at each other knowing full well where we were headed. I knew I was getting in those panties. The next move would be for us to explore the time and place where we could make it happen. She asked me if I lived nearby. I told her both my parents had died and left me their house a few streets over on Camwood Dr. Before I had gotten the words out of my mouth good, she asked, "By yourself?" I told her my nephew and my sister stayed there as well. This was when I learned she stayed with her daughters a few streets over. She was keeping the girls while her daughters worked. I told her it wouldn't be no problem to help her take the groceries in her house since we both lived two streets apart, and afterward she could drop me off at my house.

She was interested in hearing more of my story and agreed. I can't remember the name of the street, but it was around the corner from Camwood. As we were taking the groceries in the house, she ordered the girls to go in the backyard and play; it was early winter but unseasonably warm. She told the girls she didn't want to see their face until she called them. As soon as she locked the back door, we went at it, attacking each other with pure lust, dancing and spinning until we landed on the living room couch. Freedom never felt so good.

Selisa

After all those letters we had written to each other when I was in the joint and she was pregnant, Selisa and I both knew there was nothing else for us to say. It was now time for us to meet face to face and confront the truths that we had confessed to each other in our letters. From the moment I came home we both had used one excuse after the other not to meet.

She pulled up in a big black Lincoln Continental to pick me up at my house. I remember having a "nigger what took you so long to get with this girl" moment. It passed when she told me the car was a rental.

We had dinner at the Brown Derby in Warrenville. The reason we didn't feel the need to rush to get with each other was we both knew that the truth would be complicated, so we gave ourselves time to get our things in order. We knew after we certified our truth there would be commitment, and commitment was complicated because deep down inside I knew I wasn't ready for complication and commitment. Commitment meant a world in a mother-and-father structure where the man provided for his family, and he was committed to that institution at all cost. I longed and craved for my father's world. Without even realizing it I had taken the values of my father in the letters I had written to Selisa. How ironic life was.

I was going on thirty-five years old, and I felt an internal pressure to catch up with my life's clock and the simple, no drama world that my father had lived. But my father's world 2.0 would be much better.

I had been locked up for twelve years. I understood incarceration had stunted my maturity and social development. I did not have too many do-overs left. I had never had a true man-and-woman relationship. Commitment and dedication, family at all costs. I was sure Selisa was the woman, but I wasn't ready to transition into this period of my life where commitment and dedication would be my goal, my end game: the main ingredients and measure of success for my life. The way Selisa and I had outlined it in our many letters.

But there was no truth behind bars, and now the bars were no longer a hindrance to my free will. I realized an overwhelming desire to explore and experience the lies behind bars just as much as I did the truth, so I decided to put commitment and dedication on hold.

Selisa Rita Tell was my sister Lillie's best friend. She was also Freddy Foxx's first cousin; her father and Foxx's mother were brother and sister. Aside from those family connections, Selisa was the baby mama of my baby mama's brother, which meant our children were first cousins. Our families' tie never was explored throughout our correspondence, so I didn't have a clue. Selisa had assumed that I knew all about our family connections and figured everything was cool. But no matter how much I tried to explain that I had no clue how closely we had been connected she would never believe that I didn't know during the process of us getting together. It was hard for her to understand how disconnected to family and relationships an individual becomes when they are incarcerated. Trying to explain how it felt to be incarcerated was like a dead man explaining how it feels to be dead.

I believed Selisa and I had perhaps never discussed our family tree in our letters because we were afraid of the outside noise messing up what we were hoping for. By the time we had finished our dinner we both knew, or I should say had confirmed that the content of our letters was authentic. I was going on thirty-five years old and after having spent a decade behind bars I was a hopeless romantic searching for an old-fashioned kind of love, the kind my mother had given to my father. The kind of girl every boy wanted to marry, in the spitting image of his mother. It made no difference what kind of woman the boy's mother had been or is for that matter because every human being finds a measure of comfort and sometimes love, in personal familiarity.

Selisa was six years younger than me, mature beyond her years. I was certain she was searching for the things I was willing to offer to my woman. She had an old school flavor that I recognized as a dying trait among young women her age. These women grew up in an era of exploding women liberation but weren't in no hurry to burn their bra or stop cooking dinner and not have their doors opened by a man. She was the type of woman who wanted her man out front, without being under his foot. Her appearance was unassuming from across a crowded room. She had a quiet personality and a certain kind of reserve about herself. On the other hand, she was the kind of girl who wore her emotions on her sleeves, but they were her emotions and not meant for anyone else. She wasn't the flashing fake smiling kind of girl. She was always a lady. From a male perspective, the closer you got the more her unique beauty shouted out for masculine attention, but at the same time appeared antagonistic and a bit challenging to females.

Her eyes were light brown and she had a small gap between

her teeth. She wasn't a big-chested woman, but her curves were more than satisfying. She had a nice round ass, and legs to die for. Occasionally, when she had been standing for a while, she would do this standing thing where she'd pop back on her knees in a double-jointed inverted posture, thrusting her pelvis out. There are perhaps several reasons why one woman's sex is different than other women for a man. Whatever the reasons the man will feel that difference immediately, for the bad or the good. Selisa's sex was different, and I felt it immediately.

As far as I could tell she wasn't a complicated woman, but I would learn early, she was dedicated to a fault. I learned her mother had recently lost a battle with breast cancer. They had been very close. Their relationship was more like sisters than mother and daughter. Her immediate family consisted of three sisters, Robin and the twins Micky and Tia. A cerebral and somewhat aloof brother named Tony. She also had two stepsisters on her father's side, DeDe and Phray. Her mother and her father had been in the life, her parents were more street hustlers than they were nine-to-five working people. By the time Selisa was twenty-five she had sold drugs, had her own record store, and booked numbers at the money exchange for one of the biggest Black Numbers bookies in Cleveland, Virgil Brown. She had always been a woman who as a child would take care of her younger siblings for days and sometimes weeks with their parents nowhere to be found.

Once her young twin sisters, for whom she was the legal guardian after their mother's death, had turned eighteen, we moved in together. It was a cozy little two-bedroom apartment in Shaker Heights. Even though I wasn't ready for structure and commitment, I recognized Selisa was a keeper, the kind of woman you lock the door behind and swallow the key. I had no problem playing house with her.

Cocaine

I was only home two months before I started robbing the young drug dealers who were on every corner in the Black neighborhood. I knew all the cocaine money had corrupted every police department in the country, especially those in the Black neighborhood, so when I went to work I would have on a suit and tie and played the detective role. Back in the day we called it our uniform. All the young dope boys were used to getting shook down by rogue cops so my presence on the block was business as usual.

When I stepped down Mike was into finesse robbing mode, by that he used words rather than a heater. It was clear he didn't want nothing to do with the heater after doing a decade behind bars for armed robbery. I kind of felt responsible for us going to prison in the first place. Had I not been so thirsty coming off my Mansfield bit we would not have caught the case in the first place. Don't get me wrong, I am not taking the blame for us getting knocked and going to jail because with every sting there is always a 50/50 chance that shit can go south. I am just stating the fact. But had I taken my time and chilled, for say, ninety days after Mansfield, Goodnight would have been in prison and there would not have been an opportunity for us to have robbed him.

So, as I reflected, I wasn't in no hurry to convince my friend to rob drug dealers with me again. Anyway, Mike was doing just fine without a gun. In the height of the cocaine drug scene everybody was a sting to Mike. I couldn't blame him because everyone was trying to get theirs.

The meaning of dog eat dog had risen to unprecedented heights in the cocaine pandemic. The money was plentiful for these new-age would-be hustlers. The rules had changed. "Get down first" was the name of the game. Hustlers that had taken thousands from their own people would be invited back into their houses the next year. And these dudes would snitch on one another without any repercussion. It was a different world than the world Mike and I had left. There was only one hustle, all the other hustles were derivatives of the sale of cocaine. I suspect the reason was tied to the abundance of money. Everybody in the game felt that cocaine money was a bottomless well. Therefore, revenge had lost its value and if someone felt they needed to serve a measure of revenge, they served it hot rather than cold. Having to hustle for '70s dollar value is much different than having to hustle for late '80s and '90s dollars, it was like taking candy from a baby. Mike felt it, as did I the moment we both stepped down.

Because of my family ties my sister being married to one of the biggest drug dealers in the City at the time, Freddy Foxx. I had access and was able to establish a nice little small cocaine operation that was keeping money in my pocket. But it was always my nature to not give weight to low hanging fruit. My mind was on the bright shiny apple at the very top of the tree.

Everyone thought I was selling cocaine, but from the rip I was taking way more cocaine than I was selling. I had purchased a fake police badge and a nice Crown Victory that I had painted all black. The police look-alike car sealed the deal in the neighborhood I was working. I was officially a cop and if there was any lingering doubt that I wasn't a cop, no one wanted to bet their freedom on it.

Mike had fallen in lock-step with all the other hustlers; he was not turning down any hustling opportunity, he was doing it all and everybody was a sting, myself included. Every time I looked up the nigga was in my pockets for one get-rich scheme after another. Sometimes the sting was about real paper, and sometimes the sting was nothing but smoke and mirrors. It was a new laissez-faire attitude in the air when it came to hustle in this new cocaine era. "I'll take care of it," and "Don't sweat it," were phrases I would hear often. It took me a minute to get used to it. I was still in gangster mode. I was like, these niggas better get my money. But the cocaine money was coming back too fast for me to sweat the small stuff, so I learned to accept it and fell in step with the attitude of getting down first. As for Mike, like I said a part of me felt I owed him a free ride.

My sister Mary had five girls and one boy. When it came down to her children, some days Mary acted like she had been cursed and then there were days when she acted like she was blessed, depending on her economical and emotional state of mind with the men in her life.

Mary must have hated the man who fathered her only son because she used to give that little boy the blues. No one knows the depths of someone's personal relationships but from afar, I knew my sister did not have an ounce of emotional satisfaction in the brief relationship with her son's father.

She would leave her little bad ass boy to be raised by my parents. His name was Lionel, we called him Jabs. When my parents passed away, Jabs' bad ass was raised by the streets. I turned all the cocaine I acquired over to this little nigga, who must have felt he'd died and gone to cocaine-hustling heaven. I hated selling drugs and never cared for drug dealers. Right around the time I came home Jabs was just learning the tricks and trade of how to become a low down, lying, conniving and selfish cocaine drug seller. Turned out Jabs was a natural. But I was cool with his skill set because it was a prerequisite for cocaine sellers.

For a lot of young hustlers, selling cocaine was a rite of passage. It was survival of the fittest in the cocaine-plagued decades of the '80s and '90s. These young dudes were the men of their households, paying the rent and putting food on the table, buying clothing for their younger and sometimes older siblings because their parents had contracted the crack head disease. My sister wasn't a crack head but her son, my nephew Jabs, whether he was ready or not, had to become the man in his world.

I never dealt with my brother-in-law, Freddy Foxx in the exchange of cocaine because mixing business with family could get messy, even though he handled most of the Girl coming through the Northeast side of Cleveland. The most I would get from him would be a small cash loan of some kind. I set out to create my own team, with my nephew as my number one lieutenant. But like I mentioned previously, I had an aversion to selling drugs and to drug dealers. And of course, I had no patience, so I was cool with my nephew handling all phases of my one-man drug operation.

Jabs would turn a quarter of an ounce of cocaine into a quarter of a key. Before I knew it, he had flipped the quarter into a key. Selling cocaine was every little nigga's dream and Jabs enjoyed it more than most. Why not? When I came home, the little nigga died and went to young-nigga-do-nothing-but-sell-cocaine heaven. I supplied him with the inventory and tried to spend the money faster than he could buy another car, with the flip money.

Jabs sold just about all the cocaine I was taking, taking for the most part from his little peers. Again, nothing had changed; I still had no patience with things that depended on a step-by-step-by-step process. Within a month that I was home, I knew I would be taking cocaine, rather than selling it.

I learned in cocaine 101 class that a cocaine habit was different than a heroin habit. Cocaine controlled your mind, whereas heroin controlled your body. Cocaine addicts were like the zombies in The Walking Dead. Heroin addicts posed a more dangerous threat to your wellbeing. Cocaine was an epidemic and no one was immune; once you hit the pipe it was over for you. Freebasing cocaine was a way of breaking the cocaine powered down from its salt base form, extracting all the additives to get to one hundred percent purity. The freebasing process represents additional expense, as it involves a lot of paraphernalia costs, such as glass pipes, ammonia, rum, butane lighter, etc. Smoking crack cocaine was more affordable; all you needed was some boiling water and baking soda and a straight shooter pipe that cost a dollar.

Bruh became one of the walking dead, a crackhead. There was nothing I, nor anyone, could do or say to help him. He would have to find the way back on his own somehow. I missed my brother and longed for the old Bruh, but he was nowhere to be found. After he had been released from prison, Bruh went hard on the drugs. I could only imagine he had taken my parents' deaths hard. And by the time I had come home, the only one who could save him would be himself.

Nonetheless, the more I watched him slowly fade into the cocaine abyss, the angrier I became with those who were profiting off his misery. One night I got a frantic call from a family member telling me my brother had been shot and the ambulance was rushing him to the hospital. When I got there, my sisters were standing around my brother's hospital bed. He was in a lot of pain but conscious. He had two bullets inside of him and the doctors wanted to operate. But he had told my sister he did not want the white doctor doing invasive, exploratory surgery on him. The doctors were contending that the bullet might have hit something vital and the effects may not be apparent to him now, or even a day from now. Bruh said, "Fuck that." He didn't want the doctors going on a search and find mission. And we all agreed with him. We knew white doctors sold Black people's organs on the black market in the same way big drug companies sold their legal drugs in a pharmacy.

My brother was average in stature, but his height was the only thing average about him. These bullets inside him were numbers six and seven. He had been shot more times than a man sentenced to death by firing squad. He was a walking miracle, stronger inside and out than any man I've ever known and would know in all the years I would be on this earth. It is believed, mostly by our family, that he was blessed with the strength of the warrior King David and the wisdom of King Solomon; but that is another story. His story to tell, not mine.

Like the many times before, after several days of waiting for his wounds to heal to his satisfaction, he would simply get up from his hospital bed and walk out. It was at this time that I was convinced my brother was a special kind of dude. He packed up his girl and their three little kids and headed to Detroit. He had made too many enemies in Cleveland. The family agreed the best thing would be for him to leave town quickly.

Within a year I was able stack enough paper for a small carry-out restaurant. My brother-in-law had bought a building on Miles Avenue and I propositioned him to let me rehab the storefront space for a restaurant, and in return he would forgo the rent payment. There was no lease agreement ... we both were too busy to concern ourselves with the pennies. I would learn the first lesson of real estate, which was never rehab another man's real estate. On the other hand, it was cocaine money, which meant I had to find something to do with it, or else it would evaporate into thin air.

My entrepreneurship was funded by my criminal cocaine endeavors but so was a third of the American economy; financing and producing fruit from poisonous trees.

Chasing the Zeitgeist

Mike was released two years before I came home. His hustling urgency had an eerie sense of déjà vu to his words; it felt like Groundhog Day. It reminded me of the time when I came home from Mansfield, when I was thirstier than a junk yard dog and pressed him every day to help me get on my feet, and to find a robbery sting which ended up being the Goodnight robbery. Now twelve years later, here we were once again. But this time, the shoe was on the other foot and he was pressing me for a hustle.

"Everybody is selling cocaine," Mike said. "All we have to do is get a couple of ounces and keep flipping it and we'll be rich in six months." The cocaine money was fast, but I knew the only way I was getting rich in six months would be if I were to jump the counter of a bank. I had seen firsthand what Mike was alluding to because my sister and her husband Freddy Foxx was living high on the hog, as the old players used to say. They had a house with an indoor swimming pool, a closet full of clothes, diamonds and mink coats with Jaguars and Mercedes in the driveway. Freddy Foxx was killing it.

When we're cast away somewhere on a deserted island, we tend to think the world had stopped and waited for us to return, so we end up chasing the zeitgeist. And the thing we ex-convicts don't realize is that all we need to do is slow down a

187

beat. This time I learned who I was inside and out, how I was wired mentally in terms of my ADHD understanding myself. This time I was able to slow down a beat and get in lock step with the zeitgeist. After I gave my sister the cocaine I had found in the back seat, I asked her to tell me about her husband, Freddy Foxx and her eye had lit up.

"Sleepy," she said, "you're going to like him. He's your type of nigga, a bona fide money-getting hustler."

She talked about how she had given him her welfare check and he started off selling ten-dollar bags of weed and within two years he had parlayed his weed profits into a cocaine empire. And she didn't stop talking about him until we rolled up at the house in Cleveland.

The thing I came away with about my conversation with my sister was that she loved the ground her husband walked on. I was like that dog that had chased cats all his life, and one day the dog's owner married a woman, who brought with her the biggest cat the old dog ever saw. The dog's owner said to the old dog, meet Top Cat, he's your new roommate. Don't fuck with him or your flea-biting ass is out of here. Who said you can't teach an old dog new tricks? Learning the family business might not be such a bad career change after all, I thought.

But for real, I knew I could never take orders from anyone. Like my mother would say, "You are hard headed, and you just won't listen." I am the type of dude who don't listen to nobody. My ears have never worked. I listen with my mouth, not my ears. I didn't believe like most people that the only way for anyone to become successful in their lives would be for them to learn how to take orders from people. It was my belief that only carried weight and/or applied to every race of people except the African American.

To this day, I don't take orders, only suggestions. Moreover, I refuse to compromise with delayed gratification because tomorrow isn't promised to anyone. There isn't a person alive who would be cast away for a decade and come back in step with the heartbeat of life, without missing a beat. Shit changes quickly.

I was under no illusion that selling cocaine was as easy as one, two, three the way Mike had spelled it out. It seemed everybody's goal was to become their own version of Freddy Foxx, except me. And since it was clear my sister's husband wasn't looking to make me his new partner, the only thing we would have in common would be family.

I was grateful to my sister and her husband for footing the bill for me. So, I wasn't in any hurry to pull up on her husband and ask him to give me his cocaine so that I can fuck it up. I was pretty sure dude knew there was no way in hell that I knew how to sell cocaine being that I was locked up for a decade. But selling heroin; now that was a different animal altogether.

I pulled up at my sister's house in Garfield Heights, my arrival had been expected. When I got there I noticed, parked in front of their house, a long Winnebago motorhome. I had never been in one, so I thought I'd peep in and take a quick look around before going up to the house. The door was unlocked so I tiptoed inside. Once inside I began to hear this familiar slapping sound. When I was a kid, I would tie a piece of plastic or cardboard to the spokes of my bike wheel to imitate the sound of a motor bike, it sounded the same. I peeped around the corner and saw this guy on the floor but I had no clue what he was doing until the slapping sound stopped and the one guy that was out of my view asked him, "How much is that now?" "267,000," was the reply.

I almost passed out right there. I supposed they were there to purchase cocaine from my brother-in-law. I do not know what I was thinking. Instinctively my hand went straight to my waistband for my gun, but nothing was there. My eyes quickly scanned around for any possible weapon but there was nothing. It didn't register with me that perhaps this was my brother-in-law's money. My mind was frozen in the moment, I couldn't get past the number "$267,000" and the weird hypnotizing feeling that pushed me to find a way to take the money.

Mind you, this was the dead of winter, but I was sweating profusely. In my mind I told myself I would never again pick up a gun and commit armed robbery, but I knew I had lied to myself. Just as I turned to leave and go find me a weapon, a stick, brick, knife something Freddy Foxx opened the door behind me. He was surprised to see me perched in the doorway of his Winnebago. In that moment I realized the money had belonged to him. We had an awkward greeting moment. He called out for the guys in the Winnebago who were counting the money, asking them if they had finished counting. The dude, whose name was Slim, came and the two of them had me sandwiched in the small space. Fred didn't seem to be concerned with Slim's answer as much as he was concerned with the motion of my hands. We had met several times before. I managed to say "Oh, here you are." And his reply was words something to the effect of, "I'll be in the house in a minute, Lillie is in the house, wait for me there."

I am sure my sister Lillie had given him the run-down on me just as she had given me the rundown on him. He knew what my calling card was. He knew I had gone to prison for robbing drug dealers, so he knew what I was capable of.

Foxx knew I had seen something in the Winnebago I wasn't supposed to see, but he didn't get bent out of shape because he was a man who dealt with the drama that large sums of money brought to his doorstep every day. Fred wasn't afraid of people taking things from him. Because for him to hold down a cocaine empire he had to be feared, rather than loved. He employed an army of do-anything-for-the-kingpin soldiers and all he had to do was give the word, and the static was taken care of immediately.

It's a good thing Foxx pulled up when he did, and snapped me back to the present. To quote the ex-President Jimmy Carter, "At some time or another we all have lust in our hearts" or words to that effect.

Lillie made small talk and asked how I was getting along at the house. I told her everything was cool; she went on to say if I needed anything don't hesitate to ask her. An hour or so Foxx came in the house and after a few pleasantries we set down for business. I spelled out my plans to get into the heroin business, and how selling heroin would be a more familiar lane for me. Always the businessman, Foxx told me he'd been talking with his dude about selling heroin. He was intrigued about the high returns you can make compared to cocaine. He went on to say this could be his opportunity to get his feet wet and at the same time help me get on. He asked me how much I needed. I told him I'd start with an ounce; an ounce taking a good three or two should cost no more than seven thousand, I said.

He started pulling bills out of his pocket and I knew right then I should've asked him for fourteen or twenty-one thousand. When I left my sister's house, I couldn't get the sound of the money machine out of my head. That old anxious addictive, sweaty, butterfly-in-the-stomach feeling had reawakened inside me. Even though my pockets were stuffed with hundreds, that slapping sound just would not go away. I told myself I would buy the heroin … after I bought a heater. I surmised that if these dope boys were out here rolling a fraction of what Freddy Foxx was doing, robbing their asses was my best option. Fuck trying to sell cocaine; I had no patience for the tedious drudgeries of delayed gratification.

It was assumed since I had family connection with Freddy Foxx, I would go into the business with him, especially Mike. Mike suggested I get in touch with Rick Fields. The Fields brothers were known in the Glenville neighborhood for years. Ronald Fields was a tough hard-nosed dude and fought at the drop of a dime. He and I got into several fights as kids. I didn't meet his younger brother, Rick, until my teenage years.

Rick always had the pulse of the heroin market. Rick's heroin connects were passed down from his old man. In fact, the first time Mike and I robbed a drug dealer it had been Rick that set the sting up for us. We took about a half an ounce of China White heroin from some wet-behind-the-ears Italian dudes who went to college with Rick. The heroin took the strongest four cut you'd ever seen. Dudes were overdosing on the shit all summer long, without a drop-off. If you did have a habit and were to touch the shit with your bare hands you got high. I remember thinking, "Damn, this is how they rolled in college?"

The days of retail China White taking a four-cut was long gone. The only thing I got from Rick for my seven grand was an ounce of tar heroin that had been stepped on a million times. Never trust hustlers looking for a hustle with your money. The dope I got from Rick, a sick addict, wouldn't buy the shit if it was the only thing he could find. Turns out the money was too much for Mike and Rick to let pass through their hands without them taking out a sucker tax finder fee. Lesson learned. Apparently, Mike had learned his lesson and didn't want nothing to do with a gun after doing a decade behind bars for it. I understood where he was coming from because no one needed a gun to rob most of the wannabe dope boys. All you had to do was tell them, "The package got knocked in 'Utah.'"

From the very first day I was released from prison and discovered the packet of cocaine that was wedged between the armrest of Foxx's big black 560 Benz, my cocaine education had begun. I learned quickly that the drug war was being waged on four fronts: drug enforcements, drug sellers, drug users, and drug hustlers. And everybody had become addicted in their pursuit.

There were two kinds of hustlers: finesse and gorilla. I was a gorilla hustler because I took what I wanted with a gun. But the game had changed from the time when I used to kick in dope house doors. Back in the day, selling dope was looked down on in the community. It wasn't something that the drug dealer wanted promoted. To buy any type of drugs, you would have to know a friend, who knew a friend. Now, there wasn't a block in a community that didn't have a drug house in it. If not a dope house, there was a kid making his rounds on his bike, selling anything you wanted.

The 1980s presented a different script, indeed. Now dope dealers were the role models, and every little Black boy in the hood aspired to be just like them. Shit was weird because some of these little niggas came from upstanding families and you barely heard them say a curse word. They went to church and had good grades in school. Yet, they were out here dumping pounds of cocaine in the 'hood as though it was a normal thing.

Not long after I was home from prison, I pulled on a crap game. There were several OGs, several young Kats. The old school dudes were putting down busters, using six-eight flat dice with more sleight of hand than a master magician. From what I could surmise from their conversation, the old school Kats had let the little dope-boy crew win the last time they played. The young crew had been set up. They were losing close to ten grand. However, what struck me the most about the game was not how much the young dope boys were losing, but the laissez faire and nonchalant way in which they were accepting losing all that money. These little niggas left the crap game laughing and joking. It was then I decided to dust off my heater. I had just got off a decade for sticking people up and not once did I have any regrets about robbing dope dealers. My only regret was the way I had went about robbing. When I left Mansfield, I was no different from a junkie feigning. This time I vowed to check my state of mind. I wasn't thirsty. I was pressed for nothing. Thanks to my family, I could take my time and educate myself, like a professional.

As weeks turned into months, I'd learned that cocaine money belonged to whoever could spend it the fastest, and if you held on to it for any length of time the money would burn your hands to a crisp. But it was never my intention to build a cocaine empire or become this famous stickup man. You can keep the fame, all I wanted was the fortune. All I wanted was those opportunities that drug-selling money afforded you fuck the status.

The first project on my list was a Jamaican drug ring out of Chicago. After about a month of planning the hook was in, good and tight. I had bought two keys previously and had put an order in for ten. I told them to give me a call when they were ready to fill the order. After a night of partying and drinking I sprung my robbery sting on Mike, and he said he was down. But I knew I had to act fast before he had time to really think about it. It was like that girl you pick up in the bar at night: the alcohol and the darkness clouds your rational mind and in the bright lights of the early morning you have a change of heart.

I loved Caddies. I never liked cookie-cutter European performance cars. I figured if I want all that performance, I'd take a 747. Caddies had style, and design presence. The cars were everything American. I had purchased a four-door black Caddy and we put it on the road that same night. I didn't want Mike to change his mind. My partner had a million questions on the way. He didn't even have a gun, he said. I told him he could use mine, a .380 caliber, because he would be getting the drop. Giving Mike the only gun reassured him that the set-up was tight.

The sting went off without a hitch and we arrived back in Cleveland in the early hours of the next day with twelve keys of pure Colombian cocaine. The sweet nectar of high-hanging fruit is like no other.

Rare Air

I bought a house in Cleveland Heights. My five keys of cocaine turned into ten keys of cocaine money so fast I was able to start a loan shark business. Mike's pockets were on full as well and we both were looking for legitimate business opportunities.

Mike came to me with an opportunity to invest in an entertainment promotion venture. Rick was starting a concert-promoting business and needed some investors. I figured promoting concerts would be a good business to get into, and just like that I found myself in a partnership to sponsor a West African tour with the jazz band, Kool & The Gang.

I did what drug dealer stickup boys were meant to do: spend money before it burned your hand. Other than the basic knowledge I had no clue about the Ivory Coast of Africa.

When we touched down in Ghana, Mike had a full-length fox fur coat draped across his arm and Rick was wondering about the country's heroin trade. And in my mind, Ghana was no different from Detroit, Michigan. To say we were out of place in Africa was the understatement of 1989. However, ignorance is bliss, coupled with the fact that we were fearless. Marco Polo had nothing on us.

Rick had some friends in Ghana, exchange students he had met while attending Wilberforce University. And as for the busi-

The calm evening surf, Accra Ghana

ness side of things, the opportunity was the brainchild of a native Ghanaian Rick had met who ran small jewelry shops in Cleveland. I called him Joe. I did not have any clue what the fuck was required of concert promoters. I knew I simply helped supply the money to make it all happen. My only concern was profit.

I had always liked those behind-the-scenes raw footage of those rock concert musicians, so I brought a camcorder with me to gather video footage for a possible documentary about our experience with these legendary musicians in Africa.

However, the moment I looked through the camcorder lens Africa initiated a coup for my undivided attention and instead of the footage about the concert experience and the jazz musicians, it would end up being all about Her, the Motherland, and Her attempt at reclaiming her wayward child.

After a day or two, nothing seemed to matter more than my connection to Her. The more the camcorder lens brought the majestic country into focus, the more I became mesmerized and captivated with the beauty and intoxicating smell of pure Black freedom. Indeed, I felt like a lost child who'd found his way back to the loving arms of his mother after spending many lonely nights in a cruel, unloving orphanage.

Pure Black freedom. No one had to tell me what it smelled like. It was instinctive, the way a newborn animal knows the smell of their mother and finds their way back to her after being lost in a herd of thousands. Making a profit from the concert tour didn't matter; nothing mattered to me but filling my lungs with the air of pure Black freedom. It was one thing to read about your African American heritage, but a whole different animal when you connect with it. To be able to fill in that empty hole and you suddenly felt connected to a part of you that you never knew existed inside of you, finally realizing your entire being.

*Two members of the Kool & The Gang band. I am holding the
camcorder and Mike talking to a native.*

Me taking a photo with the children in Kumasi Ghana

There is a different kind of joy and brightness in the smiles on the faces of Black children who have always breathed the pure Black air of freedom. But there was something illogical about their joy. How can these African children, living in a Third World country, be so happy and exude so much joy and confidence? It seemed to be an emotional incongruency of sorts. If an individual is poor, should there be a measure of despair? But no, these children were devoid of any despair or sadness. They had always conceived, comprehended, and acted in the authority of the dominant culture, regardless of their financial status; they have never been systemically made to feel hopeless and inferior to any race of man. They were simply human beings.

These native Africans only knew one freedom, which was a pure freedom, given by God. On the other hand, my African American freedom, a man-made freedom, was inconceivable to the native African, and I too felt the difference standing on the African ground. Never had I felt so comfortable in my own skin.

We all decided to go on a sightseeing tour that ended up at the infamous Fort Elmina slave castle that had been transformed into one of Ghana's most treasured museums. We walked slowly through the dungeons in the bloody footsteps of my slave ancestors. We came to rest on the fortress walls overlooking the vast Atlantic Ocean in silence, everyone in their own private thoughts. The weather had to be ninety degrees or more, but a shivering chill came over me, and my mind drifted and was overwhelmed in the moment. And I found myself shackled in the holds of the slave ships. Somehow, my ancestors had survived for me to live. The experience was overwhelming. I felt as though I couldn't go back to be the person that I had been now that I was made aware. My awareness was the connection to this extraordinary seed of survival. Going back to my old self would be disrespectful

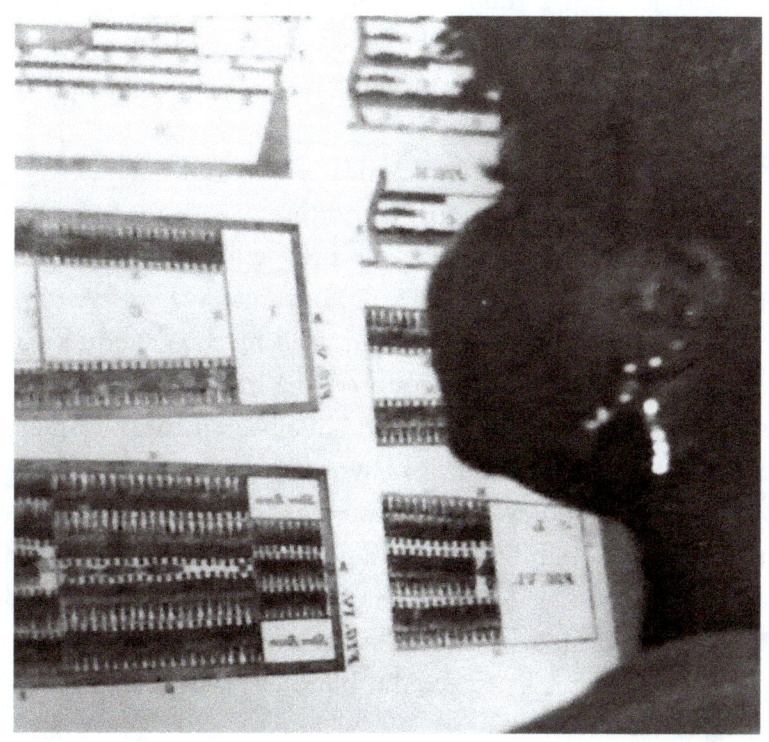

A haunting display of The Elmina Castle grim past

to the seed that had survived the voyage shackled in the hold of the slave ship and two hundred plus years of slavery.

In that moment, I felt a sense of duty as an African American to protect the seed at all cost. I couldn't think of anything more important to do with my life. I was overwhelmed with purpose and reference. For a thug who had never given a thought to be anything else but a thug, nothing else mattered to me other than connecting with my African American self. I felt extremely humble.

Mike and I had arrived in Africa with a full-fledged monkey on our backs. Rick had a gorilla, and he was dealing and snorting heroin way before I knew the drug existed. Traveling with dope fiends will surely present some drama so I wasn't too surprised to find out one of them had used my luggage to smuggle an ounce of heroin into the country. If I had been caught smuggling heroin in Ghana, that would have been it for my American ass. The Ghanaian prison, in a word, was the most inhumane place I had ever laid eyes on. Death was the norm and your freedom a remote possibility. It was a good thing we were privileged guests in the country. Kool & The Gang were some ambassadors and highly regarded by the political authorities that ruled the country. Therefore, I suspected a blind eye was directed toward our American indiscretions.

Privacy wasn't a civil right in the country, so no way had they missed the heroin in my bag. My assumption was confirmed when our military escort provided Rick with an opium connection. Aside from drugs, we bought authentic African artifacts and pure gold and diamonds. All in all, we were treated like royalty.

Having never been looked upon in such an esteemed light and then having an entire country shower you with overwhelming hospitality and borderline reverence was unbelievable. More than I could have ever imagined.

They put us up in grass huts that felt like little personal islands with customized climate control where you can set the dial to caressing morning breezes and star-lit nights. We had military escorts everywhere we went and assigned a group of women called the Jambo Girls, whose job it was to be at our beck and call no matter the time of day or night. Our promotional contract calls for eight concerts, however, we could not turn down an opportunity to meet Stevie Wonder, who had requested us to allow Kool & The Gang to join him in a private set for the governor of Côte d'Ivoire in Abidjan. Stevie had been in Paris. Of course, it was a no brainer for us.

In 1989, South Africa was constantly in the news surrounding the imminent release of Nelson Mandela. Drama was still my first love and addiction. The Motherland had me drunk with Her Black consciousness and I tried to convince everyone on the tour that would listen to me, that we should head down to South Africa to be a part of the historical moment of Nelson Mandela's release. Mike and Rick thought about it but they didn't feel as passionate about going to South Africa as I did, so they remained the voices of reason and pushed back on my idealistic suggestions that were growing each day I woke up in the Motherland.

In my mind, I was sure all that Africa needed was one dude like me, and that would fix whatever it was that had held Her back from being the most powerful continent in the world. I was certain of it and desperately wanted to give it a shot.

Monetary-wise, when it was all said and done, we left Africa broke as hell. We ended up dropping a little over two hundred thousand, but it was well worth it for the life-changing experience, at least for me. I was a changed man. It was the first time I could remember questioning my life's direction and feeling ashamed of being who I was. Every day I woke up in the Motherland my confidence grew stronger and stronger. I felt a human worthiness that I had never believed existed in me. I could feel a spirit moving toward my purpose and I began to conceive and accept my purpose with conviction. I never thought about being a promoter, but to the people of the Ivory Coast of Africa, that exactly who I was. Native musicians and entrepreneurs were lining up outside my hotel room door everyday with aspirations of convincing me to be their sponsor to America. Every morning, I would hear two or three of their pitches like in the Shark Tank TV show. There was this one entrepreneur who had invented a small little pizza oven to fit on a truck. He drove around Abidjan, smelling like personalized French pizzas. I signed an exclusive rights contract with him and had every intention to bring the French pizza maker over on a 50/50 partnership and turn my carry-out Pandora restaurant into a French pizza parlor.

The Same Soup

Shoulda, woulda, coulda. When I returned to Cleveland, my old self told my new self that lame-ass shit was for suckers, and it was as though I had never been to Africa. The couple of months after I had come home from prison, I had caught my nephew stuffing my cocaine down his pants. I felt embarrassed for the little thief and acted like I didn't see him; yet, it told everything I would ever have to know about his character in that one revealing moment of clarity. In all my treacherousness and wretchedness, stealing from family was inconceivable no matter the circumstances.

So when I got back from Africa, it was no surprise to discover the little thief had decided to do his own thing with the drugs I had left in his care. He had been selling my cocaine unchecked since day one, and for every dollar he would give me he would put two in his own pocket. Peer pressure for a young hustler was necessary as we all needed to be tested. We needed our ego stroked every so often. Being thought of as the up-and-coming next neighborhood drug king was the ultimate ego stroking, and the highest honor his little buster friends could bestow on him. It was my job to keep him level-headed and make sure he knew that the light at the end of the tunnel was a train. Like a parent, I told him don't do as I do, do as I say. I told him every day that selling drugs was a means to an end, invest your money. Go to truck driving school, buy you some trucks, learn how to drive heavy equipment but he would piss on that logic. His head blown up too big.

If you were to take the best young Black cocaine hustlers, and some old ones as well, take all their drugs from them, and drop them in downtown Salt Lake City Utah for a year, when you came back to get them, you will find that every last one of those niggas became a bum, begging for food and spare change. These young niggas weren't really hustlers. A fucking gnat could sell drugs and that's how I saw them; a bunch of brainless gnats, infesting the neighborhoods. Of course, there was hypocrisy in my rationale. Crime is crime; what made my crimes any different, one might ask. Fuck that, there are levels to this shit, that's how I felt. The true young street hustlers graduated. They had visions about uplifting their families and neighborhoods with legitimate enterprises. And at the end of the day felt a measure of shame. For true young hustlers selling cocaine was merely a means to another end for them, like getting your dick sucked; the head is good, but the head is just a prelude to the pussy. The pussy, how well the girl can throw that thang, was the true story and defining moment of the relationship, at least it was for me, a true young street hustler. All these young fake-ass cocaine hustlers wanted was their dick sucked.

No one's head was harder than mine, but my head had never gotten too big. And like every hardheaded nigga, my demise would be self-inflicted. On the other hand, I was never the monkey with a cup, dancing for passersby. I was done with peer pressure around the age of ten. That's around the time I stopped drinking my own Kool Aid, because I knew I would always make it too sweet. So, I knew from experience there would be no saving my nephew from the train, but in retrospect had I known his guts would end up spilling on me, I would have tried harder.

Confession of a Stick Man

Selling or waiting and watching someone selling cocaine was like watching and waiting for grass to grow. I could not do it. Selling cocaine was no different to me than a welfare mother with ten children waiting on a monthly welfare check, no matter how fast the check came. I reiterate that type of hustling made a hustler lazy and stunted his growth. Being a hustler was a profession; the money was only part of it. It was the doing, and if the doing did not stimulate me, I might as well get me a 9-to-5 and that shit was not about to happen. For me, wrong or right, life had to be a challenge, or why live? I got off robbing drug dealers because if you came with a fucked-up strategy, it could cost you your life. You might say that's some crazy shit well, a mountain climber isn't trying to hear that.

The ultimate rush for me was stepping in a room full of niggas with guns, and feeling this intoxicating moment, a fraction of a second perhaps, where confidence wrestle with doubt and doubt loses, and you announce, "This is a robbery." It feels like an orgasm. I would take that feeling every day than the feeling one gets from selling crack cocaine to a crackhead. But that's just me a sick stickup man with an ADHD personality.

So like everyone else, my nephew had taken my ADHD-"don't give a fuck" attitude about selling cocaine as being blind and gullible. If it wasn't for circumstance, his mistake would have cost him and his buster friends their lives. Instead, their fate was decided by a higher power, and I ended up in the hospital missing a big toe.

Some might say it's hypocritical of me, an armed robber to suggest that one crime is more honorable than the other. But there is honor amongst thieves, and to that end, I say to you, check the police records.

Most of them drug dealers folded like an envelope when the Feds put a decade or more on the table. The line was, you think if they were in your shoes, they would not give you up? For me it was simple: live by the sword or die by the sword. Armed robbers did not have snitching leverage like drug dealers.

Selling drugs as a means to an end, is for soft bitches ... yeah, I said it. When I reached the age where doing time or snitching was negotiable, I promised myself that's the day my crime days would be over. Check the record.

The war on drugs was real, it was an all-out assault on Black communities. The plan was to divide and conquer, and it worked to perfection. Every Black man in the hood was like every man for himself. No trust, no loyalty. No one could hide their blood thirsty greed. It was chaos. The word "friend" was a secret code for "hater." The players would just as well steal from their brothers and snitch on their own mothers in this fake hustler drug-selling game. I was a stickup man. Give me death or give me the honor of taking your drugs and money. You knew where I was coming from. I had no secrets. I knocked on your door and put my pistol in your face; there weren't any surprises. My robbing you wasn't personal and certainly wasn't going to be a secret in the community where you chose to sell your poison. And check this out: if the cops were to stop me with the drugs and money I had taken from you, you could rest assured I would not snitch on you. The drugs were mine. The cops would tell you I fell on my sword. Check the record.

Flip the Script

I had gotten bored living in the snake pit world of cocaine. My trip to Africa made me stop in the middle of the road and decide to give my undivided attention to the challenge of legitimacy and start focusing on my loan shark endeavors and interest payments.

I had loaned fifty thousand for sixty-five back to finance a demolition business. Mitch Miller, who called himself a resource specialist, was the go-between and the one who had introduced me to the client, whose name was Humphrey. I had hired Mitch as a consultant to help me with the formation of a nonprofit I founded called "Sport Ed Won." I had mentioned to Mitch Miller that I might be interested in giving out a few loans.

The loan was a simple collateral back loan. In exchange for my fifty thousand dollars at fifteen percent, I held their demolition equipment. I don't remember the details but the full amount plus interest was to be due in six months.

Long story short, Humphrey didn't have my money and I ended up confiscating his demo equipment: 977 bulldozers, flatbed, and an old tandem truck, which I'd planned to liquidate as soon as possible. I needed the money.

When it was all said and done, I became Humphrey's partner in his demo company. He showed me where he had all but secured a thirty-five-thousand-dollar demo contract to tear down a building belonging to Hough Baker on the corner of Euclid and Lakeview. After hanging out and listening to the old-timer demo guy for several weeks it was clear the old guy knew everything there was to know about demolition contracting in the city of Cleveland.

It also became clear to me that Humphrey's original plan was to run game for my five stacks. But after hanging out with me, the old man realized, as I did, a partnership would be more valuable for the both of us and less violent, I am sure.

We were able to put the demolition contracting company together in a few weeks, and the old man was able to secure insurance and a demolition contractor bond totaling five million. I was impressed. I named the company Caine Construction. The company's goal would be to specialize in small commercial and residential demolition. I had had flipped the script. I told myself I was finished with the robbery and drug-selling game, going strictly legitimate from here on out.

The African sun had nourished and restored my body to a point where drugs became a distant memory. After having walking through the dungeons of the slave castle Fort Elmina, my life took on a different meaning, my mind was uncluttered by meaningless worldly desires. I felt an inner worth that I had never felt before, an invincibility, like a superhero whose powers were far superior to every force opposing my path in the universe. For the first time in my life, I felt the authenticity of my Blackness, unclouded by the systemic forces that had long denied my potential.

The construction company gave me an opportunity to move away from crime. Crime wasn't a dirty garment that I was able to discard at a whim; crime was my only shirt. Committing a crime sometimes became a necessity. In the Black community, it was the type and circumstance of the crime. We knew that not all crimes were created equally. We knew there were two sets of laws, one for the Black community and one for the white community. We knew being criminalized from the womb was a way of life. For an African American family to have "made it" meant that family had risen above the Black criminalized urban ghettos of Cleveland.

The urge, if you will, to challenge legitimacy with my endeavors was not the pressure from a tell-tale heart or the punishment of incarceration, although I must admit at the point, I didn't feel like I had another long bit in me. But more than anything, I simply wanted to see how it felt to take the road less travelled. I had grown bored with who I was and wanted to see how it felt to be someone different. Crime had simply gotten old, and devoid of challenge. There were no more butterflies or excitement, and my rebellious flame had been smothered out.

Humphrey, the old demolition guy, had secured a contract with Hough Baker for thirty-five thousand, which we ended subcontracting to a company out of Akron for a grand total of seven thousand dollars. The profit margin was like drug money without the risk. I tried bringing Mike and my nephew in, and anyone who would listen to me but in the end my small circle of associates was too addicted to the fast money cocaine scene. Greed had consumed everyone like a contagious cancer. As I mentioned, I tried to convince my nephew that this was the way: learn business, learn how to operate construction heavy equipment, and we could build a legitimate business.

No matter how much money or materialism was involved, when I was bored, I had to move on. Therefore, greed was never a problem for me. It had always been about the doing. My impatience was a blessing more times than it had been a curse.

The old man Humphrey would show me that the demolition/

contracting business money was just as fast as cocaine money. He also showed me that the demolition business had a lot of seedy characters and was not without deadly risk. But compared to the cocaine business, it was a piece of cake, and wide open in Cleveland for a minority contractor.

The closest my nephew came to my company was to use my office for late-night entertainment for his little cocaine-selling crew with a private freak show. It became a nightly thing for them.

My crackhead engineer, who I let use my office for his apartment, was the main attraction. My nephew Jabs and his juvenile cocaine-selling crew, would round up a crackhead chick and pay them, engineer and the chick, to perform a freak show. It was honest entertainment, therefore, I never got bent out of shape about it. However, his backstabbing little crew who were always trying to get next to me, could not wait to tell me every detail of my nephew's every move. I told my nephew his so-called friends weren't nothing more than a bunch of jealous-hearted busters who could not wait for an opportunity to stab him in the back. Sadly, I wasn't as important to him as his friends, so he would end up learning the hard way.

It was clear from the rip that the demolition game was a young man's game. It was not much different than the cocaine business, the team with the most energy got the most money. I needed a young crew. I had a plan, but it would take time. Hard lessons would have to be learned first. Nonetheless, I did not let the inability to persuade others to join me in the business derail my vison; I became a solo act and kept it moving.

I was on speed dial and to be a solo act I had to learn everything. Like any endeavor, criminal or otherwise, the things you did not know, cost you.

I was younger than most contractors, goodlooking and stayed in uniform whenever I went to city hall or anywhere soliciting contracting opportunities. The first impression, or confidence, represented fifty percent of your chances toward achieving whatever it is you were after. Confidence had never been one of my shortcomings. Therefore, I dove into contract solicitation as though I had been doing it all my life. Can you deliver, is what the buyer wanted to know and was willing to pay for.

In less than ninety days of hustling contracts, I felt like I had been doing it all my life. I was entering the final stages of securing 3.5 million dollars' worth of demo and small construction contracts. To say I was hooked would be an understatement. My goal was to subcontract all the work out until I made enough money to buy more equipment. The Akron demo boys told me they were prepared to handle any subcontracting job I could throw their way. I figured all I would need is two new tandem trucks and a 215 backhoe, for starters, because the 911 dozer I had was a workhorse itself.

The design build engineer I had on my team was a crackhead, but dude could bid the hell out of any construction job and read any blueprint placed in front of him. Sid was a twenty-year retired veteran from the Army Corps of Engineers. But like all crackheads, Sid needed crack to function, so I owned him as though he was a piece of furniture. That is, until another guy came along with a bigger cocaine bag.

In any construction enterprise, the key is insurance and bonding. Humphrey was able to get me bonded for whatever job I wanted to bid on. I could bid on just about any demo job in the city.

There were two million dollars' worth of demo jobs on the table from the city of East Cleveland being negotiated by the money-grabbing city manager Emmanuel Onunwor. During which time, the East Cleveland Nigerian city manager made it clear he was looking for a contractor who was willing to give a huge kickback, and I made it clear to him that I had no problem with his demands.

In the meantime, I get a call from a Black contractor who had the same insurance company handling our insurance and bonding. He wanted to know if I could handle an excavation job for a proposed church on the corner of Avon and 116th, a few houses over from where Humphrey was living. The contractor had been awarded all the concrete work on a new prison construction outside of Warren, Ohio and his bond were over-extended. I told him that I would take care of the excavating, and once he realized Sid was a design build engineer, we left the meeting with an opportunity to build the entire church. Now all I had to do was convince the Church Board of Directors I was the man for the job, and with the contractor's reference that would be a slam dunk.

It was never the baller's lifestyle fame and fortune, for me it was the doing. Caine Construction became my doing. I just needed something to scratch that constant itch. I needed to be challenged every day.

In the time span of just over six months, Caine Construction was in contract negotiation for a tune of over five million. On the other hand, as the saying goes, it takes money to make money and I was finding out that Caine Construction was no different. The 50k or so I had made, my daily expense had sucked it up like a giant sponge. Notwithstanding the fact that the work was hard, it took me several weeks of daily grind to reacquaint myself with my muscles as I was in my late thirties. But at the end of the day the soreness felt good. The dirt under my nails felt good. I felt an ease and a calmness from not having to carry a gun and look over my shoulder. It was the first time in a long time I could remember waking up in the morning and the first thing on my mind was not a conscientious check of the potential threats of the day.

The East Cleveland City Manager Mr. Onunwor, along with the Akron company I subcontracted the previous Hough Baker building demo work to, both crossed me out of the two-million-dollar demo job. The Akron company had the equipment and I didn't. The money was a grant from the Federal Government. The demo job consisted of demolishing several apartment buildings located on First, Second, and Third streets off Hayden. To make things worse, two weeks later Humphrey got caught "burying the tank" on the excavating job we had secured from the Avon Church. There had been an old car workshop on the land years ago or perhaps it had been an old gas station. Nonetheless there had been a fuel tank in the ground. Basically, if there was an EPA question or situation on development land, such as gas stations, the EPA would have to come out and test the soil in a given radius which can sometimes take years to determine the severity of the soil contamination and what should be allowed in terms of development. For a small hand-to-mouth, mom-and-pop operation like Caine Construction, we couldn't afford the time or the expense.

The old man Humphrey was the only person I had who knew how to handle big machinery. Unbeknownst to me, Humphrey removed the tank and dumped five tons of sand in the hole and removed the contaminated sand. He then would repeat this process several more times, which was unethical, and more importantly, illegal. The church found out and terminated my contract.

In the meantime, I had to wear all the hats from a business

management perspective, not to mention the company's daily and pre-construction expense had drained my bank account. I had big boy bills. Caine Construction was a start-up and unable to establish any credit lines. My business ethic straddled the line between legal and criminal, so I had a guy working to create a fake company history. But there was no time. I needed immediate cash to finance the work I had on the table or else I would lose the contracts.

The cocaine money from my stash was almost depleted. My nephew had gotten used to me not giving a fuck about our coke-selling partnership agreement, so he mistakenly took my nonchalant attitude as a result of his cleverness. I would learn this underestimation to be a fundamental flaw in his character.

During the days when my cocaine was plentiful, I had given on assignment a half an ounce of coke to a chick named Debra. She called and said she had my money. I had forgotten all about the drugs I had given her because so much had happened in my fast-paced life since then. When I gave her the drugs, I probably had designs of getting into her panties and changed my mind when I discovered she was a smoker. Maybe the reason I never followed up with her was because I had just gotten married or perhaps it was my new attitude of trying to get out of the business. Whatever the reason for me not going back for the money was irrelevant.

Debra started off telling me how much she appreciated what I did when I gave her the cocaine. She thanked me for not bugging her about the long-time debt. At that point, I didn't have a clue as to what she was talking about. It had been so long I had forgotten about it. The more she talked, the more I began to remember. When I gave her the cocaine, she told me she wanted to start selling and gave me a song and dance about needing money for her daughter's college expenses. She went on to say that she was in a better place financially, so she was able to pay me back. I didn't believe her one minute, nonetheless I was blinded by my own vanity. I thought her plan was to revisit her missed opportunity to pussy whup a bigtime drug dealer but really, she was nothing but a dirty crackhead bitch. Me, I was in desperate need of cash; it was a perfect storm.

She asked me to bring her more coke to sell. All that was left in my safe was a crumb but nevertheless shoved what I had in my pocket. I decided to play her little game, with the quickness off I went to her apartment in Euclid, Ohio.

I had no clue it was a setup. I had eliminated the daily threats in my life, so I was not thinking like a baller. All I was doing was collecting money. When I arrived at her apartment, I saw several white guys scrambling around in her parking lot. Again, not threats. My antennas were not up. Nothing clicked in. When I got off the elevator and knocked on her apartment door, I had no clue what was about to happen. However, the moment I crossed her threshold and she shoved the four hundred dollars in my hand, everything became crystal clear. "Here is the money for that cocaine I got from you," she said.

Her voice was too loud, as though she was an actress repeating a line, she had been rehearsing all day. At that point everything began to unfold in a surreal slow-motion flashback, white men scrambling in the parking lot and the dude sitting at her kitchen table … her words no longer had sound and everything seemed to be in slow motion. She began to explain that the guy sitting at the table was her cousin. I automatically reached for my pocket. I realized that I had brought a quarter of an ounce with me. Why I had brought it I don't remember; perhaps I wanted to fake it like I was still in the business when in fact that was the very last cocaine I had left. On the other hand, the last thing a cocaine seller will do is allow his inventory to get down to zero, so by my calculation my nephew should have a couple pounds from the flip, but I wasn't supposed to know this.

Nonetheless, I made a bee line to the bathroom to flush the drugs. At that point, I felt like a man who had just stepped in waist-deep shit and was trying to use a popsicle stick to scrape it off. In the words of Marion Berry, "Well, I'll be damned, the bitch done set me up." In my mind I had gotten out of the cocaine business this wasn't supposed to have happened.

Years after this happened, I would often lie in my bunk, imagining Good and Evil sitting somewhere on a high cloud looking down on me, having made a wager as to whether or not I would ever be tempted to go back to my criminal lifestyle.

Good arguing with Evil, stating that I didn't get back, I was merely collecting money from the cocaine I had given to her previously. Evil making the argument that, the bet was that I could never go back and surely, I had.

I was charged with three counts of trafficking and some other trumped-up charges. I was facing no more than five years max but to a man who had just done a decade in prison, any time was too much time. Added to the fact I had checked out of the criminal lifestyle mentally, five years felt like a death sentence.

It was time for damage control. I got in touch with Luthor who had mentioned that he had a good fixer lawyer who handled cocaine cases. He was right, the lawyer was reliable and got me a flat two years, which didn't sit too well with the Euclid police department. The city of Euclid, Ohio was eating good off the war on the Black community in the name of the war on drugs. I couldn't believe I had allowed myself to get trapped in the modern-day slaver's snare. And the more I thought about it, I didn't want to do jaywalking time. In my mind there was no such thing as a minimum amount of prison time. I just couldn't come to grips with going to prison again. It was inconceivable for me to see myself behind bars and walk willingly into prison yet again.

I felt different. I was older, wiser. I was married. I'd been to Africa for Christ's sakes ... and learned about my African heritage. I had rubbed elbows with African kings and queens and had a taste of wealth and affluence. Indeed, it was hard for me to summon up the inner resolve that justified going back to prison and living in a cage again.

But it was only two years, everyone kept telling me. If you can do twelve, which I had just done, two years will be a piece of cake. It will go by in a flash, they would say. But they did not have a clue about doing time. They did not realize that prison was fifty percent physical and fifty percent mental. They didn't understand it wasn't the physical part you had to worry about, it was the mental. I just couldn't shake off the feeling that these two years would be harder than any years I would ever do in my life. Doing time, no matter how much, felt like a death sentence. So, I told my lawyer let me think about it. The lawyer said we could dance with the court for about eight months before I would have to make my decision.

I felt like a man on death row with eight months to live. Suddenly I needed to see my son, the ocean, mountains. I felt like I had to touch freedom. I told my wife I was going to California to see my son Lamar and to think about what I planned to do, which meant deciding whether or not I was going to turn myself in and walk merrily off to jail. I told her if I did not return in three weeks, she would know my decision.

Lamar was attending a junior college in Northern California. I had spent little time with him the few years I had been home. It was strange how pending incarcerations seem to always wake you up to the cost of freedom. You start thinking about all the people and places you hadn't seen and wanted to see. Life is magnified in the face of incarceration and leaves no doubt on the things that are most important.

I knew from the rip that Selisa was a special woman, but I never felt more in love with her than when I was faced with the possibility of losing her. Our marriage was young, and I wasn't sure how much her dedication would hold up under the ultimate test of incarceration. She promised me she took her vows seriously, and she was one hundred percent in my corner whatever I would decide. In that moment, I believed her. I had no choice.

Our relationship was turbulent from the very beginning. There was no script for a man who had spent half his life behind bars. The issues that made me who I was and how she believed would fit into her life, she had to decide as to whether her dedication would be worth it in the long run. Our relationship had come full circle. It was as though we both had read the ending of a novel before reading the beginning of the book. We knew how the book ended but we had no clue as to the trials and tribulations that would define the journey.

The long plane ride to California was therapeutic. When I got off the plane my decision was made. There was too much I wanted to accomplish so I decided to go with my gut. The catching would come before the hanging.

Lamar, my son, aspired to playing professional football and ranked as one of the top high school wrestlers in the state. After bonding with my son for several days it was clear to me he wasn't a football guy. Lamar was big, standing at six-two and around three hundred pounds, but Lamar was not a football guy. His weight had stigmatized and defined him in the eyes of others. To the people that oversaw his upbringing, he was a big, Black, young man so quite naturally he was supposed to play football. So that is what he was to the people.

I headed down to Oakland, California to see an old childhood friend and while there I would head over to the University of Berkeley to see Dr. Harry Edwards, the renowned sociologist who wrote the book *Revolt Of The Black Athlete*, and founder of the Olympic Project for Human Rights (OPHR) while a professor at San Jose State, and where John Carlos and Tommie Smith were students. They were the athletes who during their 1968 Olympic award ceremony greeted the raising of the American flag, with the iconic raised fists symbolizing Black Power.

At this time, I had not seen Hiawatha, my childhood 105th Street friend whom we called Hike, in close to twenty-five years. He had moved to California to visit his uncle one summer, and never returned to the mistake on the lake. He was always intrigued with street hustler and confidence games like three-card Molly or finding the pea. It was no surprise to me when I discovered that Hike was a successful confidence man in Oakland.

After explaining my situation, Hike didn't have any problem getting me some fake driver's licenses and social security card. In a matter of a few hours, I went from Willie Drake to John whatever. Hike let me crash on his couch for a couple of weeks. We got caught up on all the years but more than anything I was able to use the time to reflect and think about my next move.

All the while it felt like I had some unfinished business. I could not let go of the thought of what could have been, had I kept to my legitimate business plans when I was released from prison. Regret took hold of my entire being. I was a confident man who always lived with my decisions; doubt never control me. I move on and this time was no different. But for the world I couldn't figure out why I kept choosing over and over the path of crime instead of legitimacy. Did I fear legitimacy, the unfamiliar? Had I cleaved to the one thing that I was familiar with, crime? Or was it because I was simply afraid of failure, unlike crime, where I was comfortable because I and the world expected me to fail at being a criminal.

The air was different in Northern California. It was the first time I realized being a criminal was not worth another minute behind bars. All my life I felt rushed, but suddenly I was no longer in a hurry. I had let all my hopes and dreams dry up like a raisin in the sun merely because I had been afraid of change. Now that there was nothing to lose or fear, here I was desiring to make it happen. I knew it was too late for me to resurrect any semblance of a legit business career, but I felt the need to at least explore the "what if." I felt the need to consult with Dr. Edwards. In prison, during my research about Sports and non-profits I came to know about his work, so he became a part of my truth behind bars. I felt if I could connect with him, my truth, behind bars would not have been a lie.

Surprisingly, Dr. Edwards was sitting alone in his office. I had gotten directions from the receptionist and I just pulled up on him without an appointment. He looked up from what he had been reading with that familiar look that says something isn't right with this picture. The expression was unique to Black men living in America. After a moment of pause his body relaxed and he reached for my extended hand that had been hanging in mid-air for a couple of beats.

"What can I do for you?" he said. I told him about the proposed nonprofit organization I had planned to start, called Sport Ed Won. The concept was to get all the professional sports teams to sponsor educational excellence. In retrospect the concept was before its time. Nonetheless, rather than a discussion on my business concept, he proceeded to talk about the social economic perspective of sports, and how the collegiate sports system was broken. The more he talked, the more his intelligence lost me. Dr. Edwards was a sociologist professor. I listened to him without interruption and when he had finished, we said our goodbyes and I left. I had accomplished what I set out to do, which was to be true to initiative, and my belief that I could achieve anything I had conceived. However, the confirmation only made me feel worse than I had before, because I had proven to myself that the truth behind bars was indeed, the truth.

I moved out of Hike's house and got a small closet room across the bay in San Francisco. The hotel was full of young intellectuals from all over the world. Some of them were exchange students and some were merely drawn to the pull of an invisible intellectual force field that was resonating out of Silicon Valley. No matter what time of the day or night whenever I came back to my little room, they would have their doors open, going in and out of each other's rooms, sitting around having conversations about all kinds of subjects. The conversation mostly always seemed to end up being about the digital revolution. A phenomenon they called the World Wide Web. Computers were on the verge of taking over the world, spelling the end to the labor force as we had known it. I don't know why I was being drawn to this conversation and why it became so fascinating to me, but I would spend hours listening to all their theories and thoughts on the digital revolution.

During one of the conversations, the politics of Canada versus the United States was being talked about and it was when I got the idea to flee across the border to avoid my pending criminal prosecution. My plan would be to go to Detroit, Michigan and head over to Canada. But first I had to stop in Cleveland and tell my wife. I was conflicted about dragging her and my two little girls on the lam with me. My pockets were toast, I barely had enough money for my plane ticket back.

Once in Cleveland, I would liquidate the contract business equipment and some personal items. I would lie low with my brother who was also on the lam, living in Detroit. I would use a portion of the money to buy several ounces of drugs to sell to support me. When I informed Selisa of my decision to go on the lam, she was heartbroken; she couldn't understand why I would throw away everything I had built, just to avoid doing two or three years of prison time. Selisa and I were not married long but in these lowest moments I realized marrying her had been the best move I had made. On the other hand, in the moments I recognized this truth, I convinced myself that her love and our marriage would not withstand the test that would come with a life on the lam.

Drugs and a life devoid of morality had warped my mind. My thinking was irrational. There were no good thoughts without evil thoughts. I was hell-bent on my own demise. I underestimated the strength of my wife's love; she was not willing to give up on me that easy.

On the lam, I began to self-medicate at a higher rate, using my own supply heavily and exploring the mysteries of cocaine with a "why not, nothing to lose, I am going to prison, anyway" attitude. My demise was my mission and as it happens, every time you seek your own self-destruction, people come into your life with a mutual agenda and offer you a hand.

It was in this "What the fuck?" moment that I happened to meet Charlie and Jerry, two hustling chicks that used to buy cocaine from me. Charlie and Jerry needed cocaine the way a car needed gasoline to run. I told the two chicks I would no longer be their cocaine supplier and two hours later they had agreed to pack up and join me on the lam. I knew it would be better with the two out front shielding me from the risk of being knocked. Charlie was the alpha. She was that down for anything, "So what, nigger I did it, now what?" type of a bitch. Jerry was cleverer and sneakier. She wasn't going to burst a grape in your face but just when you thought she was soft "damn, the bitch done played me." And just when you thought she could not carry her hustling weight Bam! She would knock off a much-needed sting.

Off the three of us went to Detroit, Michigan, with the plans to get the chicks some IDs and move into Canada within the year. A month into our plan the three of us had dealers' habits, fucked up on cocaine and heroin.

Selisa kept pressing me to come along, and I was missing her love and ride-or-die dedication. Charlie and Jerry had my back, as much as two drug addict chicks could have a drug addict's back. Not that Selisa could roll with me on the lamb, it was that she would have to bring my two stepdaughters and I couldn't subject them to the lifestyle.

Leaving my wife and family was like that classic scene in the movies where the villain is cornered and after leaving a long trail of murder and mayhem in his wake, he finds himself surrounded by the police. It's that moment he looks down at his gun and realizes that he has only one bullet left — in his gun … and snatches open the door pointing his gun at the police. I knew I was committing suicide, so I wasn't about to take my family with me.

I had two sisters living in Michigan at the time and my brother Bruh and his girl and their three little children were living up there as well. Of course, Bruh and his partner were both on the lam with a cocaine habit longer than the time a Black man got for raping a white woman in the state of Mississippi.

Me and the chicks rented a house on the same street my brother lived on. Our plans to cross the border to Canada had been delayed because for one I couldn't find anyone in Detroit to get the girls some fake IDs and the fact crack and heroin didn't allow you to plan too far into the future.

Bruh would come get Charlie and Jerry like clockwork every morning, to go stealing. A drug fiend was always on time. One morning as Bruh was waiting on the girls sitting outside the house in his piece of car, some young crack-selling boys Bruh owed money to pulled up on him demanding their money. I was in the living room right by the window. I could hear their threatening voices shouting and demanding. Just when I looked out the window, dude pulled out a heater and shot my brother. I broke to the bedroom with tears running down my face, because I assumed, my brother would be dead by the time I returned, because I saw his head disappear out of view. I was in full speed; I grabbed my 45. When I burst through the front door, Bruh was still alive, pleading for dude not to kill him. Dude never saw me leave out of the house, let along bolt down the stairs. I didn't have a clear shot from the vantage point coming off the porch. In retrospect, if he did see me leave the house, he thought I was just another crack head, and the last thing a crack head would have was a gun, he must have thought. I was not a crack head; I was a junkie eating dog food for breakfast. By the time dude gave me a thought, I had jumped from the porch and come all the way around in front of the car and levelled my gun. But he was still too close to the car and I didn't trust my aim. I had no choice but to fire a warning shot.

Gun fire in the middle of the day never seemed to disturb people in Detroit in the height of the war on drugs. People were everywhere, little children were playing in the street directly in my line of fire. It was a warm beautiful summer afternoon. He had shot Bruh with a .38 caliber, and it was as though the gunshot was heard only by me because kids were still playing in the streets. But when I fired my .45 in the air, everything stopped. Baby mamas came running and screaming out of their houses for their children. I didn't have a clear shot at the motherfucker. Dude's head was all the way inside my brother's car.

The chase was on. He turned to fire in my direction. I was cursing and shouting at the top my lungs. I was full of rage – this nigga had just shot my brother and I was not going to let his little gun stop me from killing his ass. I pulled up and leveled off and fired a second shot hitting a parked car. I was not running; my pace was more of a fast walk. The plan was for my bullet to do the running. All I needed was one clear shot. I was shouting at the top of my lungs, "You dead, motherfucker! You are dead!"

The would-be assassin hugged the side of the parked cars and dashed into a backyard, which I had to approach with caution, and I lost him.

Bruh recovered from his gunshot wounds as always. This was the eight time he was shot point blank and survived. I never made to Canada, and as advertised in three months I had gone from a man with one gorilla on his back to two gorillas, and occasionally smoking cocaine on the side to come down. Again, it's a dangerous man who does not care whether he lives or dies.

I was living the classic "The catching comes before the hanging" lifestyle. Hanging with those two dirty bitches every day made me thirst for love, the way a man traveling through the desert thirsts for water. I called Selisa my wife and persuaded her to come up for the weekend. The weekend turned into forever again. We got a small house. Detroit was hard on her and my baby girls, but Lisa was a survivor. I had two gorillas on my back, three women to deal with every day, two households not to mention all the backstabbing niggas. I couldn't live this lifestyle for too long without going crazy. One day Selisa left for work and got robbed in broad daylight, in the dead of winter. All I could think about was what if she'd gotten killed. That day I made up my mind to flip the script.

I joined a drug rehab organization and just when I was beginning to get my shit together the Federal Marshals arrested my Black ass outside my job in Romulus, Michigan on the drug trafficking warrant. I had been clean for three or four months. My arrest was a relief. I was more than ready to face the piper. However, I still had this eerie feeling of uncertainty. On one hand, it was only two or three years waiting on me, but on the other hand, it was time, waiting.

The uncertainty raised its ugly head in the second year of my sentence, six months before my release date. I began to hear rumblings from family members about my nephew's friend turning out to be a Federal informant and the friend being the one who snitched me out. Moreover, my nephew Jabs was being indicted for a drug dealer we had robbed, and I would get an indictment as well.

Of course, the drug dealer was being portrayed by the Feds as an upstanding citizen in the community whose home was invaded by a couple of armed robbing thugs. I was not worried about any pending charges from the state until I learned the Feds initiated the charges and were handling the particulars of the case for the state prosecution.

My nephew had found out his friend was a Federal informant and threatened to kill the snitching motherfucker. The Feds got every word of my nephew's threats on the wire, and he probably dropped my name in his threat as well. Therefore, the Feds were compelled to protect the snitch from me as well as my nephew, by any means necessary.

At first, I had no clue all this was going on. I was locked up, doing my two years flat for the trafficking. I was in my forties; I'd had enough. But once I got wind of the situation, it didn't take a rocket scientist to figure out if the Feds were involved in my state armed robbery prosecution, my pending release was in peril.

Unbeknownst to me, the Federal Government had created this elaborate scheme that began by pre-threatening and subsequently flipping a drug dealer whom my nephew Jabs had set for me to rob. The Feds told the drug dealer if he didn't cooperate, they would charge him with trafficking. My nephew's snitching Federal informant had bought drugs from the dealer, so they had him dead to rights on the charges. The Feds believed three armed robbery convictions would mean a life sentence for me. This elaborate scheme was all devised to protect their drug snitching Federal informant because it was believed I would waste no time killing the snitch bitch when I got out.

The term Black-on-Black crime was coined in the '60s, when a Black person committed a crime against a Black person who were or had committed a crime, an oxymoronic term to say the least. Whenever I robbed a drug dealer, I was committing a Black-on-Black crime. But I am not committing a Black-on-Black crime if I am not apprehended in the commission of robbing the drug dealer. In other words, the drug dealer would not be wise to call up the police station and say he was just robbed for his drugs. There is no crime on the book that protects a drug dealer from being robbed of his drugs, or is there? The only time a drug dealer can file charges for somebody robbing him for his drugs, would be if the man being charged is Black.

As suggested before, if it wasn't for cocaine, a lot of people would have never committed a crime in their life. Becoming a drug dealer was the norm, so most of them as I said were a bunch of rubber-backed, nit-brained motherfuckers. Therefore, being labeled as a snitch was also the norm. Nothing changed. Becoming a snitch meant they would still be able to "ball out," and the only difference would be they would work for the cops.

No one played the flip-the-drug-dealer game better than the Feds. The Feds would threaten you, your grandmother, your mama, baby sister, baby brother, baby mama, everybody in your circle with a million years to life if you didn't cooperate. Right around the mid-80s, I would see dudes who had snitched on one another, hanging out together in the joint, as though nothing had happened. For the life of me, I couldn't understand it. I was old school, who came up in a time when snitches got their tongues cut out. However, after I was released and seeing this new breed of so-called hustlers, I realized it was part of their game. The Feds played a big part in creating these fake ballers because they offered them a parachute, in some instances a higher level of balling. A cocaine snitch for the Feds is one of the best jobs a fake baller could have. A fake baller would literally kill your ass, to prove his loyalty to the Feds and keep his fucking job.

My case was a state case. I never threatened my nephew's Federal informant, snitching-ass booster friend. Therefore, the only way the Feds would be able to get to me and protect the welfare of the snitch, would be to create a false state charge, whereas a drug dealer would masquerade as a respectable citizen whose home had been invaded and robbed by me.

The so-called war on drugs allowed law enforcement authorities on every level a directive to disregard the law when it came to the rights of African Americans. There simply was no rule of law or engagement: "By any means necessary" was law enforcement's motto. Therefore, it was not unusual for a state prosecution office to hand a case over to the Federal Government to prosecute, regardless of jurisdiction, if the Feds work out the state prosecutor's office.

My record was long as a motherfucker, my conviction would be assured with an indictment. Indeed, the Feds could have pinned a M1 on me, and it would not have made a difference if I had several alibis and eyewitnesses saying it wasn't me. I still would have been convicted. I would learn in my long hours of studying American Law, it's not an exact science, therefore the "definition" of jurisprudence could just as well be defined as "the manipulation of the criminal judicial system in the pursuit of the Black man's genocide in the form of incarceration." Statistics manifests this definition more than any other absolute. My case was par for the course.

They gave me a state lawyer who was literally dying from cystic fibrosis. He had gotten a recent double lung transplant and his body was rejecting his transplant. He was given six months to live. To say he had other things on his mind would be the understatement of the decade.

I was amazed by the little lawyer's courage, his hope, and his faith. Every time the little frail sickly lawyer would visit wearing the same black suit, we would end up talking more about his situation than my case. It was as though we both knew that both our predicaments and situations were exercises in futility. I learned more about cystic fibrosis than a medical intern would. And when the lawyer left, I felt as though I had just gotten a visit from the Grim Reaper. Nonetheless, even with one hand tied behind my back, I was looking forward to my day in court.

A lot of cocaine dope boys were under the illusion that they were legitimate businessmen. The Feds had hyped this dude in be-lieving he was legit. Nigga please, how dare you bring a drug beef to a court room for street justice? You are nothing but a criminal with snitching license. You piece of shit! But I wasn't aware how deep I was being played. I would learn that the mark in the movie The Sting had nothing on me, and that my nephew Jabs played the catch man, John "Kelly" Hooker, better than Robert Redford.

The Feds had set up a wire sting and got my nephew on tape making his murderous threat against their undercover snitch, and when he admitted to carrying the threats out against the Feds snitch, the Feds nabbed him. The Feds had my nephew dead to rights and were able to press him into flipping on me, or else he would be charged with attempted murder on a Federal witness. My nephew felt his only chance would be to flip on me. In return, he would be offered a five-year for armed robbery rather than the twenty years for attempted murder on a Federal witness.

Aside from providing more than enough information to the Feds to build a solid case on me surrounding the dope house rob-bery, which was being portrayed by the prosecution as a home-invading robbery case against an upstanding family in the com-munity. I asked my nephew to testify on my behalf; his testimony would reveal to the court that dude was nothing but a drug deal-er. He told me the stipulation of his plea bargain forbade him from testifying. It was then I realized my father's seed had stopped with his girls.

Therefore, without a shred of evidence or testimony revealing my accuser to be a fraud and a lying cocaine-selling piece of shit, the jury found me guilty and the court sentenced me to yet anoth-er fifteen to thirty-five years. Again, I stood a chance of doing every day of the thirty-five years, again. Ohio didn't have a three-time loser act on the books, but it was present in the parole board decisions.

In all the years of committing crimes, my victims were faceless. But after the jury read the guilty verdict it seemed the faces of everyone I had ever stolen from or robbed were sitting in the jury box. Dope dealers, numbers bookies — indeed, a jury of my peers had convicted me.

I was brought back to Lima Correctional. When I went to court, I had been only six months from the streets, and when I returned I had a life sentence. The whole prospect of it left me feeling utterly numb.

In fifteen years, I would see the same parole board I saw for the armed robbery convictions that sent me to Mansfield. The same parole board I saw for my armed robbery conviction that sent me to Lucasville. I was forty-two years old with a fresh fifteen to thirty-five. My only consolation was that the judge ran my sentence concurrent with the drug trafficking, so I had fourteen more years to go before my first parole hearing.

After my sentence, I began to have this recurring nightmare about the parole board for several months after I got back. I would be sitting in the waiting area waiting to be called for my parole board hearing, when a faceless inmate would come pass pushing a serving cart with a huge pot of coffee and Styrofoam cups. He'd stop and asked me was I going to the parole board? I would tell him yes and he'd go on to explain that he was an expert in figuring out whether the parole board would give an inmate a parole or some more time. The reason he knew, he would explain in the nightmare dream, was because he had been the parole board coffee server for one hundred years. He knew every member and could tell what they were thinking before they said a word.

During this time that I had been brought back into the system and sentenced, Ohio sentencing laws were in the process of being changed to a flat-time law system. The talk was that the new flat-time system would do away with the need for the Ohio Parole Board. For a guy who was a three-time loser, I didn't want to see the parole board on a third straight armed robbery charge and my fear of the parole board and spending the rest of my days behind bars was no doubt the reason for this recurring epic nightmare about the parole board.

After the faceless inmate got finished setting up the coffee for the parole board he would come out and sit down next to me and we would wait for the parole board members to walk past us so he could tell me what each member had in store for me.

"That's Ms. Crymes, she's the Chairperson for the Ohio Parole Board Northeast Region," he whispered in my ear. We watched a tall Black lady approach. Her physiognomy and solemn countenance manifested her vocation. She was an imposing figure. She looked to be in her sixties, carrying a briefcase, wearing a dark conservative suit and orthopedics shoes. Her clothes were perhaps fashionable during the early twentieth century but now seemed to be a statement in austerity. The faceless inmate told me for thirty years Ms. Crymes had worked for the parole board, arbitrating flop-time against the criminal's degree of remorse, nature of crime, the victims' suffering, and material losses. She tirelessly decided the public's revenge. This she felt was her duty, dispensing time and freedom with the indifference of a mortician, and the piousness of a clergy. "That bitch is cold-blooded, brother," said the faceless inmate. "She's going to give you every day of those thirty-five years."

"Check it out, here comes Mr. Druggers," the faceless inmate told me. Mr. Druggers was a large man and seemed to have a nervous mirthless little laugh at the end of his sentences. He stopped to greet us before he entered the parole room. I thought his laugh was evil sarcasm, but it was who he was. His presence and soft personality seemed to be the total opposite to Ms. Crymes." "How are you two gentlemen doing?" he said with that mirthless, dry laugh. I didn't know how to respond, so I just nodded.

And then there was Mr. Robbers, a medium-built man with a military disposition. Arrogance made up his entire being. He didn't acknowledge our greeting. It was as though we weren't even there. Mr. Robbers was followed by Ms. Sexton, an elfin little white lady with the presence of a third-grade schoolteacher. She wore wire-framed glasses and constantly straightened her clothes with a religious attention to her appearance. I would imagine her whole life was a constant attention to detail. Sometimes, the faceless inmate and I would be sitting outside the parole room and sometimes he would be waiting on the parole board's decision with me. Sometimes the faceless inmate would bring the parole board's decision on a small piece of paper and stare at me intensely.

The dream was satirical as far as the names and even the parole members' faces were concerned, but my fear was real. I used to wake up in a cold sweat, petrified about having to face the parole board a third straight time for armed robbery.

The war on drugs in the 1980s and '90s allowed the white-run United States of America judicial system to fill up the penitentiaries with young Black boys and men by any means necessary. Becoming a criminal lawyer or getting any job in the criminal judicial system, for a young white person coming out of college, was the quick way to the land of milk and honey in America; it was like shooting fish in a barrel.

I exhausted every appeal remedy I had available to me. In the end no one cared about a career criminal's accusations of an FBI frame-up. Next case.

I told my wife to go on without me. She had her whole life ahead of her, plus she had two little girls to think about. I was certain I would have to do at least twenty of the thirty-five-year sentence. Selisa Rita Drake was a stubborn woman, as she would reiterate many times her love wasn't a faucet that turns on and off. It was going to take more than words to push her away. She told me she would be there every step of the way. No matter how long it took she'd be there when they release me. I believed her and that belief only made the pain worse.

Six years into my sentence, the epiphany of 9/11 caused me to flip the script. A light came on, or was it simply that point where doing time had gotten too hard to do? My breaking point of incarceration. Nonetheless, change had drenched my being. At that point I became a different man inside and out. On the other hand, I was a Gemini, flipping the script was who I was. Therefore, no declaration of change was going to be enough for me. I had to put in some serious work. I had to get my hands dirty and get ready to put in a physical effort, like building a house from the ground up, with no help from anyone.

A lifetime criminal like me could not expect to go to sleep one night and wake up the next morning and declare to himself that he was no longer a criminal. Shit doesn't work like that. No, the only way I was going to change, that is to say, the only way my endeavor for good was going to triumph over my evil criminal mind, is for good to be bigger than myself ... that is to say, bigger than my evilness.

My world, the world of crime and all its derivatives, is manifested in my physical earthly presence. In this world-bound wickedness, my evil lives and dominates. If this is truth, as I believed it to be, then it can be said that the evil in me, and I submit any man, is characterized and manifested by his earth-bound self, the physical. Indeed, evil is the ruler of this earthly realm of the physical, and as my wicked deeds symbolized in the walls of my incarceration can surely attest. From that rationale, I came to realize that my goodness has to be waged in the physical, on evil's earthbound manifestation. Even though I knew for certain that no man's good would be able to defeat his evil in his earthly realm. Goodness can only triumph in its spiritual realm, where Goodness resides. But the war had to be waged, against evil on his own turf, in the physical, an evil sword against a righteous sword. I was in search of a righteous sword.

The Lima Prison Education Department had gotten new computers. The epiphany of 9/11 struck me big time. And one day while sitting on my bunk searching for answers, I remembered the deep conversations the young intellectuals in San Francisco were having about computers taking over the world, and at that moment I knew this pursuit would be the righteous sword I would wield in the earthly realm against the Prince of Darkness.

Every inmate wanted to put his hands on the magical machines that had the power to transfer you to places beyond the prison walls. Only a few inmates in the prison understood the difference between an Internet and Ethernet network system. But there was this one guy, his name was Larry, who was ahead of the curve and his time when it came to inmates (or the average person for that matter), understanding the hardware and software of computers. Larry took to computers and the understanding of binary electronics like a fish to water. He was one of only a few inmates who had training in the short-lived Binary Electronics Training Vocational School at Marion Correctional Institution before it had been terminated. Every inmate who was fortunate enough to have taken the classes was white. Larry was doing a manslaughter bit. He was a natural mechanical engineer, one of those guys that no matter what broken machine you put in front of him he would be able to fix it. Larry was from Southern Ohio, somewhere near the border of West Virginia. Free vocational training to Larry was like stealing. He knew more about computers than anyone in the prison system and leveraged his computer operator's skills to become one of the first inmate computer maintenance men in Lima, if not the only one.

Computer knowledge was like a gold rush claim, and Larry was not giving up this valuable knowledge, especially to a bunch of Black inmates. Dude was a redneck and I suspect a racist. Nonetheless, I was able to pick up bits and pieces from him being that I was a fellow tutor and was able to hang over his shoulder whenever his services where called upon. And some days he would give in to my insistent questioning and drop his computer knowledge to me while acting as though he was sitting in a dentist chair.

Larry explained to me that computers uses a binary system, represented by an electronic on or off signal. The way Larry explained it was this signal, which was a more in-depth decimal system, that basically elevates the concept of the telegraph to a higher level of communication. I was beyond fascinated with these magical machines. On the other hand, I wasn't too concerned with the mechanical workings of the machine as I was with its functionality. What were the benefits to the public and business were my concerns?

I began to read every article and literature I could get my hands on about computers. Most of what I would read were public disputes about electronic privacy and copyright infringements and then one day shit hit the fan, as we say. I remember the headlines as though it was yesterday: "Internet Explorer Wages Browser War." What did it mean? There was no literature being published that I could get my hands on that painted a clear picture for a lay person with limited digital understanding such as mine. It wasn't until after Google went public, which was around 2004, that a clear picture was formulated in my mind as to what it all meant for business. If it could be said that the Internet was the superhighway, then Google was Ford and General Motors. But how would people know where these websites were located? In the early days of the Internet the verbiage that was being use were analogous to cars and travel. An example would be a website was parked on the Internet. To get to the website you searched on the superhighway, using "Google."

The Internet was above all a communication and information medium with unlimited reach, created by the military, and now made available for the public. And like any communication media, its primary function would be to advertise and sell services and products.

The Internet made the world small and after 9/11 the world got even smaller and smaller.

The Internet was the new frontier. And just like a new frontier, carpetbaggers and claim jumpers were everywhere. The law of the land was that there wasn't a law of the land. I was beginning to see why Larry had kept his digital knowledge close to his chest because the more I learned about computers, the more I felt freedom.

Digital technology training was being systemically denied to low-income individuals, of whom the majority were Black, because of economics. The white males were yet again getting out front. It wasn't their fault; it was just the way of the world. Minorities and women were being relegated to the back of the digital technology training bus.

Of course, there were minority and women exceptions to the rule, and these exceptional people were filled with the tenacity and the fortitude to endure the roadblocks that were put in their training path.

Make no mistake about it, technology and the Internet was the new gold rush, a race for knowledge, and knowledge produces the spoils of valued discovery. Time has met opportunity. This was my challenge. All I had to do was figure out a way to defeat the bars that had systemically denied me access to knowledge. Only then would I be able to seize the opportunity.

Around the turn of the twenty-first century, I had exhausted all my appeal remedy. I was at my lowest point and then 9/11 happened and I found a spiritual strength in my quest for change, which I directed the energy in a self-challenge to conquer the mysteries of the digital world, or perhaps it was merely an escape from my harsh reality. Nonetheless, I was certain that the only thing that could defeat the old me would be if the new me were to do something that wasn't criminal; something that was legal, something extraordinary, a technological innovation that changed the world, like Bill Gates had done with Microsoft, Larry Page with Google, something that would make the world forget the old me.

The hardship letter my wife had gotten a member of the church, a doctor, to write on my behalf sealed the deal and I was transferred from Lima Correctional Facility to Grafton Correctional in 2007. The old joint was literally crumbling to the ground. The Federal government ruling was that the joint was inhumane and ordered its closure immediately. The state allowed us inmates to submit requests to the social service department for the place we would like to be transferred. If there was a compelling argument the placement would be approved. I picked Grafton for three reasons: closer to Cleveland, digital law library, and T.C. Programming.

T.C. were initials for Therapeutic Community Programming. This time I wanted to do some serious mental soul-searching. It was seven years after the epiphany of 9/11. I had changed. I was slowly but surely discarding the old me. For the first time I could remember being incarcerated, I was doing time and time was not doing me. I still had a razor focus about getting rid of the old me.

Grafton Correctional was the only joint in the Ohio prison system that was receiving jurisprudence digitally, which meant every Internet dispute and legal precedence would be right off the presses. I had spent the last ten years reading criminal case law and what I learned was that everything, everything in the world is predicated on the rule of law. The Internet was no different. Therefore, I had no doubt that the best way for me to become knowledgeable about any subject matter would be for me to study the legal history of the disputes that came into question. And there was only one way I would be able to do that. I had to find a way to get a job in the law library. I had worked in the prison main library and school system throughout my bit, so I had acquired several influential staff reference letters. No matter how many prison staff reference letters I had, if I wasn't qualified and connected, I had no chance at getting the law clerk job. This was the one job where your qualification had to be certified by inmates. Eventually I was able to get in touch with the right people. I was qualified and connected. But first things first.

Before I got transferred from Lima, my wife and kids had moved back to Cleveland from Detroit. Mostly because Selisa wanted to get closer to me, but she had also gotten fed up with

Detroit. The city had caused her nothing but drama, tragedy, and hardship the moment she set foot in it. Lima was all the way west, a three-hour drive across the state and now I was less than an hour away.

When I arrived at Grafton, faith was once again on my side. The only cell beds available to the new transfers were in the T.C. Program cells block. Cells were always preferred over dorm beds.

The program was a comprehensive self-awareness program that put emphasis on forcing the inmates to look inside themselves and face their demons. And once you stop running from yourself you can put strategy together for change. This was done with workshops, seminars, drug counselling, AA programs, spiritual insight, etc., designed basically for the inmate to take responsibility for his behavior.

Personally, for me, the T.C. Program was a cleansing mechanism. I had built up a lot garbage in my brain. I was desperate to try anything that would wash it out. So, every morning I would get up and recite the T.C. Philosophy as though it were the Lord's Prayer. Repetition is the seed of perfection.

"I have come to realize how my criminal thinking and past behavior need to change. I need to stop running from myself and stop my criminal behavior. I must investigate myself and commit to my family to help me to change. This is my challenge and my commitment. My family offers me awareness, trust, love, and an opportunity for me to transcend into the needed self-actualization. This challenge and commitment I accept. Remember: Honesty and hard work equal self-esteem and self-worth."

The program wasn't for everyone and most dudes couldn't get past the stigma, which was you were weak if you admitted mental health problems. I was long past what people thought of me, who, as I said, didn't even exist anymore.

If there was a flaw, it was the fact incarceration (steel bars and barbed wire fences) was still the control stimulus for my self-defined change. An inmate's behavior and recidivism rate after having been through the T.C. Program wasn't a significant change, if any. You can lead a horse to water, but you can't make him drink. I was thirsty.

Program was just what the doctor ordered. I never had dedicated as much time to soul searching as I would do in the two years or so I spent in therapeutic control. I knew there wouldn't be any short cuts to change. I had taken the long road. I was in my fifties, but time was no longer important to me, at least not as much as truth. I felt like I was thirty-five, with a do-over. Indeed, the world and all its possibilities felt new. But I was not under any illusion. I was aware that I was in the fourth quarter and God had decided to give me the ball one more time. If I fumbled, the game would be over. Reinventing myself was my only option.

I read every litigation and law that was connected to the Internet; if I didn't, it sure as hell felt like I did. The Internet was being promoted as the new frontier and every piece of the digital landscape that was being claimed was being challenged by someone else. Copyright, Electronic Privacy Rights, Government authority, and everyone's inability to find common ground the nexus if you will, between privacy, copyright, electronic ownership, government intervention, and overall innovation. But everyone knew at the end of the day it was all about the money, billions of dollars to be made. I followed the money; namely the ad companies. I discovered that the ad industry seemed to be a part of every Internet legal dispute that came across the wire. There was no shortage of opinions and predictions about what the Internet's potential would be moving forward. However, there was one dominating consensus, the Internet was a communication medium with unlimited range. A communication media. Everybody had a story; therefore, everybody stood a chance to get rich.

Every morning before I would go into my Law Clerk Office, through the General Prison Library, I would stop and check out the New York Times. On the front page of the business section, the headline read, "Google Buys DoubleClick for $3.1 Billion." It still seemed weird to me that something that wasn't being produced in a brick-and-mortar factory could be valued so much.

DoubleClick was founded in 1996 (the same year I was sentenced to thirty-five years in prison), and provided display ads on websites like Myspace, *The Wall Street Journal*, and America Online as well as software to help those sites maximize ad revenue. DoubleClick also helps ad buyers, advertisers and ad agencies manage and measure the effectiveness of their rich media, search, and other online ads. But what caught my eye the most in the article, was the line, "DoubleClick recently introduced a Nasdaq-like exchange for online ads that analysts say could be lucrative for Google."

I had a lot to learn about advertising, the engine that drove capitalism, socialism, communism, and even religious dogmas. There was no part of the human experience that was not touched by some form of advertising, whose sole purpose was to influence the minds of men the world over. Now here comes the Internet, a platform that offers advertising the biggest microphone it could ever imagined. I thought about all the evil scientists in the movies plotting to destroy the world. Anyone who did not have a stake in this communication platform, would find themselves behind the eight ball. The digital war was on. And it became clear to me that a digital divide would emerge between the haves and the have-nots. I would be the hero.

I thought about Dr. Martin Luther King Jr. and how much he would have accomplished with the internet medium at his disposal, or any of the great leaders of men and orators of the past, whether they were champions for the good or evil. The possibilities of the Internet were huge. It made me conceive and perceived through a wide lens, what the internet means in the context of the world view. Every man must recognize his calling and embrace the challenge, no matter how big the mountain is in front him. The rights versus the wrongs of the Internet was a mountain for me to conquer. I would challenge myself to become the hero and slay the internet dragon.

It was simple, a tale of good and evil, two roads. The views that controlled the podium would have the ear of the world. Governments could not be trusted to be the steward of the podium. In that moment, it came to me to conceive a non-profit organization, that would regulate the digital right from the digital wrong. The organization would be a champion for user rights, the rights of people. And it was clear this was my calling, my purpose.

The devil, my evil twin, reminded me that the truth behind bars was a lie.

The devil in me was confident in the work he had put in over the years. I was still one of his prize pupils. The devil was confident that any challenge in the pursuit of righteousness would be an exercise in futility. The devil would not let me forget that this was the same path.

The devil was a lie. I knew this road was different. I told myself not to waver no matter how it may have looked, I had never come this way before.

And I was made to believe and convinced to transform myself into principalities, with the understanding and knowledge that

Satan was not of flesh and blood. And it had been proven that no man on earth can defeat the devil in his worldly playground of flesh and blood. The only way to defeat him, I would have to step out of myself, discard that self as though it was an old worn-out garment and put on the garments, of principalities and hold the shield of righteousness firmly. Only then will I emerge from the bloody battle victorious. In that moment I threw down the gauntlet for my life.

We are all fallen angels but how many of us have the courage, the fortitude to get up and fly with broken wings? What was there for me to lose? I had nothing to lose so I welcomed the challenge. It wasn't about trying to change the world as it was about finding something to believe in that was bigger than the selfishness of self. I knew I couldn't beat Satan at his own game, my life was a testimony of his wicked powers. But from that day forward I knew I was no longer his pawn. I couldn't remember ever feeling more liberated than I felt in that moment. There was no other challenge I could think of that was bigger than taking the reins of my own destiny, piloting the ship of my life, a responsibility that had been in the hands of the Prince of Darkness as long as I knew myself.

Redemption in the physical realm is through deeds; a man can't one day wake up and announce to the world that he is now a changed man. He must pick up the sword of righteousness.

Selisa, my wife, had my release papers in her hand, but when she came down to pick me up, she would get a rude awakening. The first was on a Saturday and the parole offices were closed on the weekend so unbeknownst to Selisa, she had to wait until my effective date, which was the third of the month, that following Monday. It was against the Ohio penal code to release a convict on parole without them being able to register twenty-four hours of their release with the parole authorities. To say the mix-up about my released date was stressful would be an understatement. Neither of us got any sleep the entire weekend sleep the entire weekend. For fifteen and a half years we had dealt with hardships and disappointments but through it all we remained hopeful and persevered.

Monday finally came around and hope and faith had once again prevailed over despair. She had kept her word. She had promised me that the day I walked out of prison she would be there to pick me up. Fifteen years and nine months later she was there to take me home.

I came through the last gate and watched her rise from the bench; everything was happening in slow motion, it seemed. She was glowing like a radiant star. A manifestation of dedication if there ever was. We embraced and I kissed her lightly on the lips; the kiss was quick, without the passion. To see us kissing in a prison parking lot one would expect I had done just one or two years at the most. But for us, the most important thing was distance, as much as possible from the walls of incarceration. It was as though we feared the guard would come running through the gates shouting, "There's been a mistake, Willie Drake was not supposed to be released!" Therefore, getting off the premises was the most pressing thing, not a kiss, as we made haste to freedom.

It was an early typical August day, it seemed to have been ordered especially for me. There was a small summer breeze blowing in the air and there wasn't a cloud in the sky. Nothing but blue skies above. She had on a soft light, grey chiffon dress that fell just below her knees. She looked like a dream. We embraced again in the parking lot before I got into the car but this time, we held onto each other much longer. We didn't say a word because the moment was too overwhelming for words, we allowed the moment to do all the talking. I never knew a moment exist like that. How could such a feeling be possible? Living in darkness for so many years I couldn't fathom such a moment being real. But it was, and even though I had just walked out of prison, I felt a sudden embarrassment of riches. I was humbled.

When I got in the car, I put on the outfit Selisa had bought. It was simple jeans and a shirt. She put in a Jaheim CD and off we went up Interstate 71 to Cleveland. The trees, the white lines on the tarmac, the empty fields, everything in my view never looked so beautiful. There wasn't a big black 560 Mercedes Benz and a package of cocaine under the back seat of the car's arm rest, like the last time, foretelling my freedom this time it was the simplicity of a black Chevy Cavalier and the dedication of a ride-or-die wife.

Adult Parole Authority
1050 Freeway Drive, North
Columbus, Ohio 43229

CERTIFICATE OF PAROLE/RELEASE
AUTHORIZATION

DATE: **4/2/09**

To: Warden, GCI Correctional Institution
You are hereby authorized to release this individual on parole with the Ohio Parole Board Minutes:

GRANTED TO: Willie Drake, OFFENDER# A293-911
PRD DATE: 8/1/09
EFFECTIVE: 8/3/09
INSTRUCTIONS TO OFFENDER: To Go Immediately Following Your Release Directly To:
Approved Residence: 2208 east 87th Street, Cleveland, Ohio 44106

****You are not to change residence without permission from your parole officer****

Your Arrivals There Must Be reported to: **Todd Liggett,** Adult Parole Authority, In Person On: 8/4/09 – at 9:00 a.m. **or the FIRST** business day after release. If released at an earlier date Lausche State Office Bldg., 615 West Superior Ave., 10th Floor, Cleveland, Oh 44113, (216) 78-3015

****YOU WILL NEED YOUR PHOTO ID TO ENTER THE BUILDING***

This parole will always require you to maintain conduct in compliance with the rules set forth by the Ohio Adult Parole Authority and with any Special Conditions or Instructions Imposed by the Ohio Adult Parole Authority or your Parole Officer as Indicated below:

Your substance and Mental Health Programming and Screening will be discussed with you during your first visit with your Parole Officer.

This parole will start upon your release from the institution and will continue:

For a period of not less than 1 (one) years(s), when you will become eligible for Final Release Consideration provided that you have maintained satisfactory conduct and adjustment, your parole may be extended or revoked if you fail to comply with the requirements.

This parole is a privilege granted to you by the State of Ohio to allow you to complete your sentence outside of confinement. It will give you an opportunity to demonstrate your good intentions – direct your living towards goals acceptable to society and to direct all efforts towards the achievements of good citizenship. We hope that your adjustment will render complete success and satisfaction.

Very Truly Yours,

LIND S. Mario
CHIEF, ADULT PAROLE AUTHORITY
Anne James, Unit Supervisor
Cleveland Unit A0910